Chapter 1

"Uhhh! Is that a rat?"

Sonny's foot sinks into a soft, shrieking body. He's been in the subway tunnel for 15 minutes, yet his eyes haven't adjusted well to the darkness and even if they did he wouldn't have a good view of the black mess between the train tracks. Turning his pen flashlight towards his feet, the "rat" is actually a little girl's squeeze toy, likely cast from a speeding train like the other trash lining the A train's tracks between 14th and 23rd streets.

"Hurry. The last train was 15 minutes ago. There are still two blocks to go before 23rd Street. Another train will be coming soon. It's time to get off the tracks."

Sonny plants each foot on a wooden tie, avoiding the gooey muck oozing between the tracks.

Part hobby and part commute, exploring subway tracks in the predawn hours is a weekend routine on his way to the club. Wading through a subterranean swamp isn't part of most people's party-prep regime, but Sonny doesn't consider himself an ordinary party person.

"One block to go."

Sonny's heart beats harder, kind of frightened, yet exhilarated by the possibility of seeing a distant headlight appear in the darkness. A slow rumble rises from the tracks through his boots.

Quickly skipping from one tie to another, the glow from the 23rd Street subway station on Eighth Avenue begins lighting his surroundings, though not enough to warrant putting away his pocket flashlight. As the station's florescent glow grows brighter, a tussle bursts from the darkness.

"Fuck you, asshole! I hate you," someone yells.

Already tense, Sonny's heart jumps a bit more. There are other people on the opposite, southbound side of the tracks and real fear washes over him as sweat flows.

"How do you like this, you fucking faggot?" growls a voice from the darkness. Grunts puncture the tracks' putrid silence. "You like this?"

Sonny stops walking, afraid of moving closer to the unseen dispute. He looks back and there it is, a distant headlight. The tracks make a slight clanking, bracing themselves for a heavy onslaught. It's time to get out of that tunnel and there are only a two minutes before that train arrives at 23rd Street.

Sonny has no choice. He resumes his track-tie tip-toe. Like the rats he dreads and strangely admires, he quickly scampers along the rail and as more light splashes into the tunnel from the nearby station. Sonny sees the source of the yelling. The sight freezes him temporarily. Across the tracks, through the metal columns he sees two shadows, one hovering over the other with something in its hand.

"You like this better?" a kneeling man says to an obscure figure reclining against something.

The tracks begin their slow rumble, as the distant headlight grows brighter. Fearful of the train, Sonny takes another step and crushes an aluminum can. He slips, but regains his balance by flinging his right hand out, causing his metal lunch box's contents to clang loudly. The noise disrupt the stranger's rage. The angry man looks up and around, seeing a day-glo silhouette in the tunnel's twilight -- a waif with yellow hot pants and a matching t-shirt, black combat boots up to his knees and orange goggles on his forehead. The stranger drops his switchblade, surprised and frightened by the day-glo green bandages taped across half of Sonny's face.

Sonny locks eyes with the malevolent assailant, who stands up as he glares from beneath a sea captain's hat. All Sonny sees is the black hat and a menacing goatee because the stranger is half-hidden in the dark alcove. The increasing rumble shakes Sonny's feet and he runs towards the station platform, about 40 feet away. Surprised by the intrusion, the stranger hesitates for a moment, unsure what to do. He moves six feet towards the platform before noticing blood on his right hand.

Confused by the sight of Sonny, the stranger retreats into a humid murk in the black alcove, where he watches the waif run on the platform, the orange strap of his goggles pressed against his green hair and a pink Hello Kitty backpack violently bobbing up and down. The uptown A train roars as it approaches the station and the stranger drags his limp friend into the forgotten alcove. The fleeing waif's silhouette sears itself into the stranger's memory.

"What is that freak doing in the tunnel?" the stranger mumbles.

Chapter 2

The humid summer air vibrates outside the club by the time Sonny approaches. It's almost 3 a.m. and he runs most of the way from the subway station to the nightclub at W. 27th Street and the West Side Highway. He's shaking, out of breath and sweaty, so he pauses half a block from the entrance to open his lunchbox. The pen flashlight is still in his hand and it feels good letting go of it. He pulls a few tissues out of a package in the lunchbox, then he opens a compact to powder his face and apply some lipstick.

"What was that in the subway? What was that scary homeless guy doing? Was he killing someone?"

Sonny isn't sure what he'd just seen. It didn't look right and the kneeling homeless man had a sinister glare, so running was the best response, Sonny figures. There's still a crowd outside the entrance hoping to get in the door woman's good graces. The late-night hopefuls don't realize that there's no use trying to cultivate Cookie's favor. Her shift is almost over and she isn't in the mood to talk to anybody. Her job is to be selective and maintain a good balance in the club, which often means keeping groups of five guys from coming in. She's also supposed to limit the number of big-hair women who often wait outside the velvet ropes, hoping for their lucky break. Sonny approaches the no-luck clubbers and blows a whistle, drawing Cookie's attention.

"Darling, come in!," Cookie squeals in a scratchy voice.

"Muaah, Muaah," Cookie mumbles, pretending to kiss Sonny on both cheeks after he pushes his way through the small crowd. "You're here late. You missed the open bar!"

"I had costume drama," Sonny lies. "I couldn't decide what to wear."

"Child, in this heat you should have come naked," said Cookie, affecting a not-quite southern accent she often uses on stage during her drag shows.

"Oh no girl, that's tomorrow's look!" Sonny shoots back.

"Well if it is, find a prettier crotch cover. That dirty mop you trimmed last week was nastier than just letting your piece hang out," Cookie says, as she whips a long lock of her pink wig over her shoulder with the fairy princess wand she uses to point people out of the crowd.

She then waves the wand and gentle thrusts it into the waiting crowd, parting it. Then she ushers Sonny through the crowd and past the rope. The wand is Cookie's trademark and she typically carries it no matter the evening's look. When Cookie was a crack whore last week, the wand was a slender glass pipe she sucked at one end. With last week's slutty nurse ensemble, the wand was an anal thermometer she playfully shoved into clubbers' butt cleavage. Sonny laughs once he passes the rope. He takes the ticket that gets him into the club and Cookie returns to work.

"You're not getting in this club unless you bring a woman with you, and I'm taken," Cookie tells a group of men still waiting outside.

Once inside the club Sonny feels a huge relief. No need to run or look over his shoulder. He's safe. It's time to abandon all concern about what he might have seen in the subway. He's now at the Tunnel, one of New York City's hottest clubs where he's a minor celebrity. Sonny is thrilled that Cookie remembers last week's crotch wig. That means others either remember it or discussed it during the week. The scene he caused showing up in his repulsive getup overjoys him and adds to his petty self-satisfaction.

"Not bad for Cliffside Park," says Sonny, snapping his finger three times for each syllable in Cliffside Park, his northern New Jersey hometown just across the Hudson River from New York City.

He mouthed the words Cliffside Park, but he never acknowledges that place publicly. Certainly not at the Tunnel, where he's known as Sonny Delight from the East Village and not the former Sunil Beg from Cliffside Park, an identity and place that embarrass him.

"Sonny! Sonny! Make love to my camera!" orders Amanda Watson, who every night travels through clubland taking photos that sometimes appear in the newspapers.

Sonny obliges. He puts his hands on his hips and thrusts out his crotch. Then he makes a V with his fingers and wags his tongue between them.

"Ouch! You're hot," Amanda yells.

Sonny vamps some more, completely forgetting what he's seen just 30 minutes earlier. He's walked through a door, an alternate reality where he's no longer a struggling retail worker taking the subway at 2 a.m. to save money. He's a starlet. Amanda's fawning delivers a taste of the celebrity, even if all he does to achieve it is make a spectacle of himself. Amanda suddenly loses interest in Sonny's poses and plows into the crowd. Sonny is thirsty and ready for an escape after working all day until 8 p.m. He's off on Sunday, so tonight is a chance to escape his far-from-ideal fashion industry job in a downtown boutique with bitter queens hawking outlandish clothes to tourists.

"Sonny! You look fabulous!" yells Eagle, the evening's host.

Eagle pretends to kiss Sonny on both cheeks while he places something into his hand.

"Remember, I promised you a special party favor if you came and danced on the go-go box."

"Thank you!" Sonny squeals, clapping his hands and jumping a tiny bit. "I'll do it in a minute, as soon as a get a delicious cocktail" says Sonny.

"Sure, just don't get anything with liquor, you'll ruin the high. This is good stuff," Eagle promises about the ecstasy tablet.

Sonny swallows the pill before he even gets his ginger ale. Drink in hand, he passes by the coat check to drop off his Hello Kitty backpack, which contains all the clothes he'll need later to make it home on the subway without getting gay bashed.

"Sonny! Where have you been? I'm lonely on the go-go box and Eagle said you'd keep me company, darling" says Mount St. Helen with feigned affection. "Come, honey, come."

There's no resisting Helen, a seven foot drag queen in platforms, a towering bouffant wig and school teacher's glasses. Sonny shoves his coat-check ticket in his boot and lets St. Helen pull him towards the dance floor.

She picks him up, spins him around, and someone takes a picture. Both mug a little more, and Amanda comes by to take more pictures. Sonny revels in the attention. His behavior is the opposite of his journey to the club, where he avoids bright lights, wears a floor-length trench coat while on the trains and seeks the darkness of the subway tunnels to avoid judgmental gazes, or worse, violent homeboys. Once in the subway tunnel for the final stretch of his journey, he packs his coat in his bag so it doesn't get muck on the bottom hem.

"What did you do tonight?" St. Helen yells into Sonny's ear

over the blasting throb of the house music.

"Nothing. I came home from work and took a teeny disco nap. Then I had outfit drama. I almost came naked, hee-hee-hee," says Sonny with a practiced giggle.

The giggle is an exclamation point, a affectation, a nuisance. The giggle accentuates Sonny's Saturday morning, sing-song diction. It's part of Sonny Delight's new nursery school, childish persona.

The subway incident intrudes on Sonny's childish banter.

"What was that guy doing?" Sonny wonders again. "Was he killing somebody? Should I tell St. Helen? Would being known for running through subway tunnels be considered fabulous?"

Eagle comes by, waves to Sonny and St. Helen and then points to the go-go box. The ecstasy tab is taking hold, so Sonny and St. Helen obediently head to the go-go box under the DJ booth and climb on top. Once there, St. Helen grabs Sonny's hand and twirls him. The dance floor's lights get blurry as a cigarette haze forms around Sonny, comforting him.

Just a few blocks away, Pedro sits in the dark alcove with Steve for at least two hours after their dispute. With the heroin in full effect, all his rage dissipates. Pedro isn't sure what happened to Steve. Maybe the stab wounds aren't so bad.

"Steve always snorts more than his share, the greedy fuck."

Pedro doesn't flee the scene or recoil in horror from having a slouching, bleeding body lean on his right shoulder. He sits there, staring at Steve's outline in the darkness. After coming down a bit, he removes the shirt he wiped Steve's blood on and collects his belongings. Once the heroin wears off, a drugged buddy's head resting against the shoulder doesn't feel so snuggly. Pedro puts the bloody shirt in one of two bags hidden in the crawl space near the alcove where he and Steve often hang out when getting high. Nodding off in public is too dangerous because cops might try to make an arrest, or other homeless men might try to rob you.

"Wake up! What the fuck is wrong with you?" Pedro asks impatiently, shoving Steve's limp torso, which falls away from Pedro into the alcove's corner.

Even though the stabbing seems like a reasonable response to Steve's rejection earlier, Steve's stillness frightens Pedro. He gets up to leave.

Ever since meeting Steve three months ago at the homeless shelter's soup kitchen, Pedro wanted him in a way he hadn't felt since high school four years ago, when all he thought of was a former buddy. Steve's personality clicked with Pedro's and they laughed at each other's jokes. They both call themselves suburban refugees who came to the city to escape people who ostracized them. Pedro's desire for Steve was agitating. They spent most of their time together, but Pedro was reluctant to tell Steve he was gay for fear that Steve would shun him, as former classmates did in New Hyde Park on Long Island. Pedro and Steve spent most of Saturday, their last day together, collecting cans and begging in Washington Square Park. The arch at the park was a good place for panhandling because a lot of tourists go there.

It hadn't been an easy day because Pedro feelings for Steve were bothering him, and Steve, who was normally kind with Pedro, was in an abusive mood. By the end of the day they'd collected $30, enough for a $20 bag of heroin, some Mountain Dew and chips. After scoring some dope earlier that night, Steve suggested they go into the subway to party. Neither Steve nor Pedro had a long history with heroin. Both started using it about a year ago and neither liked shooting it, which is too hard to do anyway in a dark subway tunnel. In any case, their dealer on the Lower East Side had good stuff, so they conveniently snorted it.

Before taking their first snort, Steve took a switchblade from his bag and placed it between himself and Pedro. The understanding is that if some homeless asshole tries to steal from them, either one can grab the weapon and threaten the thief. Steve was fiending for a good high all day, so he took the first big snort from the bag once they settled into their alcove, a rail workers' hutch that originally allowed subway staff to stand at a safe distance from passing trains.

The subway tunnels have hutches throughout the city, but like much of the subway system, they were forgotten. By the 1980s many of them served as cubby holes for the homeless. Pedro heard about these hutches at the shelter and two months ago he convinced Steve to explore near the 23rd Street station after Steve's money got stolen at a municipal homeless shelter where they spent the night.

Their subterranean refuge is a retreat from the world, despite the filth and vermin crawling there. They use it as a place to get high and spend the "nodding" hours, when they get so wasted that they can't walk or function.

Pedro took the second snort from the bag, then Steve took another, emptying the glassine bag. Pedro was anxious and horny, unsure how he could be closer to Steve, who finally stopped berating him once they were settled. They opened the soda bottles and waited for "the wave," which hit Steve first. The heroin felt like stepping into Jello, and Steve's head slid on to Pedro's shoulder. The wave hadn't hit Pedro and he was aroused by having Steve's blond head on his shoulder, yet he was still feeling a simmering anger because of the way Steve treated him earlier that day. Still, Pedro tilted his head a bit until his cheek touched the top of Steve's head, which hurt a little because of Steve's spiky hair.

"That feels good," said Steve, referring to the wave.

Pedro's heart leapt even as the wave crashed over him, though less intensely. Aroused, Pedro put his hand on Steve's inner thigh. Pedro's heart beat faster and the anger turned sexual, aching for relief. Steve, wafting through heroin clouds, slumped a bit more on Pedro's shoulder. Pedro rubbed his cheek against Steve's head and then slowly moved his hand on to Steve's groin, caressing the object of his desire. Steve didn't respond and Pedro nervously stopped for a moment. The heroin wave, however, lowered Pedro's inhibitions and he continued exploring Steve's body until he'd passed his hand inside Steve's pants and on to Steve's soft cock. Steve's numbness diminished a bit and he became aware of what was going on.

"What are you doing? Don't get freaky on me, you fucking little faggot," Steve slurred, weakly pulling Pedro's hand out of his pants.

"Fuck you," said Pedro, slurring a bit himself. "I'm sick of your shit."

Pedro stumbled a bit as he got up.

"What the hell is wrong with you?" Pedro stammered, as he tried to kick Steve in the leg, knocking the switchblade against the wall.

"Get away," Steve mumbled.

"You want me to go away?" Pedro said, his numbed voice cracked.

"You go away, you fucking closet case," said Pedro, his anger penetrating the narcotic wave and sexual arousal swirling in his head.

He picked up the switchblade, not sure what to do, but wanting to hurt Steve, at least a little. He approached Steve, knelt, and vindictively thrust the weapon towards Steve's crotch, hitting Steve in the inner thigh.

"I'll go away. I'll leave you alone," said Pedro, pulling the blade from Steve's thigh. "You like this better?"

Steve didn't respond to the puncture, he was too high. Then Pedro hears the clanging of metal, and it wasn't the tracks bracing for the arrival of a train. He turned around and saw what he thought was a hallucination on the uptown tracks, which caused him to drop the knife.

Gathering his things to leave, Pedro realizes that there is a large amount of blood on the ground. Pedro didn't think he had stabbed Steve that hard. In fact, Pedro's attack was serious. He punctured Steve's inner thigh, slicing into his soft flesh about three inches, enough to sever the femoral artery.

The femoral artery is one of the body's superhighways for blood. Once it's severed, a person can bleed to death within minutes, which is what happened to Steve. Pedro doesn't know anything about physiology or femoral arteries, but that's what he's done, though he was so high he thought he'd simply cut Steve a bit. Three hours later it's too late to help Steve.

Pedro slips out of the alcove after an A train leaves the station. Peering on to the nearby 23rd Street platform, he makes sure no one is still on the tracks. It's around 6 a.m. on Sunday morning, so there is very little possibility of being seen by a commuter. Pedro carefully slinks through the turnstile so as not to awaken the token booth clerk, who's fallen asleep. He quickly walks up the stairs into the breaking dawn.

In the hostile daylight Pedro wanders towards the Hudson River, seeking a leaky fire hydrant. He has some of Steve's blood on his hands, and the dark stains are sticky. They scare him.

"Did I really stab him that bad? Why?"

Pedro doesn't have a good answer. He doesn't know why. It's another unanswerable question. In the past year he hasn't even tried to explain such questions. Nobody at the shelter, the Y or on the street ask for explanations; there's no reason to give excuses. Those are the obligations of a previous life he replaced last year with heroin.

Explanations are for the former Pedro Torres from Long Island, the artsy high school misfit with impulsive streaks, although he wasn't good at offering explanations back then either.

"I could use another bump," Pedro thinks in response to a familiar craving.

Heroin offers Pedro an impulsive path without worries. Heroin is his off-ramp. He doesn't have to deal with apartments, a job or his family. No need to act on inconvenient sexual longings. The numbing comfort makes everything wonderful.

"Finally," Pedro sighs at 10th Avenue, where he bends over the leaky hydrant.

The area is empty save for a few passing cars on the avenue. Luckily, the hydrant is on 24th Street on the south side of the street is about 50 feet from the corner, so the few passing northbound motorists barely notice him washing up, not that a driver would pay much attention to a dirty-looking homeless druggie washing up on the street. Pedro doesn't have any soap but the blood rubs off under the cool water flowing into the industrial street's gutter.

"Hey baby!", a hooker yells to a passing car on 10th Avenue ahead of him.

Pedro avoids potential trouble by walking on 24th Street all the way to 12th Avenue. A soup kitchen operates on the far west side in midtown and his cravings include breakfast. Twelfth Avenue is the most direct route. Steve pops into his mind.

"Why did I kill him? Was it the dope?"

Again, no good answer.

"I should go home and stop using. It's too rough out here. Why am I nodding off in tunnels when I have a nice house in New Hyde Park? It's not that bad, and I can go back to school."

Heroin makes it easy to fall asleep in a subway tunnel and it helps Pedro forget about dropping out of college, a big disappointment to his parents. It helps him forget about becoming a painter, not that he's painted anything recently. The homeless life doesn't allow for paints and brushes in the backpack, yet Pedro always describes himself as a painter when he meets people. He can prove it, too. The art supplies are in his locker at the YMCA. He actually hasn't painted anything in months, since leaving the School of Visual Arts.

"Why don't I stop using and go back to my art?"

Pedro doesn't answer his question, but there's a response he won't acknowledge. His main pursuit recently is chasing heroin, which is hard, but not as hard as art.

"What if they won't let me back into SVA?"

He sits on some warehouse steps once he reaches 12th Avenue and he stares across the road to the Hudson River and New Jersey beyond.

"Why did I stab Steve?"

He thinks about Steve's spiky blond hair and his pale blue eyes. He's a beautiful junkie, sexy, with a hint of danger. Pedro felt instant attraction when Steve struck up a conversation at a church soup kitchen. Pedro wanted him the way he'd wanted another blond guy in high school, though back then he was horrified by that desire. New Hyde Park High School wasn't the friendliest place and he already felt like an outcast because of the dark music he liked. He didn't have many friends, so he found refuge in eccentricity. Getting high with the stoner kids offered some relief, but it never lasted long. Still, he craved the relief and he slowly devoted himself full-time to seeking the comfortable numbness after starting college. The pursuit eventually required leaving school, falling out with his parents and postponing an art career.

"I'm not getting high anymore," Pedro promises himself after the cascade of memories shuffle through his sobering mind. "I'm going back to school."

With that flash of resolve, Pedro gets up and resumes walking north on 12th Avenue. As he approaches 27th Street, he notices a commotion ahead. He stops near the corner to watch two outlandish drag queens stand in the dawn's glare vamping and screaming. A black drag queen in a pink wig screams.

"Sonny, Sonny, the taxi's here and we're hungry. Hurry, bitch!"

Pedro gasps. A freaky waif bursts out of the warehouse, down the stairs and into the waiting taxi. Pedro doesn't get a good look. All he sees well is green hair and a pink backpack before the taxi bolts up 12th Avenue.

Chapter 3

Sonny doesn't work on Sundays, so he accepts Cookie's

invitation to crash at her place after breakfast. They wait almost 40 minutes to get paid at the Tunnel as the patrons begin filing out. That's often the case. The club owner uses clubbers like Sonny and Cookie to lure patrons seeking a circus. He doesn't pay them until the end of the night so they don't leave early and deprive the party of its color. Sonny doesn't mind. He's still high on the ecstasy, so waiting in the line is just another opportunity to vamp with the other go-go dancers. Cookie screams, affecting a faux southern accent and fondling her "breasts" as if she'd just turned a trick.

"Where's mah muhney! Mama needs some shuh-gah!"

Sonny squeals with forced laughter.

"Here you go, bay-bee!" Sonny yells in response as he pretends to slip a bill into Cookie's "cleavage." He slides his body against Cookie and then feigns going down on her. "Now I want my SHUH-gah, bitch!"

"Ooooh child!", Cookie yells. "Mama needs a tip for that kind of treat!"

They both laugh as others in the employee line and some of the remaining clubbers sitting on nearby sofas watch, some smiling or laughing. Others just stare blankly at the horseplay and showtime isn't over. Sonny spent at least three hours on the club's go-go boxes, high on the pill Eagle gave him. Cookie took one of Eagle's pills right before her shift ended at 4. Even though the sun is dawning, the show is reaching its climax for Sonny and Cookie. They'd spent hours showing off for the paying customers. Now that the party is over, they're discussing breakfast options. They're not particularly tired because the drugs haven't quite worn off. Since the club is half empty they'd lost some of their steam; there aren't enough spectators to fuel their antics. Without the ogling crowds, Sonny's and Cookie's lust for partying wanes somewhat.

"Let's go to Moonstruck," says Cookie, suggesting the restaurant with burning excitement.

"Yes, of course, daaah-ling!" says Sonny, bowing as if worshiping at an altar.

Cookie and Sonny generally speak to each other in this tone, whether they're high or not. Every suggestion is a dramatic exclamation or breathless statement. It doesn't matter where they're standing. Someone might be watching, so there must be a show. The ostentatious behavior isn't the fruit of any conscious decision or secret understanding between Sonny and Cookie or among any of the club kids. It's an unstated code of conduct, a mask as outlandish as any makeup the club kids misapply. Do they need to go the bathroom? Yes! It becomes a pilgrimage through the club, gathering others along the way until the arrival in a bathroom becomes a homecoming. Cookie's effusive suggestion that they eat at Moonstruck isn't even an original idea; they eat there all the time. Nonetheless, they both gush with excitement at the prospect of once again sitting in a booth with ripped seats and unflattering lighting.

The pay line finally starts moving and Sonny gets his $75 go-go dancing fee. It really isn't much considering how much time and energy Sonny spends assembling his outfit and makeup. Still, he needs it for the rent, which was due four days ago. Cookie gets $250, a fee she feels is too little considering her job, which is basically to make it difficult to get into the club and ensure that as many people are intimidated into paying full price. Cookie figures the club owners make tens of thousands from her work, so she's resentful that she doesn't make more. Still, she's unable to argue for more pay because what choice did she have? It's not as if eccentric transvestites have an abundance of job opportunities.

"It beats hooking," Cookie reminds herself as she receives her pay, watching the club accountant lay it out in front of her.

Cookie thinks she's a celebrated diva of the night at the club, but she knows what it's like to turn tricks. Many of the drag queens resort to prostitution in a fix. New York City is a paradise for tranny hookers and there are several neighborhoods where "women" like Cookie strut and raise some cash. There are even bars that facilitate such transactions. Trannies are able to easily turn tricks because the city's police department doesn't place much importance on the activity. Money in hand, Sonny and Cookie head for the coat check to retrieve their belongings. It's the middle of summer, so the coat check isn't particularly crowded, yet there's still a need for the service. Clubbers like Sonny have bags to check, along with the young gays from the outer boroughs and the suburbs who leave their neighborhoods covered up and change in cars or the club's bathrooms.

Cookie retrieves her long overcoat but doesn't put it on. Sonny didn't change either and simply straps on his Hello Kitty backpack. St. Helen is chatting near the coat check, but she doesn't have anything checked because she lives in Manhattan and simply takes a taxi.

"Let's go to Moostruck!"

Sonny excitedly claps his hands over his suggestion.

"I'd looove to," says St. Helen, raising her hand above her head and then slowly slithering her hand down and around her face, as if posing for an invisible camera.

It's not clear what St. Helen is on tonight, but Sonny jumps with joy that she accepts the invitation. The trio heads for the door, but not before bidding farewell to the lingering club kids, all of whom are invited to the restaurant. None accept because most are either too high to eat and not hungry, or they're drunk and not hungry. Others won't come because they can't afford a breakfast, since they spent all their money.

The club kid farewells aren't quick. They walk around at the end of the night and bidding each other elaborate goodbyes, as if someone were taking a long, dangerous journey with no guaranteed return, like when the Pilgrims left Europe for the New World. After streams of air kisses, Cookie and St. Helen walk outside to the waiting taxi. At this early Sunday hour, a lot of the cab drivers know that waiting by the Tunnel is a sure bet for fares. Some of the cabbies expect something other than cash when drag queens who spent all their money that night climb aboard. In the blinding sunlight, Cookie calls out to Sonny, who's still making his final, parting kisses. Sonny triumphantly bursts out of the Tunnel's side entrance on the West Side Highway, as if he's a superhero breaking through a wall. He lands on the sidewalk in a kung-fu pose after jumping from the top of a five-step staircase. It's another show for no one in particular except the taxi driver. The audience is larger than Sonny realizes.

The drag queens laugh and bark the directions to Moonstruck at 23rd Street and Ninth Avenue. The taxi heads north on the West Side Highway, turning right at 28th Street as a bedraggled man stares from the southeast corner of 27th Street, shaken by a flash of recognition.

"Fuck. Fuck," Pedro mumbles to himself, the words echoing through his head, crowding out other thoughts.

He's confused, frightened and crashing. The narcotic embrace releases Pedro. He sits on a warehouse step across the street from the building where he just saw the subway freak with the backpack as pain shoots up his lower back.

"That's him. What's he doing here?"

Pedro scans the building's facade and notices a small placard above a door with the word Tunnel.

"What did I do? Fuck. Why does my back hurt so much? I can't nod off in the subway anymore. Fuck. Fuck! What should I do?"

Pedro repeats the question like a prayer, as if by chanting the question some god will send an answer. There's none.

"That freak saw me kill Steve. How could I be so stupid? I didn't mean to kill him. It was an accident."

Pedro rises from the step and passes the Tunnel, noting its location on 27th Street and 12th Avenue. Hunger gnaws at him and he doesn't want to get to the soup kitchen late or he'll miss their breakfast.

"What should I do?"

Paranoia descends. Pedro checks to see if he's being followed, then he checks his clothes in case they're bloody. They aren't. Still nervous, he checks his reflection in a window and he's slightly repulsed by what he sees: an unshaven young man with tired, dark eyes, yet he's still attractive in a dangerous way.

"What if the police come for me? If they find Steve, how will they know I did it? They don't know who I am. The only person who saw me in the subway was the freak. Would he tell the cops? Would the cops believe him? Fuck."

He stops walking uptown.

"Maybe I should go back to the subway and check on him. He might just be really high. Maybe I didn't wake him up right? He might be awake now, and he's gonna be pissed that I cut him. Why did I do that? I wasn't that mad at him."

Pedro stands motionless on the sidewalk, vaguely staring at the Hudson River, but not really seeing it. For the few passing drivers on 12th Avenue, he's just another crazy homeless man doing something peculiar. None of the passing cars' occupants pay enough attention to slow down.

"Why did I do that?"

The question is unanswerable for a person who has spent the past year avoiding questions. Heroin is a good way of avoiding uncomfortable questions, because he doesn't ask himself any when he's high. No need to struggle for answers while floating in a blissful present, with no nagging future or past.

"What am I gonna do?"

Pedro resumes his path to the soup kitchen. There's no point in returning to the subway. He knows what he's done. His feelings for Steve well up again, a combination of sexual attraction and resentment.

"Why doesn't he want me?"

Pedro is confused by his emotions, as tears form in his eyes. He continues walking to midtown, only passing the occasional early-morning worker. Like his crash and hangover, he can't shake the feelings.

"Shit. Should I tell the cops? Maybe they can help Steve? How am I gonna tell them that I accidentally stabbed my friend in the subway? Should I tell them I was high and I didn't realize what I was doing?"

Confessing isn't an option. Pedro hates police and he won't speak to them.

"Maybe when Steve wakes up, he'll go to the emergency room and they'll take care of him. We've done it before, and it wasn't a problem."

Pedro recalls when Steve was really high and fell on some stairs two months ago, gashing his head on a handrail and needing stitches.

"That's what he'll do, and then he'll be back at the east side soup kitchen around dinner time. He's gonna be pissed at me. What am I gonna tell him?"

Pedro feels reassured. Maybe Steve isn't dead. He's just really high and Pedro will argue with him later over the wound. Steve's trip to the emergency room makes sense, until he walks into the westside soup kitchen.

"Where's your buddy?" asks Zoom, a can collector who sometimes eats with Steve and Pedro.

"I don't know. He's high somewhere," Pedro mumbles.

Sitting at a table by himself, Pedro eats his stale bagel and banana, served with a cup of coffee. He's nauseated, but forces himself to eat, staring into his coffee.

"How is he gonna climb the steps if he has that cut in his leg?

Should I go back there and help him?"

Pedro stands, then sits again, still contemplating a series of questions about how Steve will leave the subway. He's comforted by the imagined scenarios.

"It's time to go," a volunteer says, gently knocking on the table surface near Pedro.

Pedro snaps out of his reverie, gulping the last of his coffee with the bagel. Exiting the church basement, the sunlight amplifies an incessant question echoing through his mind.

"What now?"

There's a decent crowd at Moonstruck around 6 a.m. because other clubs in the area are also disgorging their customers, so drunk suburbanites trying to sober up sit across the aisles from rowdy college students, a few early-riser senior citizens and some prostitutes done for the night. Cookie walks into the restaurant as if taking the stage with a spotlight focused on her. She dramatically pushes the restaurant's door open, bursts through and juts her right shoulder forward, cocking her head back until she's looking up at the ceiling.

"Woooooork!" she yells to no one in particular, turning her face slowly away from the ceiling.

The many of the customers turn to check who's yelling, which is what Cookie wants, as if her makeup and outlandish attire weren't enough of an attention grabber. She struts down one of the aisles, as some of the customers gasp and whisper "Oh my God," others laugh and more look but say nothing. Cookie hates the silent ones and she's intent on getting them to react. Sashaying up the aisle, past an empty booth, to the end of the dining room, she turns around as if on the catwalk and returns to the empty booth, puts her foot on the bench and then runs her hands along her leg, ending the gesture with a slap on her ass. One of the silent customers shakes his head in disgust and Cookie is satisfied, beckoning to Sonny and St. Helen.

"Girl, you're in no mood for eating," says St. Helen.

"Of course I am," Cookie motions indiscreetly towards a table of young suburbanites. "I'd looove some Italian sausage!"

"Ooooh, they don't serve that here, you naughty girl," says St. Helen said, cooing like a mourning dove.

The waitress approaches the table and impatiently asks the trio to order. She's in no mood for the club kid show. The waitress has seen it before, she wasn't entertained the first or last time she saw it.

"I'll have a Monte Cristo," St. Helen coos.

"How can you eat that and keep such a pret-ty, pret-ty figure?" Sonny squeaks, referring to the cross between french toast and a ham and cheese sandwich.

Such a heavy dish is too much for Cookie's and Sonny's ecstasy-suppressed appetites.

"I'll have a fruit cup with a dab of whipped cream, darling," Cookie orders.

"I'll have the wheat toast with butter and some heeerb teeeeea!" Sonny orders.

"Excuse me," says St. Helen, getting up to visit the bathroom.

"Yes, girl, go wash those hands!" Cookie yelled, disrupting the dining room again. "I know where those hands have been and they are NOT clean."

One of the prostitutes in a nearby booth raises her hand in the air and nods her head, as if in church offering an amen to Cookie's wisecrack. St. Helen's trip to the bathroom isn't as loud as Cookie's entrance romp, but it's no less dramatic. Channeling tipsy divas, St. Helen takes a few steps forward, then totters a little as if she's about to fall off her six-inch platforms. Customers in the booth next to her "show" recoil. Bracing herself on a chair and startling a diner, she adjusts her school teacher glasses to make them completely crooked on her face. She then takes a few more careful steps forward, adding a little wobble to her gait as she holds both arms aloft for "balance." St. Helen gets what she wants, which is the attention of several diners in the restaurant, who possibly wonder if the green-hair Frankenstein will tumble face-first in a plate of home fries. St. Helen arrives at the bathrooms and disappears around a hallway.

"She's not high," Sonny protests to Cookie. "I didn't see her take anything tonight."

"She's a glamorous mess, but not messy," Cookie observes. "It wouldn't be cute if she was really fucked up, but her messy walk is fabulous. It's drunk starlet realness."

Sonny takes a prolonged drink from his glass, emptying it by more than half. He'd realizes that he hadn't taken a sip of water in hours and his mouth feels dry with a disagreeable minty film from the gum he's chewing, which he now spits into a napkin because it's beginning to disintegrate in his mouth. Drugs like ecstasy, coke and speed have that effect on gum.

"Did you have fun tooo-niiight?" Sonny asks Cookie.

"Hell no. You wouldn't have fun either if you had to stand at the door for all those hours trying to get all those annoying people to go away. But I shouldn't complain, since it pays the bills. I was hoping Andre would show up tonight so I could spend some time with him," Cookie says of her current heartthrob. "But that shady boy didn't show up, even though he said he would."

"You're always chasing those straight boys. Give it up, girl, you'll never get them in bed," says Sonny, wiping imaginary tears from his face.

"Oh yes I will. Remember Dougie? He's straight," Cookie said triumphantly.

Sonny replies, singing a jingle.

"Sucking off a straight guy--in a bathroom stall--with a limp dick because he's wasted on ecstasy isn't the same as getting them in bed, nana-nana-na!"

"Can you keep your chit-chat down," the waitress asks in an annoyed tone as she delivers the trio's orders. "You're disturbing the other customers."

St. Helen returns from the bathroom as the waitress finished delivering the food.

"What took you so long? Were you douching?," Cookie said.

"Voices down, ladies," said the waitress, shooting another annoyed glare at Cookie.

Cookie tones herself down a bit. She doesn't want to risk the waitress asking her to leave, which was what happened at the diner across the street last month when she was tweaking just a bit too hard.

"So, did anyone see any good scandals tonight?" Cookie asks in a hushed tone, as if discussing a secret.

"I saw Sarah Sunshine making out with that techno boy Dougie," St. Helen said.

"Do not mention his name or that slut's name," Cookie interrupts. "I'm over him."

"You're just jealous," says St. Helen, pouring syrup on her Monte Cristo. "You can't compete with a real girl and it burns you up."

"Oh please," says Cookie, dabbing her dessert spoon ever so slightly into the whipped cream on her fruit cup and then giving the spoon a dainty lick, as if testing it for poison.

"I met this French guy who was captivated by my look," says St. Helen, touching her pendant earring. "He bought me a drink and chatted me up, but I couldn't understand much of what he was saying. Anyway, after we danced he told me it was his first time in the United States and he wanted to know what we American girls are like. I told him I'm a lady and invited him to the lounge, where he bought me another drink. When we were sitting on the sofas he put his hand on my leg and pushed up my skirt a bit. I play slapped his hand and told him I was a nice girl."

St. Helen recounts her tale with excitement between bites of the gooey sandwich. Sonny and Cookie play with their food, awaiting St. Helen's next revelation.

"Eventually he put his hand on my leg again and pushed my skirt up just a little bit, then he invited me to spend the night at his hotel. I took his hand and led him to the dark part of the club, where I put my hands down his pants and felt his hard dick. He was big. Then he reached into my shirt to touch my chest, and that's when he found my tape and socks. He acted surprised when he didn't find the big boobies he wanted and he started yelling in French," says St. Helen, laughing.

The surgical tape she wears around her chest and back, just under her nipple line heaves up her chest flab and makes her look like she has a nice cleavage.

"He told me 'I know you're a she-male, but I at least expect something up here. I don't like this.' Then he pulled my hand out of his pants left me there by myself! I wasn't artificial enough for him. Can you believe that?" St. Helen asks with indignation.

Cookie and Sonny both laugh with glee at St. Helen's misfortune.

"Living in Americaaaah," Cookie sings, lampooning the James Brown hit.

Cookie can't let St. Helen's French tourist story be the evening's highlight, so she embellishes an incident she witnessed while touching up her makeup after her shift ended.

"You should have been in the bathroom when I had to call security," Cookie says dramatically about her favorite stage, the Tunnel's bathrooms.

There is invariably a gaggle of drag queens and club kids in the bathroom. Ostensibly they're adjusting their makeup, but in effect it's another lounge with easily accessible stalls for a quick fix or sex. During Sonny's breaks, he goes right to the bathroom to see who's hanging out there. He didn't see any incident requiring security tonight, so he feels excluded as Cookie begins her story.

"Everybody is in the bathroom around 4 and I'd gone up there for a face adjustment after my shift ended. I was a mess because it was so hot outside and the antiperspirant I put on my face wasn't working right. I guess I didn't put on enough before beating my face. Anyway, I had my napkins ready for a touch up when Jett Girl walks in. She was a mess, and of course she was working on a full drink in her hand. She must have decided to take a little vacation from the ecstasy."

Cookie dabs more whipped cream in her mouth before continuing.

"I don't like hanging out with her when she's drinking because she gets mean, so I knew there might be trouble when she walked in because she was looking aggressive. Then she screamed 'Where's Twinkie?' I told her I hadn't see Twinkie since she arrived at the club hours ago. I also suggested that she was looking a bit messy and she needed to put that drink down, but she didn't."

Cookie arches her left eyebrow, always her facial sign that she's delivering scandal.

"That's when Twinkie comes out of a stall with Andy, and Jett Girl flips out! 'You fucking bitch! I'm a cut you,' Jett Girl said. She threw her drink at Twinkie, but she was so wasted that she missed and hit some of the queens by the sink. It was like turning the lights on in the projects and watching the roaches scatter. There was screaming as some of the queens ran out. Jett Girl then hit her glass against the wall to break it. I guess that's what she was going to use to cut Twinkie, but she was so wasted that the glass smashed into small pieces. That's when I notice a big red splotch on my outfit. Some of that bitch's vodka-cranberry landed on me and I was furious. Twinkie was just standing there. Either she was scared or maybe too high to react, I don't know. I walked over to Jett Girl and pushed her. I didn't think I'd pushed her that hard but she went flying against the wall and fell on the floor, so call me Superbitch. I called the security guard who stands outside the bathrooms and told him about Jett Girl's threats. He picked her up and took her outside. If she comes back next week, I'm not letting her in. Basically, I rescued that fool Twinkie from getting her stupid pretty face slashed for fooling around with Jett Girl's man, though I don't understand what those straight girls see in that scuzzy skater boy. He's not worth fighting over and I wouldn't have sex with him unless he paid me. And he ain't got no money!"

St. Helen and Sonny laugh with glee, as Cookie puts another dainty scoop of whipped cream in her mouth.

It's Sonny's turn to share something that tops St. Helen's and Cookie's stories, but he doesn't have much to offer. Sonny wants to move up in the club world's petty pecking order and he's grateful that Cookie and St. Helen befriended him, but he hasn't yet mastered their art of ostentatious storytelling. There's something Sonny could tell them; no embellishment required.

"You're not going to believe what happened on my way to the club, but it's true," Sonny says in a half-whispered tone.

"Reeeelly," purrs Cookie, taking another grotesquely sexy lick of whipped cream from her spoon, her fleshy tongue poking between her large florescent pink lips, which match her wig.

"Yeah, you…will….gag," Sonny brags, bobbing his head with each word.

"Well come on, bitch, tell us," Cookie demands.

"Do you ever wonder why I wear these beat up combat boots with my outfits?"

"Yeah, 'cause you po'," Cookie replies, channeling her best Pam Grier imitation from the 1973 blaxploitation classic "Coffy."

"Nooooo, that's just one reason," Sonny admits, embarrassed that Cookie perceives his paycheck-to-paycheck existence. "I've never told anybody this before, but I have a fabulous, secret hobby that I sometimes do before and after I go nightclubbing and I need to wear these boots."

"Are you a dominatrix?" St. Helen asks, cooing excitedly at the thought.

"No! Hee, hee, hee. I'd probably make good money doing

that! I have this deep, secret hobby. I've never told anyone in the club scene. Nobody would understand. It's something I've been doing for the past year and I figured that if I told people in the scene they'd think it was gross."

"Well what is it? Are you into scat?" Cookie asks impatiently, tapping her garish plastic nails on the tabletop.

"I'll start at the beginning. When I was younger I didn't have a lot of friends, so I'd spend a lot of time reading. One of my favorite things to read was comic books, especially the X-Men."

"I never heard of them," St. Helen interrupts.

"It's a group of superheroes who are mutants and they fight evil mutants. How come you never heard of them? Anyway, darling, there are other mutants in the X-Men who aren't heroes or evil, they just want to be left alone, in their creepy, murky UNDERWORLD," Sonny says in a near whisper.

"They're called the Morlocks and they live in the subway tunnels in New York City."

"You read comic books? You're goofy," says Cookie, laughing and already judging Sonny.

"I don't read them any mo-ore!" Sonny lies defensively, worried that this story might affect his reputation in clubland.

"Anyway, when I finally moved to New York and started taking subways I remembered the Morlocks and all the comic books I read back then," says Sonny, who still visits comic book stores when he's bored or lonely. "The Morlocks live in underground tunnels, but, uh, they aren't the actual subway tunnels....they're below the subway. The entrances to the Morlocks' tunnels are almost always in the subway tunnels, usually between the subway stations. One night when I was waiting for the L train on Eighth Avenue I was looking down the tunnel. I could see the next station at Sixth Avenue and I thought about the Morlocks. I've seen subway workers walking through the tunnels when they're doing track work, and that reminded me of the Morlocks too. So one night at the end of last summer I was really fucked up. Remember that FA-bulous party we held on the abandoned elevated train tracks on Tenth Avenue?"

"Oooh, that one is very fuzzy," St. Helen whispers, faking a hiccup.

"Yeah, I drank a lot that night too, hee hee hee," said Sonny, punctuating his statement with a trademark Woody Woodpecker laugh. "After the police broke it up I couldn't go anywhere else because it was already five in the morning and I didn't want to waste any of my go-go dancing pay on taxis to the after-hours clubs. I decided to be thrifty and take the subway home, since it was only a few blocks to the L train station at Eight Avenue and 14th Street. It was really hot that night and I'd left my overcoat home because it was too much to wear. Usually keep it in my backpack to wear on the subway so I don't get hassled. That night I got dressed at Jello's house, so I didn't need the coat. After I got in the subway I realized I'd just missed the train and there was no one on the platform. I waited for the next train and I started staring into the tunnels, thinking about the Morlocks and their MARvelous world. Then I heard all this yelling. It was a bunch of rowdy homeboys coming down the stairs. I immediately walked all the way to the east side of the tunnel, hoping that they wouldn't come over to that side."

"I smell trouble!," says Cookie, half singing.

"You're right!" says Sonny, pleased that his tale is entertaining Cookie and St. Helen.

With luck, in the next few days they'll tell others some version of this story, exaggerating the highlights and forgetting the boring elements.

"I'm not sure how many homeboys there were, uh, uh, it sounded like there were at least FIVE of them," Sonny gasps. "I hid behind a stairwell so they couldn't see me. I could hear they were throwing something at each other, maybe a hat. I could hear that they were running around the platform and I started getting nervous because I didn't want them to see me. I can't remember what I was wearing that night, but it was last summer when I had the shaved eyebrows replaced with the evil unibrow. I was probably wearing something skimpy, hot pants for sure, so I knew there could be trouble if they saw me."

"Oh God, I hate those situations," says Cookie. "That's why I carried mace, but it kept getting confiscated by security in the clubs, so I gave that up and just started taking taxis. It's less drama."

"It's more expensive, too!" Sonny interjects. "I was nervous that it was only a matter of time before the homies saw me and I was too high to deal with them. I heard one come close to the end of the platform where I was. Then I did it! I ran on to a little staircase next to the platform that the subway workers use to go into the tracks!"

"Weren't you afraid of getting electrocuted?" St Helen asks, looking genuinely alarmed.

"I was so scared! But I'd seen the subway workers walking on the tracks all the time during their track work, so how dangerous could it be? I ran into the tunnel, it was so SPOOKY. I was trying to step on the wooden track ties and avoid the rails. The is the dangerous one, but I wasn't sure which of the rails was the dangerous one, so I avoided all of them. I could have been killed, hee hee hee!"

"You could have been killed," St. Helen whispers.

"But not by a train. You have to remember that the L train station at Eighth Avenue is the end of the line and I was on the track headed to Brooklyn, so I knew there wasn't any danger of a train hitting me because there was no train at the station, otherwise I would have been sitting in it."

"I can't tell you how exciting it is going into the tracks. Remember the time we broke into the public pool in the Lower East Side in the middle of the night to go swimming? It's just like that, but not as fabulous! It's also scary, because when you're waiting on the platform in the station at night you see so many disgusting things....giant roaches, mice and rats, yuk! I was more worried about stepping on a rat than on the third rail! When I was midway between the Eighth Avenue and Sixth Avenue station, I, uh, uh, heard the rumble of a train. Then I did get really scared, even though I knew it was coming in the other direction. I got near the wall so a conductor wouldn't see me. It's probably against the law to be walking through the tracks, but do they ever arrest people for that? Have you ever heard of any of the homeless people who live in the tunnels getting arrested? The train passed me and then pulled in to the Eighth Avenue station. That's when I knew that I had to hurry up and get to the Sixth Avenue station before that train started up again on the way towards Brooklyn. Fortunately, I knew that when that train pulls into Eight Avenue the conductor has to take his gear from the front car and then walk all the way to the opposite end of the platform to get into the new front of the train before heading back to Brooklyn. Do you know how many times I saw the conductor do that after waiting so long for that fucking train? And those bitches walk so slow! Anyway, the waddling conductor gave me time to reach Sixth Avenue, waddle, waddle!"

"You're a real life Warlock," Cookie says laughing.

"They're called Morlocks, girl, and they're FIERCE," Sonny replies, snapping his fingers. "I tip-toed, tip-toed real fast towards Sixth Avenue. It's really not as far as you'd think, and it's not pitch black in the tunnel either. Once I stepped in this disgusting puddle and it left my boot covered with a disgusting muck, so nasty, I was gagging! Luckily, the club was so crowded that nobody could see my boots. AnyWAY, I eventually made it to the Sixth Avenue station and I found the little worker staircase to get back on the platform, but then I realized I couldn't just stroll up the stairs and into the light as if nothing happened. I was worried someone might see me. Luckily, since it must have been 5 a.m., there wasn't anyone at that end of the platform and I quietly stepped out of the darkness. I hid behind the nearest stairwell and checked my boots. Nothing really happened to them and then I hear the rumble of the train. I immediately walked towards the other end of the platform so I could be in the front of the train, since the homies always like to ride towards the back. I almost made it to the front of the platform by the time the train rushed into the station and I got into a car with just a few people who weren't troublemakers."

Cookie slaps the back of her right hand against the palm of her left hand.

"That's a cute adventure, but what does it have to do with anything that happened tonight?"

"I'm not DONE! You're so impatient! I'm giving you background info. I'm painting a picture, diva, so you don't think I'm crazy."

"You are crazy, queen. Normal people don't go walking through subway tunnels."

"You can't imagine how exciting it is. My heart was pounding like I took a giant hit off a crack pipe. It also saved me from having to deal with a pack of homies. I felt like a fabulous SUPERhero. After that first time, I started exploring the tunnels because I realized it wasn't so dangerous. That's what I was doing earlier this evening before I got to the Tunnel. I was exploring the tunnel between Eighth Avenue and 23rd Street because I had just missed the train and I figured it would be a good way to kill some time and get to the station without having to wait for the next train. I've had a lot of practice walking through the subway tunnels in the past few months, so I'm pretty good at hopping from tie to tie. I decided to go through the tunnel fast because it's about nine blocks from one station to the other, and I didn't want to linger in case another train came. There wasn't anything weird about my run through the tunnel, which is still exciting every time I do it. My heart was pounding, and not from hurrying through the tunnel. Not knowing when the train is such a rush that feels like drugs."

"You could be killed," St. Helen whispers.

"No, I've got it figured out. At that time of night, so few trains are running that the two times a train did come and I wasn't near the platform, I just jumped into the tracks on the other side. It's fun, tee-hee-hee! Anyway, earlier tonight I was only about a block from the platform when I heard some shouting in the tunnel. In all the times I'd been in the tunnels, I'd never seen anyone down there, although I did fantasize about meeting a Morlock. I think it was a homeless bum on the other side of the tracks. He was standing in these little rooms in the tunnels that I guess the subway workers stand in when trains are coming. Anyway, he was yelling at someone, maybe another bum. I couldn't tell because it was dark."

"What did he do when he saw you," St. Helen asks.

"He didn't see me at first. He was yelling and cursing at someone. That's when I saw the KNIFE in his hand! I gagged! Then I got scared, because I felt the clanking of the rails, which means a train is coming. He couldn't see me because his back was turned to me. In my rush to go by unnoticed before the train arrived I slipped on something, maybe a soda can. I almost fell except that I had my lunchbox. I swung to help me keep my balance, but the noises from inside my lunchbox caught his attention. He turned around and saw me! I didn't know what to do. I panicked. Maybe he'd kill me! I couldn't see that well because of the darkness, but he was wearing a sailor's cap. If he was a Morlock, I'd call him Capt. Zero. After he saw me he dropped the knife and I got more scared and ran towards the platform. I climbed on the platform and ran towards the stairs. I tore through the turnstile just as the train was pulling into the station and I didn't look back. Up on Eighth Avenue I ran to 24th Street and then headed west towards the Tunnel. Luckily he didn't follow me. I was safe. I survived a horrible ORDEAL!"

"That's crazy," says Cookie. "Are you sure you saw a knife?"

"Yes, yes, I couldn't see his face that well, but I definitely saw the knife."

"What was he doing with it?" St. Helen asks.

"He was cussing at someone, calling them a faggot. I heard grunting from the other person, who must have been a man. I don't know what he was doing with the knife and I wasn't going to hang around, especially when I heard him yelling about faggots. That's a cue to get the hell out of there."

"You did the right thing. Girlfriend, ain't no one gonna top that adventure tonight," Cookie says laughing as the trio pull out their money to settle the check. "You win tonight, Sonny, but just wait 'til next week."

"If Andre shows up at Tunnel when I'm working, nobody's drama is going to top mine," Cookie says, hissing and flexing her hands to display her claws.

Chapter 4

"Where should I go?"

There's no one to respond and Pedro usually keeps to himself anyway. Normally he talks with Steve because it isn't safe to be too friendly with the bums. The shelter's drama can be dangerous, so it's easier to shut up. That silence is superficial; an inner chatter continues, with no one to answer his questions.

Like a fly hit with bug spray, Pedro stumbles after leaving the soup kitchen.

"Should I go uptown, downtown? Which park should I take a nap in?"

It's a beautiful, sunny morning, which only makes Pedro feel worse. After a couple of trips around the same block, he decides to walk downtown and sleep in Madison Square Park by 23rd Street. There are lots of nice trees and benches there, and since it's surrounded by offices, not many people. On the way to the park, Pedro can't resist the urge to see the subway station at 23rd and 8th Avenue.

"Has he come out yet?"

It's about 8 a.m. and most of the people walking around are a mix of churchgoers and joggers. Feeling numb, Pedro walks like a zombie among them and he's ignored. He's another vagrant in a city overrun by bums, beggars and squeegee men vying to wash car windshields with dirty water. Pedro takes great offense when New York lump him in the same group with homeless bums. He's an artist and he dresses like one. In fact, he dresses differently from a typical homeless man. Pedro has the disheveled, heroin-chic style popular among New York City's art-school set. Besides his trademark black captain's hat and goatee, Pedro's long, black sideburns and skinny black jeans with scuffed black combat boots suggest that he's slumming. He's a slightly dirtier version of his fellow students at the School of Visual Arts, where he dropped out last semester after failing some of his classes. He thinks the drugs make him more creative, but they didn't get the homework done.

Until recently, Pedro and Steve maintained a modicum of style and cleanliness by begging up enough money to pay for the showers at the YMCA. The Y is better than a shelter because it's less dangerous.

The Sunday morning sun isn't kind. Pedro feels like shit and the passers-by avoid him. He smells too, since he's been getting high in the subway tunnels, basically a drier version of the sewers. Walking east on 23rd Street, Pedro approaches the movie theater near the subway tunnel.

"What if there are police?"

Pedro feels a lump in his throat, a knot in his stomach and his heart palpitates. His breathing gets shallow and sweat forms on his upper lip. Pedro continues walking towards the subway.

"Just walk like there is nothing wrong. It's Sunday morning. I'm just goin' to the diner to get breakfast."

Pedro practices an alibi if some cop jumps out of a stairwell to question him. Reaching Eighth Avenue, he looks to all the entrances at the four corners, seeing no cops. He dares not go down into the station, as a morbid dread slips down his spine. Instead, he continues walking, crosses Eighth Avenue and heads towards Madison Square Park three avenues away.

"Fuck, fuck, fuck. What am I gonna do?"

Pedro walks faster, then slower.

"I need something to calm me down."

He takes a deep breath, but a swirling anxiety prevents the air from reaching the bottom of his lungs. Heroin would help, but Pedro doesn't have any. His breathing grows shallow. He gasps for air and feels tired, more so mentally than physically, though he can barely walk when he reaches Madison Square Park. He lies down on a bench under a big tree. A Giuliani for Mayor campaign placard protrudes from a trash can, which Pedro grabs to cover his face and block the sun. He passes out immediately, but there will be no restful sleep.

Chapter 5

Sonny feels a mild hangover after leaving Cookie's apartment. The afternoon sun pierces his eyeballs, stinging his brain. He's tired and bereft of the cosmetic or charismatic flashes he sported the previous night. With cosmetics absent from his pale face, Sonny doesn't evoke the previous evening's striking figure. In plain shorts, t-shirt and sneakers, he's nobody worth noting, except for the crazy hair, which is messy. It's a uniform for walking about the city or taking the subway without getting hassled.

The scary drug dealers have retired for the day and Sonny doesn't perceive any threatening looks from people on the street. He takes the A train from Washington Heights where Cookie lives. Sonny takes a window seat facing south, the same direction the train is traveling.

"What will I see when the train reaches 23rd Street?"

Sonny devoted a good part of last night passing out invitations to a small party he's organizing and hosting in the Tunnel's basement on Thursday. It's his first party and he anticipates the event with insecurity and exhilaration. The party is actually inconsequential to the club owner and his managers who need to churn out more than a dozen parties a week. Yet Thursday's basement party is a make-or-break moment for Sonny.

He's eager to become a nightlife celebrity known for parties and looks. He wants to be photographed and discussed — an outrageous the center of attention. He can't play an instrument, act or sing.

"I'll be a celebrity."

He's good at dressing up and making a spectacle of himself. That's enough for recognition in clubland, which is like elementary school because the children who scream the loudest get the most attention from teachers. He deserves the attention, just not the kind he got growing up in Cliffside Park, where many kids hated him for being a fag.

Sonny knew he was different and after all those years of peer abuse, he came to New York. Sonny used those years of alienation to turn himself into a real alien. He dyed his hair, shaved some of it, painted his face and got new clothes, becoming a strange nocturnal creature. Yet sitting on the A train this morning isn't so fabulous. He's tired and he has to repeat last night's party all over again at tonight's go-go dancing gig at the Tunnel. It will be another opportunity to distribute party invitations, and he needs the extra cash for the rent.

"Maybe Eagle will give me another ecstasy."

The 34th Street station's signs jolt Sonny out of his hungover reverie. The next stop is 14th Street, his stop for a transfer to the L train. Sonny feels a tickling fear stroke his abdomen. He looks out the window and practices scanning the darkness as the A train pulls out of the 34th Street station.

"Will I see anything?"

The train hurtles south, slowing to pass the 23rd Station. Sonny fixes his gaze to the local train tracks, which run parallel to the A train. As the A train re-enters the tunnel's darkness he strains to look across the gloom to a little alcove from last night.

"I can't see anything. I not telling the cops. Why should I? Maybe they would arrest me for being in the tunnels. That's probably illegal."

As the A train pulls into 14th Street, Sonny gets off, transferring to the L train. Sunday shoppers overheat and crowd the train. Nobody pays attention to Sonny, who stands in a corner, hoping to soon arrive at his exit on 1st Avenue. He needs to start working on tonight's look.

"Who was that guy in the tunnel. What was he doing? Maybe he didn't kill the other guy. Maybe they were just homeless bums fighting. I can't be bothered with their problems. I'll bet Cookie and St. Helen will tell everyone about it. Everybody will be asking me about it at my party. What will I tell them? I was chased by a murderer? No, then they'll ask why I didn't call the police. I should just keep it mysterious, and that way people will be more likely to believe it."

Sonny's concern about what he saw in the subway will become a badge of distinction. The encounter becomes a thrilling adventure.

"It's kind of fabulous. I shouldn't have kept my search for the Morlocks a secret. I should have played it up."

Taking a chance encounter with a murderer and turning it into a thrilling story fits the club kid logic. The group of extravagantly dressed young men, mostly gay, and women, mostly straight, emerged at the party scene in the Tunnel around 1987. Their antics appear in the celebrity pages in the tabloid newspapers and on some of the trashy local television newscasts that send camera crews to the Tunnel to record their exploits. Sonny was smitten by the club kids when he saw them on television. He instantly recognized them as kindred spirits who would understand him, unlike his schoolmates in Cliffside Park.

After graduating from high school he took the graduation money he received from his relatives, got an apartment in the East Village and enrolled at the Fashion Institute of Technology to study fashion marketing and design. Instead of studying, Sonny sought out the club kids and began following their antics at the Tunnel, which he legally wasn't old enough to enter. The greedy club owners don't care about checking anybody's identification, unless they don't want to let the individual enter. Laws aren't so strictly enforced.

Sonny saw his first club kids at the Tunnel. He fell in love, not with any particular person, but with an idea that he could be the biggest misfit reaping petty adulation and rewards. Sonny instantly resolved to become a club kid, who in his mind resembled his beloved Morlocks in the X-Men comics. The Morlocks' grotesque features, outlandish attire, subterranean society and strange superpowers were just like the club kids. Sonny entered a real-life fantasy world he cherished in high school, starring the club kids as his surrogate Morlocks.

Sonny spent his high school years trying to be invisible so that nobody would pick on him. He didn't enter the club kid's world with a loud voice or flaming personality. He built it from scratch in college. His new persona was one of the few projects he finished in school before dropping out. Storytelling was a skill Sonny hadn't yet mastered, so it didn't occur to him to immediately start bragging about witnessing a possible murder. In club kid thinking, the more perverse, the better.

Sonny didn't have a hard time befriending the club kids,

many of whom share his age and social discomfort. Together, the club kids created their alternate society where they could be the stars, though they were just as mean to each other as their former high-school enemies had been to them. The scene is very judgmental and it's important to impress the club kids with words and deeds, not just extreme fashion statements.

"What will I say to people tonight about the homeless guy in the subway? Did I tell Cookie and St. Helen that he chased me?"

It's important to remember what he told the drag queens so he can embellish the story without contradicting what he said earlier this morning. Sonny whispers to himself excitedly as he arrives at his apartment building on a dilapidated block on Avenue B.

"This story is FABulous. Everyone will be talking about me."

Chapter 6

Sweat softened the campaign poster Pedro has on his face as a sun shield; it's now stuck on his face. Although he picked a bench in a shady part of the park, Pedro is soaked and he has to pick pieces of the Giuliani for Mayor poster off his face.

"Fuck, I should have gotten a room at the Y."

Sitting up, the bench jabs at his back and he remembers there isn't enough money for a room as he sees locals walk their dogs. Staring blankly, Pedro feels a momentary vacancy. It's around 3 p.m. and he's had about six hours of sleep. He doesn't feel refreshed. Watching the dog walkers is strangely soothing, until he sees a flash of Steve's face.

"Did they find him yet? Maybe he overdosed. I have to take a shower. I'm starting to look like a wino."

Dehydration leads him to the Wendy's across the street from the park, where the air conditioning feels so good upon entering. He orders a large 7-Up and then gets unnerved by the cashier's weird smile.

"Is he laughing at me?"

It's too hot to go back outside, so he sits in the half-full dining room, where some of the customers uncomfortably stare at him and they whisper to each other

"Do they think I'm gonna rob them? Do they recognize me from the subway?"

Pedro fixes his gaze on the table.

"How would they recognize me from the subway?"

Pedro's heart starts beating faster. He looks up and catches another patron staring furtively.

"Why are they looking at me?"

Pedro reflexively reaches for the little fifth pocket in his jeans, but it's empty. Still groggy and now paranoid, he can't remember if he has any drugs on him. Grabbing his soda, he approaches the counter again to borrow the bathroom key so he can search his secret compartments discreetly. Once inside he unbuttons his pants and searches his groin, where he typically hides money and drugs when sleeping in a park. There's nothing hidden. Still panicky, Pedro turns to the sink to splash some cold water on his face, and then he finds a mark on his cheek, an upside down red G from the Giuliani for Mayor poster bled onto his face. His knees almost buckle with relief, as if cops had been banging on the bathroom door ready to arrest him and they were now gone. He washes his face and immediately leaves the restaurant.

Pedro doesn't have a regular place to live, but he isn't truly homeless. The homeless are bedraggled; he has style. His homelessness is a choice, an art project, an escape, an experiment on life in New York without the burden of an apartment, but he ensured domestic comforts like showers with a YMCA membership.

He bought the membership after stealing $500 from an older tourist who picked him up for sex. The guy took Pedro to hotel, sucked his dick and when he went to the bathroom to take a shower Pedro grabbed his wallet, removed all the cash and fled. It was easy. Instead of spending all of it getting high, Pedro invested in a Y membership that entitled him to a locker, unlimited showers and a discount on a rooms when he wants a real place to sleep. The Y on 23rd Street and Sixth Avenue is just two blocks from the subway tunnel where Steve is "sleeping." Walking towards it, Pedro feels a lump in his gut, but not as badly as before.

"I'm done with him. Why did I hang out with him so much anyway? He's an asshole. Fuck him."

Anger bubbles up his throat. He spits and it lands on his right leg.

"Shit. Why doesn't Steve want to be with me? Why did I leave school? Why didn't the teachers like my work? Why was so hard? Is anyone gonna ask me about Steve?"

No one asked. The Y is a transient place with people coming and going all day long, who'd notice that Steve isn't with Pedro? There are two bags in Pedro's locker, one for dirty clothes and one for clean clothes. He takes his shower, shaves and changes into clean clothes, picking another pair of black jeans and a light blue polo shirt that gives him an arty, preppy look. He sniffs the captain's hat and it doesn't stink, so he keeps that on. It will help him make better money tonight. Begging won't do today, it takes too long to make decent money. Instead Pedro opts for the merry-go-round, a block on the Upper East Side between Lexington and Third avenues where male prostitutes hang out watching the cars drive around the block.

Pedro learned about the merry-go-round at one of the soup kitchens. Two guys were arguing with each other and one accused the other of being a faggot who sold his ass on 53rd Street. Pedro doesn't think of himself as a homosexual, even though he's only attracted to men. That's one of the reasons he left Long Island. It's easier finding sex with guys in New York City, where no one questions why you don't have a girlfriend.

The soup kitchen accusation intrigued Pedro. He'd seen female hookers on plenty of streets, and he'd even seen guys dressed like women on 14th Street near Ninth Avenue, but he didn't know there was a place where guys did that without dressing up as women. One night, roaming around high, he explored 53rd Street. Not knowing where the boys were, he walked almost the entire length of 53rd Street, from the far west side until he notice a bunch of guys hanging around on 53rd Street. Some of them were really cute. By the time Pedro discovered the merry-go-round, he had just been evicted from his apartment and he was staying at the Y, paying by the week. He didn't have a job and his parents cut him off from any money because they were furious with him for dropping out of SVA. They thought that would force him to come home, but he didn't.

Pedro didn't know what to do when he first encountered the merry-go-round. He decided to sit on a step and just watch what the others were doing. He noticed that cars were driving around the block with male drivers surveying the various young men, who either loitered or slowing walked against the flow of traffic. At times a car would pull over and one of the guys would walk over to the car to speak to a driver. Sometimes the guys would get in the car and it would drive away.

There were also some older men walking around the block, smiling and nodding or saying hello to the young men. It was creepy at first when these overly friendly men approached him. Being from the suburbs, Pedro remembered all his parents warnings about speaking with strangers, especially in New York City. That was his mom's number one warning before he left for school. That warning echoed through his head on his first visit to the merry-go-round, but he didn't heed it. He was so high that warnings didn't matter. If they had, he wouldn't have gotten high.

After watching for about half an hour, a skinny old man came right up to him.

"I'll give you $40 to suck your dick. That's all I have," said the slightly sloppy man, who looked too old to be interested in sex.

"Here?"

"Hell no. My car is around the corner. We'll go there and drive somewhere private."

"I can't leave Manhattan," said Pedro, who was vaguely frightened by the prospect but too high to reconsider this dangerous trajectory.

"We'll go to the west side."

Pedro got up to follow the old man, relaxed about the destination, since he was familiar with it and the desolate areas around there. The man drove to the garment district between Eighth and Ninth avenues, which was completely deserted. He parked his car and reached for Pedro's pants, unzipping them and then ordering Pedro to pull down his underwear. He sucked Pedro's dick for about 15 minutes. Pedro was so scared. He kept looking around to see if any police or people were coming, but the block was desolate. The paranoia sobered him up a bit and he got an erection from the sucking. He felt panic welling up inside of him as he became more aroused. The man, who smelled bad, noisily sucked his cock. Shooting his load down the old man's throat was more a nervous relief than sexual satisfaction.

The old man gave Pedro his $40 dollars and offered to drive him where he wanted, but Pedro just wanted to get out of the car. As the man pulled away Pedro felt more at ease and he marveled at the fact that someone had just given him $40 for something that only took 15 minutes.

"That was so disgusting, but so easy! Maybe I can charge more."

Today is Sunday, so the merry-go-round starts earlier than other weekend nights. A lot of the regular customers will likely be in the vicinity as some of the gay bars in the area open for Sunday afternoon happy hour. Pedro decides to arrive at 6 p.m. It's still too early to go to the Merry-Go-Round, so Pedro leaves the Y to get something to eat.

He walks east again, still feeling angry at Steve and at school. He wants to break something, but he doesn't want to call attention to himself. He's still feeling paranoid about what happened in the subway, recalling the waif across the tracks.

"Who was that freak? Does he work at that club? Did he call the police?"

Pedro can't tolerate the people inside the Wendy's by Madison Square Park, so he goes outside and heads east, towards a block he usually avoids: 23rd Street between Third and Second avenues. That's the site of SVA's main building, and usually Pedro is too embarrassed to go by there for fear that someone he knows at the school might recognize him. He doesn't want to answer their questions. Since it's mid-August and Sunday, there's little chance that anyone he knows will be there. The building probably isn't even open. Pedro sits on a window sill across from SVA as he eats his food, studying SVA's windows and entrance and recalling his arrival at the school.

"Why did I drop out? I should have been more creative."

Pedro avoids SVA because he didn't like seeing former teachers or classmates. His meal is filling but unsatisfying. Combined with the dread over what had happened earlier, Pedro feels a little nauseated.

"Shit, what the fuck am I doing? What's gonna happen to me?"

Pedro stares at the SVA entrance, once a portal into a world where Pedro imagined a future as a successful artist. He's not sure what kind of artist, but when he arrived he thought he'd become a painter or illustrator. The excitement of passing through SVA's doors made Pedro's heart beat faster and it made him feel so creative and accomplished. Ideas coursed through his head, too fast to jot them down. Ideas for paintings, drawings, films or three-dimensional constructions. It was an amazing feeling having those ideas rush through his mind, so many possibilities and so many opportunities for recognition in the New York art scene. Pedro loved that feeling.

About three months into his freshman year, the realities of school began clashing with idealized notions. Homework and class assignments were big problems. Teachers disapproved of his work ethic because Pedro didn't like to work. Although Pedro dreamt of attending art school and maybe becoming a celebrated artist, he never considered the possibility that art school would be just as hard, if not harder, than attending a regular college and studying something boring like accounting. Art class in high school wasn't so hard and he never really spent much time on his drawings or paintings. He didn't think much about them or conceive grand concepts before picking up a pencil or brush.

Art school is different. Teachers want complicated concepts and ideas, followed by what seems like an excessive amount of time to execute them. Pedro didn't have time because he was finally in New York City and he wanted to explore this giant playground. There were clubs, bars, parks and parties, all of which left little time for homework. There were drugs too, wonderful drugs like coke, ecstasy, acid and heroin. Pedro was in love, and his new, jealous lover wouldn't share him with art school.

Pedro looks up to SVA's third-floor, where one of his drawing classes was held. He hated the teacher and the feeling was mutual, though the teacher didn't dislike Pedro personally. The problem was his laziness. For Pedro an hour or two on a piece was more than enough when there are adventures awaiting.

He eventually failed the class because he was hungover too often to arrive by 10 a.m. When he did show up, the teacher ripped into him.

"There's nothing here for me to grade. What is this? This took you 10 minutes," said the teacher, waving his hand with dismissal and moving on to the other students.

Pedro felt like ripping his work to pieces right there in the classroom. But he didn't, fearing that if he destroyed his work, the teacher might tell the class that it's the best thing he could have done with it. When Pedro did spend a few hours with his art, he sometimes stared at the paper or canvas motionless, no inspiration motivating his hand. Often he got high before doing his work to stir up his inner creativity. He'd still sit there with a blank mind. How was it that so many ideas coursed through his head when entering the building and partying with friends, but in the studio, sitting in front of a blank canvas, there was nothing. His mind was still, no activity. He grew impatient with his work and regularly quit in frustration.

"Why wasn't I more creative?"

Pedro turned his gaze from the third-floor classroom. He was disgusted.

"I should have worked harder."

In fact, Pedro works very little. He hates working so much that he'd rather let some stranger suck his dick for quick money. Pedro sits there, staring at the pavement, listening to the inner voices. His father and mother, nagging and questioning. His own voice, cursing, asking what he should do next. Steve's voice, suggesting they get high.

Pedro aches with a combination hangover, drug craving and sleep-deprivation.

"Tomorrow I'm gonna the academic advisers' offices to talk to them about returning."

Pedro realizes he's been sitting on the step for almost an hour and his ass hurts from the concrete. He walks towards Third Avenue on his way to the merry-go-round. He'll walk there to save the subway fare, plus it's still early, so by the time he gets there the customers will be in the mood. He looks back at the SVA building and his eyes burn.

Chapter 7

"I'm going for the space-age chef look tonight," Sterling Silver boasts to Sonny after arriving around 6 p.m.

Sterling lives in Brooklyn and he often comes over to Sonny's or other club kids' Manhattan apartments to get changed. Like Sonny, he doesn't like the dangers of subway commuting when dressed for clubbing. Sterling can't really go on the train unnoticed with his namesake silver lamé outfits. He can't fight either. Even if he could fight, such skills aren't any good against the armed thugs who roam New York.

"I got the idea last week when I was watching a cooking show and the chef was wearing one of those tall hats. I figured it must be easy to make those hats because if you think about it, all it is is a big tube that you put on your head and it's held up by your ears. How hard to make could that be? Umpf!"

Sonny nods in agreement, pulling bags out of a closet containing the raw materials for the evening's creation.

"Sooooo, after I made the hat, I needed an apron. I was cooking up glamor! That wasn't hard either. It's just a big bib with a couple of straps. I think the whole outfit took me about two hours. It's a new personal outfit-making record, hiaaah! I should watch TV more often, hiaaah!" Sterling exclaims, punctuating his statement with a nasal yelp he makes whenever he thinks he's clever.

Sterling's yelp was one of his attention-grabbing gimmicks, in addition to the silver lamé. Another Sterling gimmick is glitter. He'd carry it in tubes and toss it around the club, though he's toned that habit down after a hostile encounter last month with a muscle head who got a fistful of glitter in the whiskey sour he'd just purchased. Sterling had to give the guy his last drink ticket to calm the situation and avoid getting the glitter tube rammed down his throat by the pissed partier.

Sterling's piercing yelp is high-pitched enough to be heard above the bass-heavy din permeating the dance floor. The club kids and drag queens have many versions of yelps, similar to the screams of school girls when they realize how loud they can yell and then try to outdo each other.

Cookie's gimmick is the fairy wand she uses at the club entrances. St. Helen's gimmick is her half-whisper voice, which is not particularly attention-grabbing, but it works for her because of the rest of her package, which typically consisted of thick glasses and her giant stature. Soft voice, loud look; a perverse yin-yang for a drag queen that forced clubbers to huddle around her just to understand what she's saying. That made conversations with her look even more intriguing and interesting, even when she was simply telling someone that she was thirsty.

Sonny doesn't have a gimmick, yet. He can't decide what it should be, and it worries him. Picking a gimmick is like getting a tattoo, which Sonny doesn't have either. If Sonny has any gimmick or identifiable trademark, it's the Hello Kitty backpack he wear to store his long overcoat and club gear.

"I'm glad you whipped up something new. It's cute......for you. Remember, it's my first party at the Tunnel on Thursday and we have to deliver a big turnout so that the managers will ask me to host again. This will be a make or break moment."

"Oh please, queen, it'll be FAAABulous! Hiaaah!"

"I'm worried, Sterling! The hardest aspect of hosting a party is promoting it ahead of time. That means we have to really dress up and pass out thousands of invitations. That's so much work! The more we serve outLANDishness, the more interested clubbers will be in my party."

Sterling shrugs his shoulders indifferently, touching up his eyeliner.

"Tonight we'll barely have to push invites on clubbers; they'll want one. Why wouldn't they? We're FIERCE! Having some of tonight's gay Sunday crowd come on Thursday will make us STARS!"

"All you really need for a fierce look are two good pieces that work together," Sterling says excitedly, waving his left hand in a grand gesture and pulling his ensemble out of a big black trash bag he uses as luggage.

Sterling fancies himself a fashion designer, but he can barely sew or sketch a design. In fact, most of his designs are barely wearable and mostly uncomfortable, yet not in a glamorous suffering-for-fashion sense. They are simply painful to wear, with the safety pins that hold the contraptions in place often popping open and drawing blood. The outfits hurt and the wounds, depending on where they are, typically become conversation pieces. He carries Band-Aids in his lunchbox, just in case.

"Silver lamé isn't sturdy enough to make a chef hat, so I used that hat netting they sell in midtown and then put the lamé on top of it. It worked perfectly. I just used glue for the rest of the hat, no need to waste any time sewing, hiaaah! The only part I really had to sew was the finishes on the apron and the straps. I'm just wearing my silver spandex shorts underneath and my silver boots, which I touched up yesterday so they're perfectly shiny. The best part of all was that this look only cost me about $20. Can you believe that?"

"Work the budget, bitch," Sonny said in a squeaky, whiny voice. "My outfit tops yours by being cheaper."

"I doubt that."

"Yes, I'm serving Easter abortion trash, eeeouw!"

Sterling says nothing in response, furrowing his brow with

skepticism.

"That's right, Sterling. In the springtime the drug store on First Avenue threw out their leftover Easter decorations and there was a bag with a ton of plastic Easter eggs. I got a huge bag of them and now you have to help me put them together. I've already done my shorts. I took the trashed Easter grass and glue it to my crotch, so now I have green pussy! Eat it! Your job is to take the Easter egg halves with the holes I put in them and help me tie them to these straps I safety-pinned together."

"You'll get a big, bloody jab from this costume when one of those pins unfastens," warns Sterling, secretly wishing it happens more than once, ignoring how awful it is when safety pins stick him.

Sterling isn't in the mood for helping Sonny, but he grudgingly obliges because Sonny lets him come over to change. The straps Sonny pinned together are made of a black elastic typically used for the inside of waistbands. As they finished each strap, tying the Easter egg halves with heavy-duty thread strung through sewing needles, Sonny puts on the straps over a neon yellow stretch spandex t-shirt.

Assembling the costume, Sonny tells a new version of his subway adventure. He's been thinking about it earlier in the day since traveling home from Cookie's and he concluded that the story should be dramatized a bit more for extra appeal. Sonny regrets that he told Cookie and St. Helen about the Morlocks and the X-Men. He worries that it makes him sound dorky, like the many grown men Sonny sees at the comic book store Forbidden Planet on Broadway. Sonny looks upon those young men with scorn, assuring himself that he's better. To Forbidden Planet's clerks, Sonny isn't particularly different from the other customers in their early 20s, except that Sonny has dyed hair and sometimes shaved eyebrows.

There's no discussion of comic books in the new and improved version of Sonny's terror tale because Sonny sticks to the lurid details.

"You'll NEVER guess what happened to me last night," Sonny starts, as Sterling looks up without responding, clearly bored with the outfit assembly.

"When I left home last night I decided to take the subway to the Tunnel because I wanted to save some money. I don't get paid until Friday and my go-go money from last night will barely get me through the week, so I needed to cut corners somewhere."

"Mmmm-hhmmmm," Sterling replies in a long, sing-song drawl.

"Anyway, I took the subway figuring it wouldn't take that long. I was really dressed up so I put on my black trench coat and my big sunglasses to try to blend in and when I got on the L train it was practically empty, so no problem there. But when I was waiting for the E train at 14th Street, something SCARY happened."

Sterling looks up, intrigued.

"I decided to wait for the train by the far end of the platform closer to 16th Street by the stairwell because I figured nobody would see me there, when I hear a wolf pack of homeboys come on to the station. They were drunk and cussing at each other, fuck you faggot. One of them says."

"OK, I've been in that situation on the L train coming from Brooklyn. I can tell this won't end well," interrupts Sterling, who stops tying the Easter eggs on the straps.

"You'd think so, but in DESPERATE panic, I did something I've never done before....I ran into the subway tunnel so they wouldn't see me."

"No you didn't," Sterling says dismissively.

"Yes, I did. It was HORRIBLE," Sonny continues. "The subway tunnel was so dark and I swear I felt this disgusting cobweb hit my face when I ran in. Thank God I was still wearing my sunglasses, but I had to take them off in there because it was so dark. Inside the tunnel you could hear all this rustling. It was the sound of rats running around, looking for food. I was so scared! All I wanted to do was get away from the wolf pack, so I quickly stepped from one of the wooden ties to the other, trying to ignore the smell. Since I only needed to get to 23rd Street I just quickly ran along the tracks towards that station."

"How could you do that? What the fuck were you thinking?" says Sterling, now a little less still skeptical.

"Look at my boots. See those discolored stains on them? That's from accidentally stepping in the nasty wet spots in the subway tunnel."

Sonny's not sure what really caused the stains; he suspects it was spilled cocktails.

"That wasn't the worst of it. You know there are people

living in the subways. Just last week on the TV news they were talking about a fire some homeless bum started in the tunnels. They were trying to cook something. Anyway, I saw someone in there near the 23rd Street station. I felt a rumble on the track and when I looked behind, there was a distant light that I knew was a train coming down the same track! I had to hurry or it would kill me."

"The thought of a train hitting me made me run even faster until I heard a scream. It was this low, grunt-like scream, like an animal made it, but no normal animal. It was EVIL and I instantly felt a chill. It came from across the tracks, and I heard this guy cussing. Then he turned and looked at me with angry eyes. It was like a horror movie, he had this monstrous expression, like a savage cannibal. His staring felt like ICE on my back. I think he killed someone or something in the tunnel. Maybe it was one of those satanic rituals where people kill animals. I'm not sure. It was so dark I could barely see, even though the subway platform was less than a block away and light was coming into the tunnel."

"What did you do?" Sterling asks, somewhat engaged though still skeptical.

"I ran towards the platform and when I climbed the stairs onto the platform I ran to the exit and then I could hear the train coming into the station. I didn't even look back."

"How do you know the bum killed something?" asks Sterling, still not convinced.

"I don't, but something was going on there. Something hideous that I didn't want to know about. Why would he have looked at me in that evil way and try to follow me?"

"He followed you?"

"Well, he tried to follow me, but the train came and he couldn't."

"That's incredible," says Sterling. "It's FABulous, hiaaah!"

Sonny drew his hand across his forehead as if wiping off sweat with relief.

"Don't tell anyone about this."

Sterling picks up another Easter egg half to tie on a strap.

"Why don't you call the police?"

"Why would I call them? Can you imagine? 'Hi officer, I was walking through the subway tunnel and I think I saw someone get killed.' Wouldn't that get me in trouble just for being there?"

"I guess so. What are you going to do then?"

"Nothing. I don't know what really happened there. Maybe he was just killing a cat, that's not big deal."

"I can't believe you'd go walking through the subway."

"I told you it was an E-mer-gen-cy situation," says Sonny, with a hint of annoyance in his voice. "It was a desperate act of self-preservation. I had to get away from the wolf pack. You've told me about your run-ins with the homeboys on the L train, why would I want to let that happen to me when I could just as easily escape through a tunnel?"

"It's the fucking subway tunnel, darling. It's not like you're walking into the back of the Tunnel nightclub where they left the rail tracks for show. It's real trains going on those tracks and they run fast. You could have been KILLED!" says Sterling, his raised tone showing a faint spark of concern.

"I could have been killed last night when I took that second hit of ecstasy Eagle offered me, tee hee hee. I took it and I was fine. That's no less dangerous than running through the subway."

The argument makes strange sense to Sterling. Recreational drug use is something Sterling understands, and it hadn't killed him either, especially his favorite combo, cocaine and liquor. It's fun. Maybe running through a dark subway tunnel isn't so dangerous. Just as quickly as Sonny broaches the subject of having seen someone kill someone or something in the subway, he flutters to a topic of lesser gravity, but greater urgency.

"Sterling, you have to help me pass out as many invites tonight as possible. You can't just spend your time on the dance floor or in the lounge. This week is very important to our nightclub careers and if Thursday's party isn't a big success, then we might not get another chance to throw parties."

"Don't be such a drama queen," Sterling replies. "Of course Thursday's party will be FABulous. How could it not be. You're giving people free ecstasy, they'll all be there kicking each other trying to find the pills in the balloons. It will be MAYhemmmm, hiaah!"

"It's genius. I'm fierce!" Sonny says of Pop Goes the Dance Floor, Thursday night's party theme.

Last month Sonny suggested to the club's event coordinator that all the club kids would turn out for his party if the Tunnel gave him 10 ecstasy pills that he'd insert in balloons that would be mixed with about another 100 balloons to create confusion and pandemonium. To his surprise the club's coordinator liked the idea, though he had a lot of rules for the party so that the club wouldn't be legally held liable if something were to go wrong or if the cops caught wind of the event. For starters there could be no mention of drugs on Sonny's invite, which wasn't really a problem. Sonny simply wrote the invite saying that there would be "prizes" in some of the balloons. The club coordinator gave Sonny some cash to buy the pills, but he made Sonny sign a sheet of paper saying that the money was an advance payment for his promotional services. Sonny didn't care. The police wouldn't find out about his party; they were too busy with other things.

"Anyway, as brilliant as my idea is, we still have to pass out invites. We can't just allow a promise of free drugs do the work for us! What about people who don't realize what the prize will be? We can't tell strangers what the prize is, but we still need them to come to the club with our invite so that we get the credit at the door. That's how they'll judge our party, not by how SCANdalous it is. You have to help me pass out as many invites as possible tonight."

"Alright, stop nagging," says Sterling, putting his hands over his ears.

"Sorry, but you don't understand how important this is. This is our chance to become big nightclub celebrities. STARS! We can do more parties and maybe you'll even be asked to do the door with Cookie. Wouldn't that be incredible? Then you'll really owe me because you got your start doing doors at my basement party."

"OK, let's not get carried away. I'm the one who's helping you throw a fabulous party. You'll get most of the credit because I'll just be doing the rope at the entrance and you're having all the fun inside."

Sterling feels indignant, even though Sonny really is doing him a favor because he could have asked someone else to be the doorman. Sterling is resentful that his stature in the club scene is not as high as he wants it to be. He'd only moved to New York City six months ago from Ohio and he'd instantly fallen in love with nightclubs, where he was determined to work. So far that means bussing, which wasn't at all what he had in mind when he saw the club kids and drag queens prancing atop go-go boxes and getting paid for it. He's stuck picking up empty cups. Sterling ties the final Easter egg half to an elastic strap.

"You're right. This party is important. I'm fed up with bussing and it's not glamorous. It's embarrassing and I'm over it, but I can't quit because I have to pay the rent. I think I'd be a perfect door diva. I should be working the front entrance."

"Well you won't get that job until you pay your dues. Why did you move here, anyway?"

"I was meant to be here. I remember seeing pictures of club kids in New York magazine and I was instantly convinced that I had to move to New York. I didn't know anyone here, but I figured I'd make a lot of friends in the clubs, so I saved my money and made a reservation at the YMCA. I took Greyhound from Ohio and it was so exciting and scary getting off the bus at Port Authority Bus Terminal. It wasn't hard finding the Y and I immediately started looking for a cheap apartment before I had a chance to spend my security deposit money. I found my basement studio in that run-down house where I live in Williamsburg in the first week I moved here."

"Finding a job wasn't as easy," Sterling continued. "I had worked as a busboy and waiter at restaurants in Ohio, so I knew how to do that. I went to a lot of restaurants until I finally found something in a stupid Mexican restaurant. It was gross and I was so relieved when I got the busboy job at Tunnel, but it barely pays the bills. I need a promotion, hiaah!"

"You'll get your promotion, but you have to work for it," Sonny says sternly. "That means passing out a lot of invites and not wasting the evening hanging out in the bathroom or by the bar. No dancing either."

"How many times are you going to nag me about that? You're really working my nerves."

"This is so important, Sterling, to both you and me. We can't fuck it up. I'm tired of working at Runway. It really doesn't pay much and I'm tired of struggling. New York is so expensive and I can barely pay for this little studio. If it wasn't for all the free drinks and admissions we get at the clubs, I wouldn't even be able to afford going out, and forget about taxis. That's why I had to take the subway the night I saw the murderer."

"OK, we're not sure you really saw a murder. You saw a dirty bum, for all you know."

"I saw something SINISTER and VICIOUS," says Sonny in a horror-show voice.

About three hours passed since Sterling's arrival. The plastic egg shell halves are finally attached to all the straps and it's make up time. They have to leave in an hour because the gay party gets started earlier on Sundays. Sonny pulls out a pot of clown white and smears it over his face, blotting it with a kitchen sponge from the sink. Once his face is a ghostly white canvas, he draws a big black circles around his eyes and a big frown on his lips and around his mouth. The effect is an unhappy face with ruby sequins glued on to his nose in the shape of a triangle.

Sonny then puts on his yellow spandex hot shorts with the green Easter grass attached to the crotch and a matching yellow spandex shirt. Next come the elastic straps: one under the left side of his crotch and over his right shoulder, another over the left shoulder and under the right side of the crotch. Others loop around his chest and waist. He carefully positions a half dozen armband sized straps on his upper arm and a couple on his legs. The final effect is a bandoliered kook. It's less Easter detritus and more an unfortunate clown festooned with plastic body armor offering dubious protection.

"Don't I look fabulous?"

"Mmmm, hmmm," Sterling replies, without looking up from his mirror because he's applying more make-up, two silver stripes running from the top of his forehead, over his eyes, and down the face to the jaw line.

Sterling then applies silver lipstick and some dark violet shading on his upper cheeks and forehead not covered by the stripes. He slips into a black leotard, puts on some silver hot pants and then the apron and hat. With his shoes on, he struts around the little floor space in Sonny's studio, striking poses for imaginary photographers.

"Dinner is pre-PARED!" Sterling shouts dramatically, quoting a line uttered by the evil Magenta in "The Rocky Horror Picture Show."

"OK, let's go," Sonny orders. "We want to get there early so we can get at least a couple of drinks at the open bar. We're on a budget! Tee hee hee!"

Since there's two of them, they decide to split the cost of a taxi to and from the club, so there would be no need for cumbersome overcoats, though Sonny still needs the Hello Kitty backpack for the hundreds of invitations for his Thursday party. With some final preening in the mirror, the queer duo step out into the night and quickly hailed a taxi, their appearances giving little pause to the taxi driver.

Chapter 8

Pedro is sweaty again by the time he arrives at the merry-go-round. The evening is just getting started and he feels tired. There are at least a dozen young guys hanging around the block around 6:30 p.m., so Pedro sits on an office building's window ledge for relief. The cars circle the block. It's mostly older men from outside of Manhattan who come to the merry-go-round. There are a lot of New Jersey and Connecticut license plates on the mostly nice cars, some of them driven by married, family men or clergy.

Pedro doesn't come to the merry-go-round that often, yet he's weary of the place. Within minutes he feels a numbing boredom grip his mind and he stares blankly ahead, not responding to any of the eye contact initiated from the passing cars. The numbness deadens his hearing, too, and he sits there, not thinking, practically asleep with his eyes open. A blaring horn snaps him out of his numbness. An impatient driver frustrated with a cruiser's decision to chat up one of the young guys without pulling over to let traffic pass pounds his horn and shouts a few curses.

"I need to concentrate on making money. Otherwise, what's the point of coming here?"

As if dragging himself out of bed, Pedro gets up and moves to the middle of the block where he knows he can't stay long after the regular hustlers arrive because they'll chase him away from their favorite spots. It's still early, though. Leaning against a wall, Pedro fights off the lurking exhaustion that grabs at his mind, keeping himself in a noxious half-daydream.

"Excuse me. Can you tell me how to get to 53rd Street?" asks an older, balding man who suddenly approaches Pedro. "I'm looking for a friend."

"This is 53rd Street. You're standing on it," Pedro replies vacantly.

"Oh, have you seen my friend? He kind of looks like you," says the man who then smiles, which raises his puffy lower eyelids and makes him look like he's squinting.

"There are a lot of guys around here who look like me," says Pedro, who realizes where this conversation is headed, so he gets to the point. "Uh, maybe I'm the friend you're looking for."

"Maybe. What's your name?"

"I'm Jimmy," Pedro lies.

"Nice to meet you Jimmy. I'm Rick. How about we take a walk?"

Pedro just shrugs and begins walking alongside Rick.

"Why not," Pedro thinks to himself, "it's not like I'm getting in a car. I'll give him five minutes. He looks like he might have money."

"So, Jimmy, why are you hanging around here on such a nice summer afternoon? Why not a park?"

"You know why I'm hanging out here. That's why you stopped to talk to me. Where do you want to go and what do you want?" Pedro asks, trying not to sound too hostile or impatient.

"OK, I guess we don't have to spend a long time exchanging pleasantries. I'm looking for a friend and I like what I see. Let's take a ride to the west side."

"For what?" Pedro asks, hoping to keep impatience out of his tone.

"For a good time. I'm an old-fashioned man. Nothing weird, just some simple sucking and fucking."

"I don't suck dick and you can't fuck me. You have to give me $100 first."

"Alright Jimmy, we'll take care of business as soon as we get to the hotel."

Pedro feels very nervous about going off with strangers. He's not used to it like the other hustlers. Some heroin would ease the discomfort, but he doesn't want to be too doped up to lose track of business. He needs the money and he won't repeat a recent mistake where he turned a trick high and then nodded off, allowing the john to leave him in a dark alley without paying him.

"I had to park my car over on 56th Street. I hope you don't mind walking a couple of blocks."

Pedro says nothing and the pair continue walking until

reaching a new-looking Lincoln Town Car. It's a suburban pleasure craft and Pedro notices the New Jersey license plates. They get in and Rick drives to the west side.

"So Jimmy, what do you do?"

"I'm a student at the School of Visual Arts. I'm studying painting and illustration," says Pedro, forcing himself to speak.

"I can't be too quiet or I'll scare this guy," Pedro thinks.

"That's wonderful. You have an artistic look, so I'm not surprised. Do you paint with oil, acrylic or watercolor?"

"I like acrylics. They go better with the type of painting I like to do," says Pedro, realizing he hasn't really spoken with anyone since being in the tunnel with Steve.

Pedro feels a sour pool within, aching to burst forth. It's a relief to talk about art.

"What do you paint?" Rick asks.

That was a good question with no answer. It's been months since Pedro actually painted something and he can't remember what he painted in school.

"I like to paint the subway and tunnels," Pedro says, thinking about Steve and what happened to him.

"Oh, a mass transit artist. That's very interesting, but it must be hard because the subways are often so crowded. Doesn't your easel get bumped around by the crowds?"

"Not really, I prefer to paint there when it's not so crowded," says Pedro, who never actually painted in any subway tunnel, though it seems like a good idea.

"When do you graduate from school?"

"Uh, this is gonna be my last year and then I'll look for a job working as an illustrator or designing sets on Broadway, maybe."

"It sounds like you have a very interesting and exciting future. I envy you, just starting out your young life."

"Don't envy me so much. Everybody has their problems and struggles," says Pedro, again feeling the poisoned reservoir pushing up to his throat.

Suddenly discussing art doesn't feel so good as Pedro recalls dropping out of school in January. He abandoned his paintings and sold some of his art tools for drugs.

"I enjoy art myself, but I'm terrible at drawing and I wouldn't dare pick up a paintbrush," Rick says.

"It's better that you don't. Um, painting is so difficult and it's like torture sometimes."

"Are you a tortured artist or do you mean that you're a starving artist?" asks Rick, who perceives either situation as a romantic condition rather than a wretched state.

"I wouldn't be here with you if I was a successful artist."

Pedro immediately recognizes the hotel near where Rick parked at 10th Avenue and 51st Street. Other johns bring him to this hotel, maybe because it's near the Lincoln Tunnel, so it's an easy drive back to the suburbs after they get their sex fix. Rick parks the car along 10th Avenue a block away from the hotel and they walked towards it. Pedro said nothing and he didn't want to discuss art any more, since that subject could only worsen his mood. Rick pulls a small travel bag from his trunk, perhaps filled with sex toys or lube or any of the other kinky accessories some customers need in order to get off. Pedro waits in the lobby. Rick pays for the room and the two go to the third-floor room. Once in the room, Rick removes a bottle of lube, some condoms, a pint of rum and a couple of cans of Coke from his travel bag.

"You have to give me the money, first."

"I'm getting to that. Would you like some rum?"

Rick pulls his wallet from his pants and removes five $20 bills, handing them to Pedro.

"I'll just take the rum, no Coke."

Pedro takes a glass from a little table in the room and hands it to Rick, who puts about two shots of the clear liquor in the glass. Pedro drinks the entire amount as if doing a shot.

"Looks like you're a drinker."

"Not really, I just needed it to get started."

Pedro awaits the fleeting euphoria that will take him out of that room.

"Come here."

Rick sits on the bed and kicks off his shoes. Pedro silently obeys and stands before Rick, looking down on his bald spot. Rick pushes up Pedro's shirt and gropes Pedro's crotch like a little, clawing animal, which sends a tingle of revulsion through Pedro. The alcohol is kicking in and the repulsive tingle dissipates as Rick continues fondling Pedro's loins. Rick unfastens Pedro's pants and pulls them down. He runs his hands from Pedro's knees up to his inner loins, forcing Pedro to close his eyes. Rick pulls down Pedro's underwear and cups Pedro's genitalia in his hands, as if holding a precious treasure. He gently strokes Pedro's flaccid cock, petting his testicles. Pedro becomes sexually aroused by the fondling and his cock begins to stiffen, which leads Rick to put it in his mouth. He moves his mouth up and down Pedro's shaft. It feels good and repulsive. Rick continues the blow job and Pedro just stands there, imagining Steve. He's longed to be with Steve, but it never happened. Pedro longed to have Steve with him now, not an aging, chubby man. The image of Steve in the subway tunnel flashes through Pedro's mind. Pedro suddenly opens his eyes, frightened. The fear immediately dissipates when he sees Rick's balding head bobbing back and forth. Despite the conflicting thoughts, Pedro is aroused.

"I'm getting $100 and all I have to do is cum for this guy. If I did this every night I'd make $700 a week. That would be a good job."

Rick sucks faster and Pedro wants it to end. The sucking noises are like little bugs biting his skin. He wants to swat them away. With a groan, Pedro shoots his load into Rick's mouth. It's pleasure mixed with disgust.

"That was great Jimmy, you're a healthy young man, Rick says after getting up.

Pedro pulls up his pants, walks back to the table with the rum bottle, pours another shot in the adjacent glass and gulps it. Rick goes in the bathroom as Pedro stands in the room staring, not at anything in particular. The numbness is back; thoughts flash through his head, some of Steve. A dark sadness descends as the liquor's burn eases.

"So what are you doing the rest of this evening?" Rick asks after returning from the bathroom fully dressed and ready to leave.

"I don't know. I'm tired. I might just go back to my room at the Y," says Pedro, not really thinking about Rick's question or his answer because the booze has set him adrift. The feeling is like the heroin he loves, except not as powerful or effective. Nonetheless, it works well enough for a quick blow job.

"Well, I can't leave my car on the street much longer, shall we go?"

"OK, I'm ready."

"Do you want a ride?"

"No thanks, I'm gonna walk home and visit a friend on the way."

"Alright, Jimmy, it was a pleasure meeting you and good luck with your art career," Rick says as they walk out of the hotel.

Pedro walks south on 10th Avenue, thinking about where he'll go as hunger pangs slowly rumble in his belly. He notices a clock in a storefront. It's only 8:30 and yet the street is deserted as he slowly walks down the 50s and then the upper 40s. Upon reaching 42nd Street, he decides to stop at a diner in the vicinity for a real meal. He and Steve often stopped there to eat after begging money from tourists at Times Square.

"Hey baby, it's been a while. Where's your buddy?" asks the older, heavy-set waitress with bleached blond hair who always works the late-afternoon and early-evening shift.

"Um, I'm not sure. I haven't seen him in a few days. Maybe he's on a bender," says Pedro, ordering a bacon club sandwich.

Pedro is still a little drunk from the rum and he stares blankly at the TV in a corner of the restaurant. It's a movie he doesn't recognize and the volume is turned low, so he can't really hear what's going on. He stares. It's been days, or maybe weeks, since he'd watched any TV, a custom he abandoned after entering school. There was no time for it then. Steve's face once again shoots through his mind.

"Shit, fuck. What am I gonna do?"

Frustrated by his inability to summon a response to this nagging, agonizing question, he thinks again about getting high. The question won't arise when he's high. The bacon club sandwich doesn't taste so good compared with a nice baggy of heroin. He feels a craving. Pedro eats a little more slowly, now forcing himself to swallow as the heroin craving slowly kills his appetite.

"I can use this money for food and it could last me at least three days," he stared at his plate, toying with a french fry before putting it in his mouth.

He redirects his gaze out the window and his heart freezes. He silently gasps as the large police officer stands on the other side of the window, staring down at him. Pedro feels a wave a nausea, not knowing what to do.

"Should I get up? Run? No, that would be stupid. Just stay

here and act normal. Focus on my food."

Unsure what to do, Pedro puts another french fry in his mouth. It's like eating room-temperature cardboard. He takes the salt shaker and sprinkles some on the remaining fries. He puts another in his mouth and chews. It's worse and practically impossible to swallow. His heart races. Choking on the second french fry, Pedro takes a big gulp from his glass of Sprite. Some of it dribbles down his chin on his shirt. He furtively raises his gaze towards the window and the cop is gone. He coughs and a piece of french fry lands in the glass, splashing Sprite in his eye. Blinded, Pedro feels for the napkin, wipes the liquid off his face and looks for the officer again. Scanning the streetscape, he can't find the cop. Looking back to the window, he realizes why the cop was standing there: a menu is posted on the window adjacent to Pedro's table inside. He was simply checking out the daily specials. Cold perspiration glistens on Pedro's forehead. He fishes out the half-chewed french fry from his glass and takes another swig. Now he really can't eat any more. The diner's clock says it's 9:30 and he doesn't know what to do.

"I should have stayed in the hotel room. Rick might have let me."

It's too late for the homeless shelter. Their last call is around 8 p.m. They don't allow latecomers, and he's tried it only to be refused. He'll have to spend some of his earnings on a room at the Y.

"If I buy some dope I can just do that. I don't need a room," Pedro thought, then suddenly remembering that he can't go to his usual hideout.
Steve might still be there.

"I can't ever go there again."

Pedro slowly walks west on 42nd Street wondering about Steve, trying to forget about him and unsure what to do. When he reaches 12th Avenue, he turns south, walks half a block, and then sits down by a fence, staring at the passing cars and the dark void where the Hudson River flows. No solutions rise from the black river, nor from his inner darkness. He closes his eyes for a bit, but that rest offers no clarity. After half an hour Pedro's ass hurts and he gets up, still with no idea of what to do, except to go to the YMCA. He walks south along 12th Avenue, thinking about his parents.

"What's dad gonna say if I get caught? He's not gonna help me this time, I'll bet. I could go to jail. What's wrong with me? I'm sorry, Steve."

Pedro continues walking south, lost in his noxious reverie. Soon he happens upon a small group of people, some laughing as they get out of a taxi. As he crosses 27th Street, he realized where he is. It's the same club from this morning. He pauses on the southeast corner of 27th Street and 12th Avenue, watching the doorman talk to bouncers and greet people who just came out of the party. Interested in the commotion, Pedro sits on a step across the street and watches. Small groups of gay men and some women arrive by foot or by taxi. Some of them kiss the doorman, a handsome man who looks like a fashion model. Pedro feels physically attracted to him, like he feels towards many men, but he suppresses the feeling. Pedro has never been inside this club, or to any of the big New York City clubs. He's always thought that he's too cool for such scenes, though maybe he couldn't get in. So he makes up excuses for not going or not liking them. The beautiful men he sees entering the club spark desire and self-loathing. He hates them for having friends. He hates them for being unattainable. He hates them because he wants to be loved by one of them.

"These guys are so pathetic, dressing up for such a lame club. I would never line up the way they're doing."

As the small groups arrive with more frequency, a little line forms at the front entrance. Many of the patrons come for the open bar from 10 p.m. to 11 p.m. The doorman pretends to be busy and forces some of them to wait, even though the club is empty inside. Pedro just sits and stares, seduced and repulsed.

"You need to go!" says a burly white guy with shoulder length hair who suddenly approaches Pedro.

"I'm not gonna warn you a second time," the thug said as he walks across the street and joins the other door men at the Tunnel's entrance.

Startled by the threat, Pedro's heart beats faster.

"Why should I leave? I'm not bothering anybody and I'm not sitting on their property. He can't make me leave. I haven't done anything. Fuck you, asshole."

Just at that moment, a taxi pulls up and he hears someone blowing a whistle.

"Coming through! Coming through! Make way for a diva of the night!" yells a queeny guy. "Let the party begin!"

Pedro momentarily forgets the bouncer's threat, captivated by the commotion. He sees a skinny guy with a tall silver hat jump out of the taxi and then run to the end of the line, yelling "Be patient! Don't be alarmed. We're here!"

"Come to our party on Thursday. It will be extra special! Tee hee hee!" says the skinny gay guy who freezes Pedro's heart when he turned towards to club's entrance.

He's wearing the pink backpack.

"Shit," Pedro said to himself, recognizing the cartoonish gay boy from the subway. "Shit!"

"I told you to get the fuck out of here!" is all Pedro hears when he feels a sudden heave, flinging him off the steps and causing him to fall face first on the sidewalk.

All Pedro hears is the sound of front teeth crunching into lips, sending a white flash of pain across his his retinas.

"If you don't leave now I'm-a fuck you up."

"You should be the first in line at our party on Thursday. You look fabulous! All of you should come, you'll have the times of your liiives. WORK!," screams Sonny, so caught up in his own self-promotion and spectacle spinning that he doesn't notice the violence across the street.

In fact, nobody notices the assault on Pedro. It's the bouncer's job to be discreet and violent, if necessary. Terrified, Pedro gets up as quickly as possible as the bouncer quickly walks away.

"Come inside, come inside! I promise I'll suck all your dicks, ga ga ga ga," Sonny cackles as Pedro rises, taking one last look at the waif as he stands at the top of the steps before going into the club.

"He's laughing at me! He thinks it's funny, that fucking asshole. Who the hell is he?"

Pedro quickly rushes south on 12th Avenue when he realizes the bouncer is still glaring at him from across the street.

"Fuck, he broke my tooth!"

Pedro pulls his hand away from his mouth and finds a small pool of blood in his hand. He takes some napkins from his back pocket that he took from the diner and covers his mouth, which is throbbing with every step. The club is not far from the 23rd Street YMCA and he walks as well as he can, tears welling in his eyes, partly from the pain and partly out of anger.

"Is this happening because of what I did to Steve. Is this his revenge?"

As he walks towards the YMCA, no one offers him help despite his clear distress. Along 12th Avenue there are no people on the sidewalk except some prostitutes. Along 23rd Street there are more people, but most are wary of reaching out to strangers, especially if they're bloody. At Ninth Avenue the pain persuades him to take a short detour on his way to the Y. He fishes a $10 bill out of his pocket and folds it in his free hand with the expectation of seeing one of the heroin dealers that hung out at the public housing projects near Ninth Avenue and 18th Street. It's easy finding the drug thugs and he quickly walks up to one of them, hands him the money and gets his medicine. It's an uncomplicated exchange that doesn't even require hiding. The dealers know there are no cops in the area. The bleeding stops by the time Pedro reaches the YMCA, but he still looks a mess.

"What happened to you?" asks one of the attendants who recognizes Pedro because he rented his locker from him.

"Somebody tried to mug me, but they didn't get my money. I need to rent a room for the night."

"OK, but don't get any blood on our sheets. You should call the police and file a report with them."

"Uh, I didn't get a good look at the guy who did this to me, so I really wouldn't have anything to tell the cops, and my money wasn't stolen."

"Well, here's a plastic bag. Before you go up to your room you should stop by the ice machine at the back of the first floor corridor and get some for your mouth to bring down the swelling."

"Thanks," Pedro says, feeling vaguely comforted that somebody cares about what happened to him.

Distressed, Pedro doesn't even go to his locker in the gym. He takes the elevator to the fourth floor, the terror draining out of him, with guilt and dread slowly well up. The attendant gave him the worst floor with the smallest rooms. Pedro hates this floor because it's sleazy. As he walks down the corridor some of the renters of these room left their doors open because they are looking for sex. He walks directly to the communal bathroom and washes his face. Upon closer examination, his mouth is not in as bad shape as he feared. He realizes that his knees took much of the force of the shove, so his mouth didn't hit the pavement with as much force as the shooting pain led him to believe. His front teeth are intact, but they cut the inside of his lips when they hit the pavement and there is swelling. After washing up, he goes in his room and locks the door. There is virtually nothing inside the narrow room except a single sized bed, a chair and a small chest of drawers, with little space for walking about. Sitting on the bed he can reach both the chair and the drawers. After removing his shoes he opens the little heroin package, snorts about half of it and then carefully folds it up again and puts it in his jeans' little pocket.

Holding the bag of ice to his mouth he lies down on the bed. He cries about the pain in his mouth. Then he cries for Steve, his parents, his art career and his drug use.

"What am I gonna do?"

The heroin's comforting embrace eases his torment, though it also plays a trick by delivering an unpleasant flashback before Pedro drifts into seclusion.

"That asshole laughed at me when the goon attacked."

Chapter 9

Sonny and Sterling rush to the open bar as soon as they enter the Tunnel, demanding a vodka and cranberry and gin and tonic.

"I don't know why you insist on drinking vodka and cranberry," says Sterling. "How many times have you ruined your outfit or gotten some ugly red stain because you got bumped and the drink went right on you? With my drink, you can spill the whole thing and no one would notice."

"Darling, I'm barely wearing any clothes. What difference does it make?"

"Well what about the winter when you're wearing a lot of clothes?"

"Let's live for today!   Don't worry about tomorrow's outfits. It's enough work just thinking about what I'll be wearing on Thursday for my big coming out party. It has to be specta-cu-LAR, since I'll be on a new level. I'll be held to a higher level of fabulousness. Bow down before me, tee hee hee!"

"Oh, please. You'll be the same skinny queen you are today.

Don't get an attitude with me."

"Hey, this party is just as important to you, or do you want to keep picking up someone else's dirty glasses? Isn't that beneath you, Sterly Sterling?"

Sonny's testing another club gimmick tonight. He's decided that speaking in a nonsensical sing-song goes well with his wacky personal. He only uses this voice in the club and it's not his normal speech, but it might be some day. It's another childish element in his repertoire, all designed to craft a unique celebrity.

The duo quickly guzzle their drinks and then elbow their way back to the front of the open bar and order two more. Sonny isn't working tonight, so there won't be any drink tickets, the little cards that party promoters press into his hand when he works that entitled him to complimentary beverages. He usually gets three or four during a shift, but not tonight. The promoters and hosts of the gay parties don't favor him and the other exotic club creatures that hang around Tunnel. They are too queeny, too queer, too faggoty. The gay party promoters want to promote a manly environment for their parties, so a skinny young man in hot pants and Easter egg halves strapped around his body is not the kind of sexy image the beefcake-obsessed promoters seek, though they tolerate the club kids' presence and pretend to like them. The muscle gays ignore the club kids, not remarking upon or even noticing their flamboyant appearance.

Sonny and Sterling sit at a sofa in the club's lounge guzzling their second round. There is only about 20 minutes of open bar left and they're determined to pack in a third round before they start passing out the invites. There really isn't much point in doing it yet because most of the other partiers are also focused on the free drinks. Anyway, they have all night to pass out invites. After scoring their third drink, the duo relax a bit and stop guzzling. Now the challenge is to make the drink last as long as possible.

"Cocktails are like foundation, your make-up won't look good unless you have plennnnnty of it, hiaaah!" Sterling proclaims.

"You're right! The more cocktails I have, the better your make-up looks, tee hee hee."

Sonny grabs Sterling and drags him on to the mostly empty dance floor. There are maybe 200 people in the massive club by now, but it's just after 11 p.m. and the dance fever hasn't yet possessed the clubbers. They are still in that awkward high-school dance mode where the buff gay guys are too shy to be the first on the dance floor, so they stand around the dance floor's perimeter cruising each other.

"OK, it's show TIME!" Sonny barks at Sterling, as he began to spin around the dance floor. "Chase me!"

Sterling obliges, running after Sonny, catching him and then spinning around some more. Sonny begins dry humping Sterling and then lowers his body in front of Sterling. He lifts Sterling's silver lamé apron over his head and then Sonny bobs back and forth to the music's beat as if sucking Sterling off. The silly display mildly amuses the young men standing around the dance floor, who take great pains to look as masculine as possible, even though some of them also want to cut loose. Other spectators are annoyed by the vulgar, queeny display.

Sonny then crawls under Sterling's legs as Sterling gyrates his hips and waves his lunch box in the air, still matching the song's beat. They are both drunk by now, so their ability to actually follow a beat isn't perfect, yet they aren't yet sloppy. Unsure of how to end the spectacle, Sonny quickly gets back on his feet and swiftly kicks Sterling in the ass. The blow jolts Sterling off his disco cloud and he turns around angry, chasing Sonny off the dance floor, through the lounge and into the bathrooms, where Sonny locks himself in a stall, laughing.

"What the fuck's wrong with you? That hurt. If you think I'm going to pass out invites after what you've done, think again. I'm not helping you, asshole!"

Sterling hits and kicks the stall's door. He's pissed and wants revenge. Quite pleased with himself over the early evening drama he's wrought, Sonny feels a sudden panic at hearing's Sterling's threat.

"I need your help Sterling, and you'll only be hurting yourself by not helping. You know that," says Sonny, hoping manipulative logic will calm Sterling.

"Why did you kick me?"

"I'm sorry. I got a little carried away and I didn't realize how hard I was doing it. I was just playing on the dance floor and I lost control. It must have been those three vodka and cranberries. Did it really hurt?"

Sonny unlocks the bathroom stall door and slowly opens it. Sterling, still fuming, violently kicks Sonny in the right shin as soon as the door is three-quarters open.

"I'm sorry Sonny. Did that hurt?"

Sonny retreats into the stall and sits on the toilet seat as pain shoots up his leg. His open-bar euphoria shattered, all he can do is hold his leg in the area where Sterling kicked it. Satisfied with his revenge, Sterling turns to the bathroom's mirrors, opens his lunchbox and reapplies some lipstick. As a bruise and swelling begin forming, Sonny emerges from the stall, limping.

"You've crippled me. How are we spending the night passing out invites when I can hardly walk?"

"That outfit is crippling you! Don't fuck with me!"

Sterling wipes a bit of excess lipstick from the corner of his mouth.

"Is that Sonny Delight?" asks Pierrot, a long time Tunnel party promoter, with a hint of disdain. "You're early. Are you here to promote your little party on Thursday?"

Sonny suddenly forgets his throbbing leg. A genuine nightclub celebrity is speaking to him and Sonny didn't initiate the conversation. That's a first. Flushed with excitement, he doesn't notice Pierrot's condescension.

"Yes, are you coming?"

"Sorry, doll, I can't. I'm hosting a party over at MK's. There is a fashion show involved, so I'll be there most of the night."

Sonny feels disappointment that Pierrot won't attend. Pierrot is someone who goes out every night and he often organizes some of the best parties, so it would be a coup having him in the house.

"You can come after. We're serving ecstasy, tee hee hee!"

"We'll see. There are a lot of important parties that night," says Pierrot, who quickly checks his hair and turns to leave.

"I hope we don't lose a lot of the fabulous crowd to Pierrot's party," Sonny whispers to Sterling. "If I had known he was having a party that same night I would have picked a different night."

"There are parties every night of the week. You'd have competition no matter what night you picked. Anyway, he's tired. Our crowd doesn't want to hang out with him."

"He's one of the best promoters and we go to his parties. They're fabulous. Having him at our party would be a real stamp of approval."

"Why do you need his stamp of approval? We're making our own stamp of approval. It's just as good as his. Actually, it's better because we're original and he's been working his Pierrot trick with the black diamond over one eye for years, from what I hear. We're different every night and we're SCANdalous, hiaaah! People love scandal and that's why they'll come to our party on Thursday. For the free ecstasy and all the fighting and drama that 's sure to break out when you throw those balloons on the basement's dance floor. Why, we've already had a fight tonight, and people loved it. It WILL be pandemonium and we'll be famous for it. Top that, Pierrot!"

Sonny says nothing, rubbing his injured shin and then pulling off his backpack to remove two huge stacks of invites. One for him and the other for Sterling.

"We've got to get to work," Sonny says as he hands half the stack to Sterling.

They leave the bathroom to rejoin the party and it seems as if there are hundreds more people in the club. The dance floor is now half full of dancing men, some shirtless. It's not a receptive crowd for club invites, because the freak look doesn't appeal to as many of them as it does to the straight crowd at the Tunnel's other parties. It's a strange paradox: the gay muscle boys have little interest in his extravagant styles and invites, yet the straight kids that come to Tunnel on Friday and Saturday nights often clamor to get one because they're curious. Nonetheless, Sonny and Sterling walk around, offering the invites to the crowd. Some clubbers take them, others don't. They walked past the dance floor, through lounges, by the coat check and into the basement party.

"We can't take a break until we've passed out this whole stack!" Sonny yells in Sterling's ear.

Sterling rolls his eyes and they continue passing out the cards with feigned enthusiasm.

"Come to our party!" they say, barely pausing for anyone to ask about the particulars like a time or date.

They stop for cute boys, though.

"Come to our party. We're giving away free ecstasy," says Sterling to a young man who barely looks old enough to be in the club.

"Really? Isn't that illegal?" asks the young man, who's

awkwardly leaning against a wall in one of the lounges.

"Of course it's illegal! It wouldn't be any fun if it was legal, hiaaah!"

"OK, I'll try to come."

"What's your name?" asks Sterling, suddenly more interested.

"I'm Ted. Do you work for this club?

"I'm Sterling and I do work here. If you come on Thursday I'll be at the ropes leading to the basement, which is where our party will be. It'll be very exclusive, so you're lucky we met because I'll let you in."

Sterling feels pride as he tells the young man about the party. His time to shine approaches, when everyone will see him standing at the top of the basement stairs deciding who gets in and who doesn't. He'll escape from the busboy work, which bores and belittles him, especially when the clubbers he likes see him doing it. He's too good to be picking up empty glasses and he deserves better.

"How did you get that job?" Ted asks.

"It's not easy. You have to be special. Look at me! I'm FABulous and club owners need fabulous people like me to keep their clubs interesting. Otherwise, it would just be a bunch of suburbanites and outer borough trolls. We call them the bridge and tunnel crowd because they have to drive over bridges or pass through tunnels to get to the Manhattan. Basically, I'm a performer. I run around, dance, socialize and keep the party hopping. It's not enough to simply open your doors and sell some booze. Anybody can do that. You need some per-so-na-li-ties to spice things up, and if you look around here, there's a painful need for spice. Most of the guys here are just clones, with nobody trying to stand out. That's why we're so important."

Sterling's exaggerations aren't lies, it's a reality that will replace the one that actually exists. He expects to become the person he brags about. Sterling doesn't credit President Ronald Reagan for his frame of mind, yet it's very Reaganesque. Just believe it and it's true! No need for reality to intrude on belief. Sterling is a Reagan youth who knows almost nothing about Reagan despite the former actor's years in the Oval Office.

"I have to pass out more of these invites. See you later."

"I'll try to come to your party."

"Don't try. Do!" Sterling yells as he skips off towards the

dance floor feeling empowered, his stack of invites dwindling.

Sonny's stack of invites is almost gone too. He runs into Sterling a couple of times as they make their rounds around the club. Each time they bump into each other they make petty, joyful scenes, flamboyantly kissing each other multiple times on the cheeks. It's another form of self-entertainment and the conservative gay guys look on in amusement, but most quickly go back to cruising.

There are several good cruising spots in the Tunnel, especially in the back, where part of the building was left raw to remind clubbers of the venue's past as a garage for freight trains carrying valuable cargo. The management on Sunday night intentionally leaves a back area of the club unlit, and some parts of it are completely dark, where the guys feel each other up and have sex. Sterling and Sonny are intrigued by the dark area, but they don't venture in, too worried of messing their make-up or costumes, or fearful of rejection. Sonny can troll through a subway tunnel with no problem, despite the ever present danger of being killed by an on-coming train. But he can't enter a dark room full of horny men. Sonny gives up standing near the cruising area in the back and he re-positions himself at the club's entrance because there's a fresh flow of people he hasn't already approached. Later on he'll repeat that trick outside the club, standing at the exit passing out invites. There is a greater chance that the clubbers will hold on to the invites when he passes them out at the exit, even though he dislikes standing outside the club because it feels demeaning.

Sonny, Sterling and many of the other club kids mostly hold servile jobs highlighting their low social status, working as waiters or retail clerks. They tolerate abuse by their customers, so in self-defense they project out-sized egos and illusions of superiority. They think they are too good for the jobs they hold, even though they really have no skills or education that merit higher wages or better positions.

The club kids even have low status at night when they unleash their over-blown self-importance in demimondes run by cheap club owners looking for faux celebrities. The club kids fit the club owners' needs because they work for cheap, create scenes and get the clubbers buzzing about certain parties. The club owners' penny-pinching is an immense boost to club kids like Sonny, who feels like royalty go-go dancing for $75 and a hit of ecstasy. For the club owners it's a negligible expense in return for the thousands of customers paying $10 to $20 cover charges and buying $6 drinks all night.

Sonny's position by the entrance allows him to quickly finish off his first stack of invites and he pulls out another fat stack. He sees Eagle enter, dressed in a white Panama hat, a guyabera shirt and white pants.

"Hey Sonny, thanks for dancing at my party last night. You look look incredible," Eagle says laughing.

Sonny adopts a corny, sexy voice and he strokes his crotch vulgarly.

"Wanna to put your face in my green pussy?"

"You should have worn that last night. What is that on your face?"

"I'm an Easter egg abortion. Can't you tell?"

"Oh, I get it, and that's your Easter basket," Eagle says, brushing the green grass affixed to Sonny's pants.

Sonny feels a flash of euphoria that makes him forget his bruised leg. Having someone of Eagle's stature banter with him stirs immense satisfaction. Sonny quickly looks around to see if anyone notices him chatting with Eagle. Eagle is a Saturday night promoter, the most prominent night of the week for party promoters, and he is well known in New York. Suddenly, Sonny doesn't know what more to say. He really doesn't know Eagle and he stutters as he struggles to conjure a clever turn of phrase.

"My, my party is Thursday and I hope you can come," he says, handing Eagle an invite.

"Oh, I didn't know you're promoting parties."

"It's my first one, so it'll be special and FABulous. I'm putting ecstasy in a bunch of balloons and releasing them mixed with a 100 empty ones on the dance floor, tee hee hee. It's a treasure hunt, just like on Easterrrrr," Sonny growls, mocking Christianity's holiest day and fondling his green pussy.

"I'll be all over the city on Thursday, but I'll certainly try to stop by."

"Goodie!" says Sonny, hopping and clapping his hands in feigned glee.

Eagle walks away to rejoin his friends who entered with him and Sonny feels an uncertain angst. The idea that Eagle won't come to his party unsettles him. Their trivial exchange means so much. It's a validation. Now he needs another validation, Eagle's presence, since that will proclaim his party's importance. Eagle must come.

"Hey, I finished passing out my invites," says Sterling, approaching from behind with a cocktail in hand. "Everybody loves my outfit. It's the best look in the house. hiaaah!"

"That's what you think."

"That's what everybody thinks. Not just me. I can tell from their reactions. They adore me and some of them want to fuck me, but they'd never admit it," says Sterling, snapping his fingers in Sonny's face.

"Where did you get that drink? Is there another open bar?"

"You wish. I just swiped it."

"You could get in a fight by doing that."

"I've already been in a fight, with you! Anyway, darling, this is a gay party. No homo will fight me for some drink. I'm a bus boy here some nights. That's what I do. I take glasses. Granted, they're usually empty, hiaaah!"

With a fourth drink, Sterling is fairly drunk and Sonny worries that he wouldn't get much work out of him the rest of the evening, especially if he continues swiping cocktails.

"Eagle said he's coming to my party," Sonny tells Sterling triumphantly.

"Why wouldn't he? It'll be FABulous and everybody will be talking about it. I can't believe you're making me do the rope to your party. I'll be stuck outside fending off drunk bridge-and-tunnel. Everyone else will be inside having a blast. Can I at least have an ecstasy to make the job bearable?"

"No! Your job is very important and you have to take it seriously, Sterling. This is your big chance to move up in the club world, and you want to be high? What if you screw it up? They'll never ask you to do it again."

"What's to screw up? Anybody can do that."

"I'm paying you $75 to do that, which is much easier and more glamorous than walking around picking up empty glasses and nasty ash trays. You need to be a little more appreciative. I could have asked anybody to do the ropes."

"Oh please, you act like you're doing me such a big favor. Let's go dance."

Sonny sighs in frustration. He isn't used to being at the receiving end of a club kid's over-blown sense of entitlement. He's usually the one serving a superior attitude. He shrugs it off as he approaches the dance floor, now full. Sonny dances longer than he should have. During a bathroom break he realizes it's almost 1:30 and he still has half the invites. His liquor high is gone and he now feels tired.

"I'm standing by the club's exit and pass out the rest of my invites," he tells Sterling, who is completely drunk because he swiped more drinks. "Come sit on the sofa near me."

Sterling says nothing, his silver chef hat now drooping to one side because he accidentally smashed it with his wildly flailing arms during a song's climax.

"I'm over passing out invites," he says, even though Sonny only gave him one big stack at the beginning of the night.

By 2:30 Sonny finishes passing out the hundreds of invites that filled his backpack. He easily has more than 1,000 at home and there are only three more days until his party.

"Let's go, Sterling. I have to work tomorrow and I don't want to be a burned out zombie because that just makes the day drag on longer."

Sterling says nothing as they leave the club and quietly take a waiting taxi. Sonny feels an uneasy satisfaction at having distributed some invites and spoken to Eagle and Pierrot. It's important to be seen out, even though he can barely afford it. Tonight's taxi ride is a budget buster, and for sure he'll have to take the subway on Tuesday. Sterling complains on the way home, criticizing the free drinks, music, crowd and the club, as if he had no fun at all. Sterling doesn't articulate what would have made for a better evening.

Chapter 10

A crawling bug races under his nostrils. Flinging his eyelids open, Pedro awakens with the damp towel from the melted ice lying on the right side of his face, and he realizes that it's just a drop of water trickling across his face.

"Fuck you, asshole" is all he hears of some commotion down the hallway. A dull throb envelopes his head as soon as he rises from the bed, followed by a jabbing pain in his mouth. He instinctively touches his mouth and it's swollen and painful to touch. He puts his head back on the bed and waits for thoughts, but the throbbing allows for no higher thinking.

The heroin has certainly worn off, also leaving a semi-numb funk. Suddenly an echo of the affected laughter he heard last night in front of The Tunnel flashes through his mind. The skinny queen with something on his face and a little girl's backpack taunts him.

"Why was that little faggot laughing at me? Does he recognize me from the subway? Did he tell the bouncer to push me? He must work in that club. If he recognizes me from the subway, why would he tell the bouncer to attack me? Has he told the police?"

As the unpleasant numbness lifts a bit more, the unanswerable questions resume.

"Shit, Steve, what did you do? What did I do?"

Pedro stares at the ceiling, which offers no clarity or responses. The dingy white ceiling glares back, offering a blanched void. The residents in the hallway are still arguing about a can of soup someone is accused of swiping. It's another day of petty bullshit at the Y, which is one of the reasons Pedro doesn't like staying there so long. The residents get too mixed up in each other's business because they don't work, or because they enjoy the bickering.

Pedro keeps his life private at the Y, and he doesn't socialize with anyone, unlike the other druggies and drunks who spend too much time together. He stays in his room and only leaves it when he goes outside. Still, he's nervous about coming out of his room to go to the bathroom. The Y is on 23rd Street between Seventh and Eighth avenues, less than a block from the subway tunnel where he left Steve. The proximity unnerves, but Pedro likes this Y and he keeps his things here, so why should he change his habits? Wouldn't that raise suspicions?

Worry gnaws when thoughts turn to Steve. "Did I stab him? What's wrong with me?"

"I'm fucked."

The hallway yelling continues and Pedro realizes that the fight makes a good distraction. He grabs his shower kit and leaves the room. The showers are empty, to his surprise, so he quickly showers and cleans his face, though it's still obvious that he's been in an altercation. Still, such wounds don't attract much attention at the

Y because residents often show up with black eyes or bloody noses. Many of the resident winos seem unable to enjoy their highs without arguments that lead to blows. After shaving. Pedro reexamines the wound. His lips are swollen and his scraped knees still really hurt and they feel raw. He'll need some antibiotic cream, big bandages and tape for them.

"I look like one of the fucking winos in this shit hole."

Pedro returns to his room. Examining his pants, which were ripped and bloody in both knees, he rolls them up and puts them in the garbage can. There's still enough money from last night to buy medicine, food for the day and another night in the Y. It's painful to sit and rise, or to put on a clean pair of pants. His departure doesn't go entirely unnoticed.

"Hey Pedro, your mom called again. Call her! She's pissing me off with all her fucking calls and I'm not your secretary," the receptionist yells.

"Oh shit, I forgot to call her. I better do that later or she'll show up here like she did last month."

Pedro hasn't spoken to his mom in about 10 days, violating her request that he call at least one a week. It's never a good time.

"I can't call her when I'm high and I don't want to call her when I'm crashing because she'll think I'm sick. Fuck, I better call her today."

The Woolworth on the corner of 23rd Street sells Bactine and bandages, but it's above the subway stop he avoided last night on his way to the Y after visiting the dealers at the Ninth Avenue projects. Last night Pedro walked north on Seventh Avenue until he reached 23rd Street, but now he feels a dreadful compulsion to go near the subway station. Guilt, morbid interest and stupidity push him to visit the subway entrance.

"Maybe he's not dead. Shit, he's gonna be so pissed at me. How do I explain this?"

The noon sun burns Pedro's eyes, sending a wave of pain throughout his body. He stops and closes his eyes for a moment before continuing. Woolworth's entrance is only about half a block away and Pedro moves slowly in that direction. Walking towards the store, Pedro mostly stares at the ground because his eyes hurt too much from the sun. The closer he gets to the store, the more intentionally Pedro begins stepping on the sidewalk cracks. He finally looks up, and suddenly stops. There are three police cars parked at the intersection of Eighth Avenue and 23rd Street. A flight instinct seizes Pedro's body like a painful shiver, yet he can't run or even move.

"What should I do?"

Overwhelmed by alarm, Pedro quickly walks into the Woolworth. The air conditioning's cold slap gives Pedro a rush of goosebumps and a flash of pleasure, followed by a nervous chill. He stands near the store entrance, again momentarily immobilized, having forgotten why he came. The store is not very busy on Mondays. Mostly older women who live in the neighborhood walk about, one of whom rouses Pedro from his paralysis when she passes.

A slight, painful burn on the knee reminds Pedro why he's in Woolworth. Walking towards the medicinal products aisle, Pedro pauses to look at an electric room fan, then at a microwave. After an appropriate amount of time, he proceeds to the medicinal notions for some rubbing alcohol, Bactine and large bandage pads or cotton. After buying the products he approaches the corner of the store that sits next to the subway entrance at 8th Avenue and 23rd Street. He pauses about 10 feet from the door to examine some more merchandise, furtively looking at the door to watch the cops. No luck, he can't see a thing.

"Can I help you?" asks an elderly store clerk, suspecting that Pedro is a shoplifter from the Y or a nearby homeless shelter.

"Uh, no, uh, I've already bought what I needed," he responds, holding up the bag to ensure that she could see the receipt still stapled on the bag, the store's way of signaling customer payment.

"Uh, I noticed that something's going on outside with the police. Wha-, what happened?"

"I'm not really sure," the clerk says, satisfied that Pedro is not a thief, at least not today. "They've been there for a few hours and we saw them take someone, a dead body, in a stretcher. We think it's one of the homeless who live in the subway. They live in the tunnels and they even have campfires in there, according to the Daily News."

"Oh, uh, that's terrible," Pedro says, fighting the urge to run from the clerk. "Umm, do they know what happened to the man?"

"I don't know if it's a man, but I suppose it is because I can't imagine a woman living in the tunnels. How would I know what happened? I'm not sticking my nose in the police's business," the clerk says, gazing towards the glass doors.

"Oh, OK, thanks," Pedro says, steeling himself as he walks towards the door.

Exiting into the humid street, Pedro is already perspiring from the sight of the subway stairwell from inside the store and he feels a drop of sweat run down his face. He crosses 23rd Street, counting the police cars and trying not to walk too slowly or appear too interested. It feels like a dream in which he wants to stop but some force compels him to keep moving. Reaching the southeast corner of 23rd and Eighth Avenue, his mind freezes, unsure what to do, but his body continues walking south on Eight Avenue.

"I'll go around the block and try to get another look," he decides, turning west on 22nd Street.

His racing heart exacerbates the pain in his knees and mouth, which he'd momentarily forgotten.

"Why don't I just stop and stand and watch? Other people are doing that and the police aren't accusing them of anything."

Once on the corner of 23rd Street and 9th Avenue, Pedro slows his pace. He puts his thumb in the little right pocket and starts picking at the seam with his thumbnail. Halfway down the block, he removes his thumb from the pocket, stops walking and scratches his elbow. It doesn't itch. He resumes his walk towards the corner and the police activity. The police set up police tape that blocks access to the southwestern corner of 23rd Street and 8th Avenue, so he joins other spectators, but doesn't speak with any of them. Pedro's hand finds its way into his right back pocket and again begins picking at the pocket seam with his thumbnail. He presses his thumb against his buttocks and he reminds himself not to pick or pull on his pocket too hard, since he recently ripped one of his back pockets waiting for the subway and picking at the seam.

He moves a little closer to two police officers standing near the police tape, hoping to hear their discussion.

"How long do we have to wait out here?" one officer asks.

"Until the sergeant says otherwise," the other cop responds, shifting one of his feet that he reclined against a wall and putting his other foot in the same position.

The officers then discuss television and what they saw last

night. Then they start debating baseball.

"Why don't these cops care about what happened in the subway?"

Discouraged, Pedro scans his surroundings for other cops he might be able to overhear. The appropriate cop would have a few stripes on his shirt, because he might be in charge. There is one cop with those stripes, but he isn't near the tape and he's walking around talking to others. The city's din drowns out anything he's saying, and then he enters the subway station. The police start taking down the tape and a group of officers come out of the station, get in their squad cars and drive off. A pedestrian approaches an officer and speaks to him, then the pedestrian goes into the station. In about 10 minutes all the police officers leave the area and Pedro notices people coming out of the station, as if a train had just left the station.

Pedro walks to the stairwell leading into the station for the downtown trains. He tries to move his foot towards the first stair down, but his leg doesn't respond. His loses his breath and momentarily gasps for air. Conscious of his heart beat, he makes another attempt to take the first step and this time his leg moves. The roar of the passing A train makes his heart jump again. Short of breath, he takes another step into the darkness and slowly descends.

"What am I looking for?"

Once downstairs the station looks like it always looks: dirty and depressing. The token booth clerk doesn't look up as Pedro approaches the exit gate. He realizes that he doesn't have a token to get on the platform and he is too nervous to jump the turnstile, in case a cop is still on the platform or in the area. He doesn't dare enter illegally. Despite his compulsive curiosity, Pedro isn't spending money on a token. Failing to see the end of the platform on the south side of the station, Pedro walks to the other stairwell on the north side of 23rd Street and leaves.

The sunshine doesn't burn off the gloom clinging to Pedro as he emerges from the subway station. It gets worse. Like a heavy winter coat with the zipper stuck at the neck, the suffocating gloom chokes Pedro. He perspires heavily and panics. At the corner of 23rd Street and Eighth Avenue, he looks around, unsure where he should walk.

"Hey, wait a minute!" yells one of the few remaining police officers at the scene.

Pedro almost sucks the back of his tongue down his throat.

"Why does he want to talk to me? Did he see me go into the subway and not go on to the platform? Shit, why did I go into the subway station?"

"You forgot your clipboard," the cop yells past Pedro.

"Thanks sergeant," says another officer says, hurrying past Pedro to retrieve the forgotten item.

Exhaling, Pedro's aching knee buckles a bit. He needs some relief, and the cop's sudden yelling provokes a nasty craving pointing to the projects. Walking with new purpose, he feels the sidewalk rumble as a subway passes. Pedro heads south to the projects near 18th Street and Ninth Avenue.

"The dealers be out at this time"

Scoring is a mix of excitement and apprehension. There's the prospect of buying something really good that delivers a soothing disconnection. There's also danger. On several occasions the dealer thugs stole Pedro's money. Once, the dealers in the project jumped him and left him with a black eye, probably because they weren't content with stealing $20 he handed them for a fix. His heartbeat quickens as he approaches the decrepit, red-brick buildings. He walks along the south side of 19th Street heading west after crossing Ninth Avenue, slowing his pace and peering into the courtyard, looking for "Joey." It's very early in the day and none of the shady characters are hanging around. Afraid to walk into the courtyard, even though it's daylight, Pedro continues walking towards Tenth Avenue to not raise suspicions.

It makes little difference if he raises suspicions. The police don't patrol the projects with much diligence. All the junkies know that the Ninth Avenue projects are the place to score fixes. All you have to do at night is walk around the block and pushers will approach. That isn't the only part of town where Pedro shops, it's just the most convenient drug mart near the Y. If the police were serious about policing, they'd certainly pay more attention to areas like Ninth Avenue, Bryant Park, Times Square, Tompkins Square Park and Washington Square Park.

Still, a junkie paranoia stirs in Pedro. Perhaps cops don't care about the projects, but he's nonetheless determined to be discreet and inconspicuous. At least as discreet as possible for a fair-skinned young man with a swollen lip walking around the block near the projects around lunchtime. Fixing his gaze on the little playground near the projects' parking lot, Pedro scans the landscape for familiar faces. The playground at night is a good place to find the dealers, but most of them aren't be around so early in the day.

No one is in the playground so Pedro continues slowly walking on the north side of 18th Street towards Ninth Avenue, but not too slowly. To his relief he sees "Pee Wee" come out of the lobby headed towards Ninth Avenue.

"Hey Pee Wee. What's up?" Pedro shouts, trying to sound friendly and not too excited. "Wait up."

Pee Wee, a young black teenager squints meanly at Pedro even though Pee Wee's New York Yankees baseball cap shades his eyes from the sun. He recognizes Pedro as one of his posse's regular customers, though he huffs impatiently at the sight of Pedro, also remembering that he's one of the budget junkies who come looking for the cheapest bags, never spending more than $20.

"I'm looking for Red Skull," says Pedro, referring to a popular "brand" of heroin currently available in New York City.

Like any supermarket item, Red Skull is a brand with loyalists. The drug brands result from the big-time dealers and their posses competing with each other, not just with guns and intimidation, but through brand loyalty and catchy names like Red Skull, 21 and Pigeon. The dealers mark their $20 bags of heroin with little rubber stamps. Red Skull is Pedro's favorite brand for now because it has a consistent quality. Before switching to Red Skull he snorted Pigeon, symbolized by a little black pigeon stamped onto the paper envelope holding the drug. After a while dealers start diluting their brand, or competing dealers recognize the appeal of certain brands and then create their own rubber stamps to push counterfeit versions. So Pigeon fell out of favor, but the forgers still hadn't caught on to Red Skull's quality control, so that's what Pedro wanted, right now.

"Come on," PeeWee snorts impatiently. "Gimme the money."

Pedro complies with the order and hands him the $20 bill as they head to a grocery store on the corner of Ninth Avenue and 16th Street. "Wait out here."

This is the part that Pedro hates most about copping. Having a pusher take your money and then tell you to wait. Watching a pusher walk into a building is always a leap of faith. It's sometimes badly placed faith, especially when the dealers disappear into a housing project or into a large apartment building. You don't really know where they're going and you're stuck outside, usually in an unsafe neighborhood where other thugs lurk or try to start fights. More than once Pedro handed over the money and waited for up to an hour for a pusher who never returned. He can't return the next day and complain to the pusher, who might beat him or worse. Waiting in front of a grocery store doesn't worry Pedro as much. Where could Pee Wee go? He has to emerge from the little store eventually.

Pedro notes the grocery store's corner and resolves to return tomorrow to check if they're selling heroin. Buying drugs in grocery stores is Pedro's favorite way of copping. It's usually pretty quick, but the stores don't stay open long and some of them are up in Harlem where it's too dangerous for a white Puerto Rican like him. The stores usually operate like regular businesses, but often in the back there's a fake wall or a little window similar to a bank teller's. Buyers insert money under the window in exchange for a little package. Some of the stores put their drugs inside boxes of candy like Lemonheads, so there's a sweet treat to consume before the high takes effect.

Pee Wee finally emerges from the store with a shopping bag apparently full of groceries.

"Did he spend my money of food?" Pedro wonders, as he follows Pee Wee back to the projects.

About a half block away from the grocery, Pee Wee pulls a little brown paper bag out of his groceries and hands it to Pedro. "Get the fuck outta here," he barks.

Pedro turns the corner at 17th Street and walks east towards Eighth Avenue. His heart beats quickly with excitement in anticipation of the high. It's one of the best feelings, the anticipation after having safely scored some dope and then rushing somewhere safe to use it. So many thoughts swirl through the mind on the way to a date with dope.

How good will it be? Did I get gypped? Party time! Relief.

Arriving at Eighth Avenue, Pedro looks north and imagines the alcove where he left Steve. Shuddering just a bit, Pedro continues walking towards Seventh Avenue and then to the Y. Once in his room he prepares the bandages and ointment for his knees. It didn't make them feel much better, but it's good being in his room, even if it's hot and stuffy. He opens the window, snorts some of the heroin and then turns on the ceiling fan, careful to repackage his drugs before the fan scatters the precious powder.

Lying back on the bed, Pedro awaits take-off. "I need to call Mom. What should I tell her? Maybe she'll let me come home for a few days?"

Pedro imagines his father yelling at him. It isn't a good relationship, especially after he dropped out of SVA. His father resented him and accused him of wasting his money by attending college and not being serious. Just the thought of his dad raising the same accusations and complaints make Pedro tense. Pedro feels angry. He's angry at school because it didn't work out. He's angry at his creativity, which hasn't served him well. Creativity makes him miserable. He's angry at his father. He can't explain all this anger.

"I need to talk to somebody about this."

The blessed numbness returns. A warm tingle tickled the top of his skull and then slipped down his body, releasing the worries about his situation and his family.

"I'll talk to them tomorrow," Pedro promises himself, though he rarely recalls such resolutions.

Chapter 11

Mondays are usually Sonny's day off but he rearranged his schedule so he can have Thursday and Friday off for the big party. Although Sonny was so excited to land a job at Runway six months ago, he's bored of it now. Its low pay barely affords him a studio, in reality a big room with a bathtub in the kitchen, like many of the apartments in the East Village old tenements. The run-down apartment building on E. 12th Street between avenues A and B is simply a place to crash and keep clothes. It isn't a home and Sonny never bothered to decorate. It's more a workshop where he spends hours constructing outfits for the greater glory of his prized creation — the nightclub personality Sonny Delight.

There's no question about leaving Sterling in the apartment. There's no rousing him from his state of unconsciousness given the many drinks he consumed last night. Sonny washes his face to remove last night's left-over mascara and then applies some light day foundation and a little under-eye cover to hide the exhaustion.

There's no time for hairstyling; it will be a hat day.

There isn't much of a dress code at Runway. Anything goes so long as it has some style. Jeans are OK if they are paired with an eye-catching jacket or fierce pair of shoes. The problem with "anything goes so long as it's fabulous" is that there's pressure to compose an ensemble, not an easy task on hangover days. Sonny isn't in the mood for fashion or work. The daily need to compose an ensemble produces chaos, with clothes scattered throughout the room, hanging in the bathtub, from chairs at the table and lying in a pile on the floor in the corner. The apartment is a mess and Sonny rarely cleans. Why bother? All that matters is the final product that walks out the door, not what remains behind. Without looking too closely, Sonny grabs a pink t-shirt from the pile near the stove, puts on some skinny black jeans and red sneakers. That's it. He has an outfit to go with his sequin-covered baseball cap.

The sunlight doesn't perk up Sonny, it just gives him a mild headache, despite his dark sunglasses. Runway is a quick walk over to E. 7th Street between First Avenue and Avenue A, nestled among other trendy stores catering to the hordes of foreign tourists who visit St. Mark's Place one block to the north. The tourists usually find their way to E. 7th Street after walking over to Tompkins Square Park, the epicenter for the East Village's dying punk scene. Many of the old junkie punks hung out there day and night, panhandling and appealing to the tourists' sympathies. When that doesn't work they use intimidation, which also yields them a fair amount of "donations."

Sonny avoids Tompkins Square Park and he doesn't walk down Avenue A much either, especially by himself. Although people think the East Village is a "live-and-let-live" type of place, Sonny knows better. It's a nest of intolerance, especially for a queer dodo. The junkie punks begging at the corner of St. Mark's Place and Avenue A by the pizzeria sometimes flick their lit cigarettes at Sonny. The punks are so disdainful of Sonny, who they considered one of the posers ruining their neighborhood. In fact it's real estate speculators and young, urban professionals who were "ruining" the neighborhood by slowly transforming it into something stylish and sophisticated. Sonny likes the transformation because it delivers many customers to Runway, so his job depends on it, but the junkie punks somehow concluded that Sonny is to blame.

Sonny likes walking along First Avenue, which doesn't have the same menacing groups of punk rockers. Instead, it gives Sonny the opportunity to acquaint himself with the drug dealers that regularly stand on First Avenue between 9th and 10th streets. It never makes sense to Sonny how dealers choose one block and not another. What is it about this block that allows the pushers to feel so brazen? They chant their wares "weed, coke, ecstasy" to every passer-by, like a Greek chorus extolling the city's blatant lawlessness. Just a few blocks away on Second Avenue and 12th Street, prostitutes regularly work the corner with little hassle from authorities. If barely dressed hussies can openly solicit customers passing in cars, why shouldn't pushers on First Avenue just ask every pedestrian if they want to get high?

Sonny arrives at Runway with a big yawn and no desire for work. Some of the employees are already in the store, which opens at 11 a.m. Monday is inventory day, when employees count the merchandise and reconcile sales with what actually remains on the shelves. Sonny enjoys having Mondays off. Not only is most of the staff in a hangover-induced bad mood, but the job requires far more mental engagement than any other weekday because of all the counting, review of sales receipts and comparisons with old delivery invoices. Most of the time the numbers don't add up, which the staff attributes to shoplifters. Blaming theft for the faulty numbers isn't just an excuse for sloppy accounting. There's a good deal of theft from the store; Runway is expensive and it attracts young fashion devotees from uptown and the Bronx. They are expert thieves and friends with some of Runway's staffers, so they can distract employees with gossip so their accomplices can steal. The owner accepts the significant theft so long as it doesn't cut too deeply into profits. It's like a tax, and the "tax collectors" are mostly young black and Latino gay boys from uptown. Sonny even sees some of them at night in the clubs wearing items that disappeared from Runway, but he doesn't call them out for it. It's not his store and he doesn't get paid enough to care.

Sonny first realized that some of the scene queens were shoplifting from Runway a few months ago at a house ball, a party organized by drag queens in the form of a beauty pageant. One of the competitive categories was Mop 'Til You Drop, though he didn't realize at the time that mop was slang for shoplifting. After the MC introduced the competition and explained that the competitors had to strut before the judges wearing only items that they had shoplifted from stores. There were seven competitors and they came out in expensive ready-to-wear, jewelry and shoes. To prove that they'd shoplifted the items, all the garments had to have the untorn price tag or else a competitor would be disqualified. One of the contestants came out wearing a complete outfit from Runway: a shirt, pants and sneakers that the owner had accused an employee of stealing. Sonny's response was to giggle with delight.

"Good morning, ladies," says Darnell, a portly black queen who manages the store on weekdays. "It's our favorite day of the week and evvvveryone has to help. No hiding in the dressing room, bitches."

Like many Runway staffers, Darnell uses exaggerated, overly theatrical speech, even when he's reminding his co-workers that they have to count sequined socks. It's the same tone he uses on stage performing in his drag alter-ego Miss Creant. The voice works so well on stage that he uses it off stage.

"Sonny, get your skinny ass over here. You're my right-hand assistant today."

Sonny says nothing, but slowly lumbers towards Darnell, shuffling slowly and unsteadily.

"Girrrl, what's wrong with you. Not feeling perky?"

"I'm here on time, aren't I?"

"OK, you don't need to talk. You just need to follow my instructions and we'll be done by lunchtime."

The inventory check begins by making lists of the store's sections, with the three employees counting and writing down what's on the shelves. Runway isn't a big store, so the task normally takes about two hours if there aren't a lot of customers. Monday mornings are very slow, which is why the inventory is done then. The first hour at Runway is agonizing for Sonny as he slowly emerges from his hangover. He doesn't say much, focusing on the counting. By 1 p.m. the trio finishes the chore and they take turns going on lunch breaks. After two cups of coffee, Sonny feels better and chattier, as do Darnell and Corvette. Darnell spends some of the afternoon discussing Miss Creant's show at a West Village gay bar.

"This was quality entertainment, not mindless bullshit. I even hit the crowd with a new joke: 'The Republican candidate Rudy

Giuliani said last week that if David Dinkins becomes our city's first black mayor, it might be because of voter fraud in Harlem.' This is my punchline: 'No, Miss Comb-Over, I've worked the polls. There's no fraud uptown, but there are some fine brothers casting votes. Four years ago a hot motherfucker came in to vote just as we were closing. We started talking and he waited for my shift to end, so the only ballot box that got stuffed that night was right here,'" says Darnell, slapping his ass for emphasis.

"That's not funny," Sonny says, interrupting Darnell's self-satisfied laughter. "Most people don't care about politics and they don't get that."

"People get it. People laughed at it, you shallow queen! Just because you're ignorant doesn't mean everybody else is. People know about politics and they appreciate my humor because it's IN-TEL-LEC-tual. It's not just stupid drag queen jokes. I've added to my humor and expanded my boundaries and the public appreciates that because it's different," Darnell says indignantly.

"You're funny no matter what you say."

"Don't patronize me, bitch. I'll get ghetto on your ass and rip your eyes out before you can shed a tear!"

Both Sonny and Darnell burst into laughter after that threat, and Sonny decides to stop bantering with Darnell because it's getting too heated. It's best to change the subject, preferably to Sonny's party on Thursday night.

"Darnell, are you coming to my party on Thursday? It won't be fabulous without YOU."

"I don't know yet. I'm too old for that Tunnel crowd. It's nothing but children," says Darnell, who never reveals his age, but he's at least 10 years older than Sonny and the other club kids at the Tunnel.

"You need to COME. It'll be one of the most talked about nights. It will be LEGENDARY."

"I'm the legend. You are NOT," says Darnell, correcting Sonny.

"Well, just think about it. Hey, I didn't tell you about my insane Saturday night."

"What happened," Darnell asks, raising an eyebrow but not his gaze from the inventory list he's still trying to reconcile.

"I had a near-death experience."

"I told you not to take that ecstasy with the Mercedes Benz symbol on it. There is some kind of nasty shit in it and I know at least three people that got sick from it, including myself."

"Noooo, this has nothing to do with ecstasy. It's something far more dangerous and evil. I did something I'd never done before on Saturday night in the subway."

"Did you have sex in the subway?" said Darnell, this time looking up with anticipation.

"Noooo, it's not drugs or sex. It's something more outrageous. I decided to go into the subway tunnel to spray paint my name in the tunnel like the taggers do," Sonny lies, referring to the graffiti vandals who scrawl illegible names in the subway instead of painting elaborate murals.

"No you didn't," Darnell says with certainty.

"Yes, I'm experimenting. I figured there are so many graffitis in the subway tunnels that it can't be so hard. It's an art form and I'm open to exploring any creative outlet in case it's something that works for me."

"There is nothing outrageous about painting your name in a dark tunnel, little Miss North Jersey," Darnell says in a falsetto.

"No, that's not the outrageous part. I was in there looking for a place to paint my tag. I decided to go in the tunnel under Eighth Avenue between 14th and 23rd streets because it's on the way to the Tunnel. So I looked for a good spot when I was running on the tracks because I was nervous that a train might come, even though I waited for one to pass before running into the tunnel."

"Wait a minute. What's your tag?"

"It's S-Dee," says Sonny, instantly blurting out a response and feeling pride at having concocted a tag so quickly. "That's S, hyphen, D, E, E."

"What else have you tagged?" asks Darnell, still incredulous.

"I haven't really tagged anything yet. I wanted to try the subway first because I've seen so many of them down there. I'm not interested in scrawling up the subway trains the way some of the taggers do. That's no fun and any idiot can do that with a Magic Marker. I wanted a challenge, which is why I decided to go into the subway tunnel, because not everybody has the balls to do that. I also like the subway tunnels and I've explored them in the past, so I know where the good spots to tag are."

"You're exploring the tunnels?" asks Corvette, whose morning Don't-Talk-To-Me scowl is fading.

"One of my hobbies is exploring the subway tunnels. I like going in there because it's dangerous and exciting, and there are all kinds of incredible graffitis down there. All you need is a flashlight."

"You could be killed," says Corvette, though she isn't really expressing concern for Sonny's safety since he annoys her.

"Well, the graffiti guys who go in there and paint big murals aren't getting killed. You know it's taking them much longer than the time between trains to paint murals."

Darnell and Corvette nod in agreement with Sonny's logic.

"That's still not so outrageous," Darnell says.

"I haven't even told you CRAZY part yet. I was quickly running through the tunnel looking for a good, blank spot where I could paint my Day-Glo pink tag. It had to be a spot that was a little higher up so that when the trains passed the lights from inside the trains will light up the paint and flash back at the passengers. My idea is to spray paint it in a couple of spots one after another so that the passengers won't just see it once, they'll see it a few times. I'd like to have a tag viewing party when I'm done, but I'm still preparing for my big event on Thursday."

"Girl, you've got it all planned out, don't you. Maybe you ARE a closet tagger. I would never have guessed," Darnell interrupts. "How could you see in that tunnel?"

"I had a flashlight in my lunchbox," Sonny replies impatiently, as if that's the most obvious answer since the club kids typically carry supplies in their lunchboxes.

"Here's the CRA-ZY part. I was walking through the tunnel and coming near the 23rd Street station when I heard a NOISE. It wasn't the train. I was getting nervous even though I waited until an uptown train passed before going in the tunnel, just to make sure there'd at least 15 minutes to run to the next station. It's only about six blocks when you think about it, since the 14th Street platform goes up to 16th Street and the 23rd Street platform comes almost to 22nd Street. Anyway, the sound was someone yelling, or maybe two people fighting. It wasn't coming from the street either. I could hear it very clearly in the tunnel and I suddenly got so scared that I wanted to stop walking towards the 23rd Street platform, but I also knew that I had to hurry up because a train might be coming. I kept walking, but slower, just in case. I heard more yelling and cussing and then I saw this evil looking guy wearing a captain's hat holding a knife in his hand. I think he stabbed someone."

"For real?" Darnell asks.

"Yes, and then I slipped and my lunchbox hit the wall and made a big noise. That's when the guy with the knife looked over to where I was and he SAW me. Right at that moment I felt the clanking of the train tracks. You know that sound when you're waiting in the station for the train and you can't see it but you hear the tracks clicking together so you know something is coming? That's the sound I heard and when I looked back I could see the train's headlight, so I knew I had to get the hell out of there. I started running for my LIFE and the guy with the knife yelled 'Hey you, stop.' There was no way I'd take orders from some scary man in a dark tunnel with a knife. He started running after me towards the platform, but I think he also heard the train coming because he didn't cross over to the uptown side of the tracks. He ran towards 23rd Street on the downtown side and I made it to the platform first. I was so SCARED! The train was coming and a killer was chasing me. I practically jumped from the tracks to the platform and then I ran up the platform towards the stairs to the street. There were a couple of people on the platform who I'm sure were surprised to see me jump out from the tunnel. None of them tried to stop me. By the time I got to the turnstiles you could hear the train roaring into the station. I didn't even look behind me at the point.

"Didn't the token booth clerk see you?" asks Corvette, still certain that Sonny is lying.

"Unless you knock on their windows trying to get a token, they're usually asleep past midnight."

"That's true," Corvette says, still not willing to believe.

"I made it out into the street. I was BREATH-less! I ran up 8th Avenue until I got to 25th Street before I turned around to see if he was following me, but he wasn't. I quickly put my flashlight away, and that's when I got an even bigger shock," Sonny paused.

"What?" Darnell asked, by this time no longer looking at the inventory lists.

"I think some of the invites to Thursday's party fell out of my back pocket when I was climbing out of the tunnel or when I began running on the platform. They were in the back pocket of my hot pants, but I'm not sure if I really had some there or if I just thought they were there. Either way, there wasn't anything in my pocket by the time I was on Eighth Avenue. This guy might come to my party on Thursday and cause a SCANDAL!"

"Why didn't you call the police," Corvette asks in an accusatory tone.

"What could I tell the police? 'Hi, I was strolling through the subway tunnel tagging and I saw this scary guy with a knife?' It's illegal to be in the tunnel, they might arrest me, and I didn't see that guy with the knife do anything anyway, other than scare me," Sonny explains.

"I wouldn't worry about it. New York is full of scary people. What'll he do at the Tunnel in front of thousands of people? It's not like you're ever walking around those desolate street near the Tunnel. He won't find you," Darnell concludes, assuming that Sonny took a taxi.

"We have a CUST-o-mer!" Darnell announces with a trill in his voice. "Get to work, you lying bitch."

Sonny retells the story a couple of times during the day as scene queens come by the store. He adds a few dramatic pauses and changes his tone a bit, though he tries not to change the story he originally told Darnell and Corvette, since they already didn't believe it. By day's end Sonny told four people who came by the shop, strategically choosing his confidants to ensure maximum gossip. It's an investment in party promotion. It will help create a bigger buzz about his party and maybe more people will come if they think there will be an element of danger.

Sonny doesn't know if he dropped any party invites on the subway platform. It doesn't matter. People are interested in the story. It's exciting. Graffiti is the last thing on Sonny's mind in the tunnel, but now that he "confessed" his "passion" for tagging, it makes sense that he should adopt it as a hobby. He pulled a tag out of thin air, but he likes it and during the rest of the afternoon he draws little tags on paper, trying to decide which will be the best style to paint in the tunnel. There has to be at least one, so he can show it off before Thursday and add it to his debut party's hype. It's got to lead to another party celebrating his tags. After about four hours, Sonny settles on a tag that doesn't require much artistry or drawing skill, yet resembles a real tag because it has some of the exaggerated lines that make tags difficult to read. Sonny's tag consists of all capitalized letters with an S whose top part is horizontally elongated above the rest of the letters so that the top line of both E's are part of the elongated line for the S. The top of the D is also attached to the horizontal line. The top horizontal line suggests Hindi writing, which Sonny noticed on some of the Indian restaurants on Sixth Street. The hyphen for S-DEE stretches from the S through the second D, ending with an asterisk. He wants to end the tag with a star, but can't figure out how to make it look nice, and the asterisk is easier.

"No point in agonizing over something that's displayed in the dark."

Wrecked after a full day that ends at 7 p.m., Sonny endures a comatose walk back home. Mercifully, Monday isn't a very busy club night so he can stay in and plan his outfits for the rest of the week. During some of the down time in the store he made his to-do list:

1. Plan Tuesday's outfit, maybe a playing card theme on body/face?

2. Plan Wednesday's outfit???

3. Plan Thursday's outfit. Borrow the kelly green bolero jacket with black feather epaulettes from work and pair it with my black boots, black feathers on the face, black vinyl hot pants and black net t-shirt. Tie a frog purse with a zipper in the back to my black studded biker's belt.

The list gives Sonny costume anxiety because this is an important week and there are too many question marks. Even borrowing the bolero from work isn't a given, since he hasn't asked permission. He's tempted to just take it without permission and bring it back Friday. The problem is cleaning it. Clothes usually reek after a night in the smoky clubs and there is no masking that smell with any kind of freshener. The bolero isn't washable, and dry cleaners will take a few days.

Sonny thinks some more at the Chinese take-out, where he orders chicken chow mein.

"Is it worth getting yelled at? Yes, fuck work. A day job shouldn't hold me back."

After stopping at the variety store to buy two decks of cards, Sonny heads home to rest and assemble a new outfit, maybe two. Sterling is gone and he didn't leave any note, so Sonny figures he'd see him Tuesday at Trix, a fashion party on 19th Street that caters to an older, mixed fashion crowd with a big gay presence, drag queens and aspiring club kids like Sonny. Trix often draws people in expensive designer ready-to-wear, but Sonny can't afford those kinds of clothes, so he always improvises. The crowd appreciates thrift-store chic and inventive flair, one of Sonny's strengths. Trix's management also allows promoters to distribute their invites inside, so it's the perfect place for Sonny to drum up attendance for Thursday. Clearing his table from the debris of last night's Easter egg abortion, Sonny begins looking for his costume's building blocks, not so easy in a messy apartment where nothing has its place and where there is no place for anything. Sonny has little furniture or storage. The studio's one closet is full of clothes, with boxes and shoes on the floor and more disorganized gear on a shelf above the clothing pole.

"Should I prominently feature the joker or the queen of diamonds? Red or multicolor?"

He shuffles through the playing cards and then pulls some tights from his dirty clothes pile. One pair is yellow and the other red, so he cuts the leg off one of the pairs that has a run in it and decides to wear them together. Assembling an outfit is like painting. Sonny dabs color or removes it from the collage assembled on his bed. It's the only time he actually makes the bed. When successful Sonny has a little pile of garments and accessories for the featured ensemble. Sonny inserts cards all the way around the band of a black top hat he bought at a flea market. That solves the hair issue, since he's covering it up, and it also steers him in the direction of the joker. Queens don't wear top hats, he figures, so he'll glue a couple of the joker cards to his face. The rest of the costume is easy because it is a variant of what he often wears in the clubs, green hot pants with the two pairs of tights beneath, his black combat boots, a red spandex t-shirt and a vest festooned with as many playing cards as possible. That will be the hardest part of the look. Using a skinny nail Sonny punched two little button holes in about 50 of the playing cards, which he then ties on to his vest with a needle and thread, as if sewing buttons. It's a tedious chore made all the more difficult because Sonny is so tired. The goal is to sew at least the front half of the vest so that it looks finished even if he doesn't have time for the back. Fortunately, playing cards take up a good amount of space on a vest, so he finishes the front of the garment before passing out in bed, without even turning off the radio.

Chapter 12

"Check out time is at noon, so you've got to go or pay for some more nights," yells a Y attendant, banging on doors as part of his morning ritual ensuring compliance with the rules.

Pedro already woke up earlier before snoozing again, but this time there is no drifting off. He snorted up the whole bag of heroin during the night every time he emerged from his drug cloud. The drug did its work, he passed most of the night in a world removed from the one he dreads. Still a little disoriented, Pedro gathers up his shower kit and goes to the bathroom. He quickly takes a shower and shaves. Back in his room, he dresses in clean black jeans and a grey t-shirt. He counts his money, only $10, barely enough for a lunch and certainly not enough for another fix or night at the Y. Leaving the room he walks down the stairs to the locker room to put his things away, considering his next move.

"You payin' for another night?"

"Not right now. I don't have enough money. Maybe later," Pedro mumbles to the attendant.

The Y staffer has no response. It's just another day with the unlucky men who waft in and out of the building. Checking out at 11 a.m. and then reentering at 6 p.m. is not an unusual occurrence. Especially with young men like Pedro, who staffers see on the streets begging for change. Others walk around the neighborhood collecting empty cans. The staffer knows Pedro will be back. If not tonight, then tomorrow after sleeping in the park, most likely.

Feeling hungover, Pedro walks out of the Y into the blinding sunshine that his dark glasses don't block. He heads to the nearest deli and orders a coffee and donut. Sitting in the little tables in the back of the deli, Pedro nurses his coffee and donut, wondering what's next.

Unlike yesterday, there are no voices poking at him. He's blank and tired. It's a comforting vacancy that quickly fades as the grogginess fades. Steve's face flashes through his mind and he hears his voice,   provoking a longing. Pedro imagines Steve sitting with him in the deli, drinking coffee, gazing at blue eyes that served as dots under the exclamation points in his blond spiky hair. Desire curdles into anxiety.

"Shit," Pedro's eyes water.

His throat aches swallowing the last of his coffee and he can't eat the last bite of the donut. The deli's florescent lights become intolerable, so it's time to go outside. On the way out Pedro walks past the newspaper racks and sees two big words on one of the tabloids: DEADLY DISCOVERY.

The words paralyze and intrigue him. He averts his gaze, yet awkwardly reaches to grab the paper. He doesn't dare to read it in the deli. Paying for the paper, he nervously walks out of the deli, careful to fold the two ends of the front page together so that only the back sports page shows, as if nobody else hasn't already seen what's on the cover of one of New York City's largest tabloid newspapers by simply looking at the news boxes and newsstands that sit on most of the corners along 23rd Street.

Unsure where to go, Pedro instinctively heads to Madison Square Park. It's almost noon and most of the park benches are occupied by the workers from the surrounding toy and insurance office buildings. Pedro finds one end of a bench and sits down uncomfortably in the blazing, morning sunshine. Pausing for a moment, Pedro stares at the folded newspaper. He looks around to see if anyone is staring at him. He sees a number of people eating and reading the same newspaper he just bought. Reassured, he opens the paper and studies the photograph of ambulance workers taking a stretcher up the final steps of the subway entrance at 23rd Street and Eighth Avenue. The stretcher has what looks like a body with a white sheet over it from head to toe. Under the awful headline the newspaper announces: "Gruesome find."

Pedro continues staring at the photograph, as if expecting some movement on that stretcher. The image's stillness tightens a growing knot in Pedro's chest. He gasps for air. Turning the page, there is another photo of the stretcher inside an ambulance whose back door is open. A short article accompanies the photo.

"NEW YORK — Transit workers checking on the Eight Avenue line's electrical systems Monday got a macabre shock when they discovered the decomposing corpse of an allegedly homeless man.

Police say a white male in his early 20's with an apparent stab wound was found in a tunnel recess near the south end of the subway platform next to the southbound tracks.

No identification was on the body, according to police.

Workers made the gruesome discovery around 10 a.m. shortly after the morning rush hour when the work crew began its inspection of the line's electrical systems, which in the past two weeks have suffered power outages resulting in stalled trains.

Police could not say how long the man had been in the tunnel or if he died from his stab wound or from some other cause.

A police source familiar with the investigation who declined to be identified said that the man may have been a drug addict or a dealer because investigators found drug paraphernalia on his body and in the recessed area, including empty glassine baggies typically used to package drugs.

Authorities shut down all local subway service on the Eighth Avenue line between 34th and 14th streets for almost three hours during the investigation. They offered few details about the man or why he might have been in the tunnel, though in recent months the transit system has been the site of various encampments by homeless men.

"The subway system has hundreds of miles of rail lines and tunnels that are very hard to secure," said Dale Wilson, an MTA spokesman, responding to questions about yesterday's discovery. "The engineers who designed our system decades ago never imagined that people would take shelter in the tunnels, so they didn't make them hard to enter."

The bone-chilling find under a busy commercial strip sent shivers down the spine of longtime resident Bernice Grillo, 68, a retired receptionist running some shopping errands.

"I only take the subway in the daytime because it's gotten so bad down there with all the thugs and the homeless. I think I'm just taking the bus from now on, even though it's much slower than the trains," Grillo said.

Pedro puts down the paper. Confusion leaves him blank, unsure what to conclude.

"He wasn't homeless or a junkie, you fucking assholes," Pedro mumbles. "Steve is dead and this is all they have to say about him?"

Pedro takes the pages of the paper about Steve, folds them and inserts them in his bag, discarding the rest of the paper in a smelly garbage can just two or three feet from his bench.

"No wonder nobody was sitting here."

Pedro rises from the bench for a walk around the park's fountain, hoping to pass through a cloud of mist coming off the fountain. He slowly circles the park's southern fountain. He violently hits his thigh three times in quick succession, seeking an answer. There are lots of questions. He sees Steve's face again.

"What the fuck are you doing?"

Pedro winces and raises both arms, clutching his head as he looks around the park. Looking southeast towards 23rd Street, Pedro starts walking towards SVA. For just a second he feels like he's going there for a class, but confusion clouds his thinking again. He continues walking towards SVA. Once there, he pauses outside the school, unsure if he should enter.

"What am I doing here? They're not even gonna let me in. I don't have a valid school ID."

Pedro enters the building and goes to the business office, an area of the school where entry doesn't require a student ID.

"Can I help you?" a school employee asks from behind the business office's counter.

"Um, I'm a student here. Uh, uh, I mean, I was a student here and I had to stop coming, but I want to talk to somebody about coming back," says Pedro, stammering self-consciously.

"We don't have an advisor who's immediately available, but if you want to wait I think there might be one available in about 10 or 15 minutes," the young woman says.

"Uh, OK, I'll wait," says Pedro, giving her his particulars and dates of attendance, avoiding eye contact.

Sitting in the business office offers unexplainable solace. The air conditioning helps Pedro relax a bit, though he is still shaking his left leg. It's quiet in the office and even the phones ring quietly, more like an electronic purr. The setting reminds Pedro of the distant excitement he felt when first entering that office. The business office was one of the first parts of the school that Pedro saw and even that sterile room with desks and file cabinets offered him so much promise as he began his art career. It was a dream come true.

"Why didn't it work out? The advisor might ask me that. What's the reason?"

Pedro considers an appropriate answer, but can't think of one. Shuffling in his seat, he asks himself again why school didn't work out.

"The advisor is ready to see you," the young woman says, interrupting the self-analysis. "It's Mr. Avella. He's in room 122."

Pedro picks up his bag and leaves the business office, excited at the prospect of speaking with someone that can help him get back in school. He feels a tickling reassurance on his way down the hall until reaching Mr. Avella's office and knocking on the open door.

"Come in, Pedro. I'm Chris Avella. How can I help you?"

"Uh, um, I stopped coming to school last year and I want to come back to finish my degree. H-h, How can I do that?"

"If you stopped for more than a year then you'll have to reapply to the school, but it won't be as hard getting in as if you were a new student because we're also interested in you finishing your degree. What's your major?"

"I was, um, fine arts….painting, but, uh, th-, things didn't work out."

"Why not?"

"Uh, I'm not sure. I don't think I was ready….for college. I came right out of high school and it was too much for me, the independence, being in the city….the parties."

"I understand. That happens to many young people who come to college in New York City. What I'd like to know is whether you're ready to try again and really apply yourself. You got into the school in the first place, so the admissions officers thought you had talent and potential. Something went wrong along the way, but how are you different now so that you can finish your education?"

"Um, I think I'm more mature now?" Pedro responds with more of a question than an assertion. "Uh, I want to be more serious about the future and I'm tired of just living day to day, doing nothing."

"What have you done since dropping out?"

The question sends a shiver through Pedro.

"Um, nuh-, nothing really, just working stupid jobs," says Pedro, avoiding Avella's eyes and looking at the floor, scratching an elbow that doesn't itch. "I really need a….nuh-, new direction and I think coming back to school will give me the motivation to move forward."

There's a short, uncomfortable silence as the advisor stares at the dropout.

"Pedro, I'm concerned about what I'm hearing from you. We deeply regret losing every student when they drop out and we have resources in place to prevent that from happening. I don't know if you took advantage of those resources when you were here, but what you're saying right now is a cause for concern. I don't know you, but judging from what you're saying I don't think you'd be successful if you returned. The reason I say this is because you just told me you need a new direction and you think coming to school will give you motivation. You need motivation before you walk in the door. This school can't give you any motivation. Only you can bring that to the table. Can you explain to me why you dropped out?"

Pedro shuffles in his chair some more, unsure where to start.

"Uh" he pauses awkwardly, "It's not easy explaining this. I, uh, I stopped coming for a few reasons. One is because I didn't get along with my painting teacher, Mr. Stanley. Another is because I started going out, partying and it kind of interfered with homework. But I don't want to party any more. I, uh, want to be more serious. Um, I want to go back to painting."

"When was the last time you painted?"

"I don't know, um, it's been a while. One of the problems is that I don't have any st-, storage space for my art supplies. I live at the YMCA and some of my supplies are at my parents' house in Long Island."

"Well, since you were in the fine arts program, you probably took sketching, which you have to do on your canvasses when you're setting up your scene and perspectives, right? When was the last time you sketched anything? Teachers usually require you to sketch every day, and even in the summer our students who are serious about their art continue sketching. Do you have a sketch book with you that I can look at?"

The solace Pedro felt when he entered the business office and the resolve to continue his art degree drains away with each question. Pedro doesn't like thinking about painting or drawing, since it brings up sour feelings. Answering questions about it is even less appealing.

"Uh, I don't have my sketch book with me. I left it in my

locker at the Y," Pedro says, lying. "I haven't sketched in a fuh-, few weeks, I guess."

"Pedro, you need to start drawing and painting, even before you apply for reentry. The admissions officers will want to see what you've been doing while you were away from school. It's important to show us that you still have a passion for your art because it's obvious that your passion and motivation either weakened while you were here, or you didn't apply yourself. We need to be reassured that you have the necessary drive and that you'll be able to finish if we let you back in. Otherwise, what's the point? You'll only end up wasting a lot of your time and money. It's not fair to you or to other students who might want to come into the school but can't because you're filling a seat. Do you understand?"

"Yea," Pedro responds, feeling dejected and a surging anger.

"I want you to spend the next month drawing and painting. Lets make an appointment for Sept. 30 for you to come back with your new work. On that day I'll meet with you and I'll also invite an admissions officer to our meeting. That way we can discuss the possibility of you returning in the spring semester. OK?"

"OK, thanks," says Pedro, taking a paper from the advisor with the next meeting's date and time.

"Good luck," the advisor says after Pedro turns his back to walk out.

The incipient anger Pedro feels grows stronger as he walks towards the school's exit. The anger is accompanied by a familiar resentment Pedro experienced walking through the school. "Fuck art," he used to say after leaving a class when teachers reprimanded him for sloppy work or for clearly not spending enough time on his assignments. Unsure where to go, Pedro returns to the park. Staring at the ground, the anger continues pecking at him, alternating with visions of Steve's face. Pedro, puts his left elbow on his left knee and his right elbow on his right knee, clutching his face with his right hand.

"I'm fucked."

Rising from the bench, Pedro walks west on 23rd Street. It takes about 15 minutes to reach Eighth Avenue and he slows his pace as he approaches the subway station and waits by the stairwell until a group of subway riders comes up the stairs from the southbound side. He then descends the stairs, buys a token and enters the platform, heading for the southernmost end of the platform, but he doesn't get too close to the tunnel entrance. Nervously, he looks around to see if there are any police or cameras. He looks into the darkness, trying to recall how many steps it takes to reach the alcove.

"What did you do to me, Steve?"

Pedro's face moistens with with a few tears. Staring into the darkness, he aches to see the alcove and he hears the rumble from an on-coming southbound train. Drying his eyes with his t-shirt's sleeve, Pedro steps back. He doesn't sit down when he boards the train, but instead stands by the door looking out into the station through the glass. As the train pulls out of the station, Pedro brings his face almost to the glass. He looks for the alcove, but can't really see it as the train speeds up. The dark recessed area passes in an instant, unnoticed by any other train passenger.

Pedro gets off the train at 14th Street, frustrated by his proximity to a safe haven that now stirs dread. He sits on the platform's bench, unsure where to go. He's spent money on a token, so he shouldn't waste it. There aren't too many options: the soup kitchen, Times Square for some panhandling, the merry-go-round. He doesn't have enough cash to visit the projects and there's no point returning to the park. Unable to decide, Pedro's heart starts palpitating and sweat starts forming on his forehead. He feels short of breath and unsure.

"I can't take this."

Pedro jumps up from the bench and walks north on the platform, about 40 feet before slowing down as he realizes he can't actually walk anywhere but out of the station. The northbound train then begins its loud rumble into the station and Pedro suddenly considers an unpleasant option.

"What the fuck, I'm desperate."

Pedro tries again to look out the window heading north on the train, but there's no seeing the alcove from the northbound tracks with all the light flooding out of the train car. His search for the alcove is a fruitless effort. At the 23rd Street station, Pedro resists the urge to get off the train and abandon his new course. At the next stop as the train slows to a stop in the 34th Street station, Pedro has a lump in his throat. He leaves the subway and enters the brightly lit, yet dingy Penn Station concourse. The chooses a bank of telephones next to the shoe repair shop, fishes for some change and finds too little for a call. Hanging up the receiver, Pedro turns to leave, but freezes in his tracks.

"Where am I going?"

There's no answer. There's no voice in his head offering any advice. His thoughts are a hiss of TV static, so he picks up the receiver again and calls the operator to place a collect call. He scans the Long Island Railroad's departures board for the next train to New Hyde Park. The lump in his throat bulges bigger after the operator patches the call through.

"Uh, hi mom, how are you?"

"Junior? Oh my God. Where have you been? Oh my God, why haven't you called? You're killing me. Where are you?" asks Sandra, Pedro's mother.

"I'm at Penn Station. I'm thinking of visiting you. Can you pick me up at the New Hyde Park station?"

"What's wrong? You haven't called me in almost two weeks and now you want to visit? What are you doing in the city? Where are you living?"

"Um, I'm living at the YMCA on 23rd Street, but I duh-, don't have a phone in my room."

"Come on, mijo!" says Sandra, using the Spanish expression for "my son," one of the few Spanish words that Pedro understands. "There are phones in the YMCA, pay phones at least."

"Yuh-, You don't want me to visit?"

"Yes, mijo, come, come. Oh my God, I've been dying to see you."

"I'll be there there at 4 o'clock."

"Good, be careful and call me if you're late!"

"I'll be there, mom, bye."

Pedro hangs up the phone, relieved yet agonized by what's to come.

"How am I gonna tell them about what happened? Should I?"

Pedro walks past the 7-11 where he often bought cherry Slurpees when he first moved to New York City on his way to school from home.

"What am gonna tell Dad? No matter what I say to him he's gonna be pissed."

Pedro buys his ticket for New Hyde Park, the station he and

his family always used because it wasn't too far from his house. It was almost departure time and Pedro reflects on his visit to SVA.

"I really need to go back and finish my degree. Once I have that I could get a job illustrating or maybe even working for a cartoon show or something exciting. Why did I drop out?"

Steve's face flashes through Pedro's mind, dimming his hopes of returning to school.

"You're one of the reasons I left school. You made it seem so cool to be on the streets scamming and partying. Why did I even listen to you? You ruined my life."

Pedro involuntarily crumples his train ticket in his left hand. He rises from a seat in the waiting area, too alarmed, nervous and agitated to sit. He sees a bar across the waiting room and craves a shot of something, just to calm down a bit. Walking towards the bar, he remembers that he doesn't have enough money left for a drink and veers towards a newsstand. Looking up at the clock, it's almost time to leave, so he goes to the platform to check if the train arrived. Settling in his train seat for the ride, Pedro organizes his thoughts.

"I want to go back to school, that's an idea they'll like. I'm gonna get a job. I'll live with them for a while just to get back on my feet, or I can live with them and go to school and work. It's far to SVA, but if I only take classes two or three days a week I don't have to commute every day. If I'm in New Hyde Park, nobody will ask about Steve. Nobody knows him out here and I won't have to tell anybody what happened. The police aren't gonna find out and that little queen who saw me doesn't know who I am or where I live. I can start all over."

The train's soothing coolness lulls Pedro to sleep.

"Yo, buddy. Your stop's coming up," says the conductor, nudging Pedro out of his sleep.

Still groggy, Pedro rubs his eyes and looks out the window, seeing the familiar suburban landscape he previously swore never to revisit. The train slows and Pedro rises from his seat, heading towards the door. It's been two months since he visited and he feels apprehension swelling within.

"What are they gonna ask me?"

Standing at the curb in front of the station, he looks for his mom's car, rehearsing what he'll say about school, work, his recent months in New York, how he got by, where he hung out. There will be a lot of questions that need good, or at least believable, answers.

"Junior!," Sandra yells while pulling up to the curb. "I'm so happy to see you."

Sandra jumps out of the car and runs around the front to the curb to hug Pedro, who weakly hugs her. She shakes him back and forth a couple of times and kisses him some more.

"Mijo, you're trying to kill me. Right? How dare you not call me or visit for such a long time. What's wrong with you?" she says, hugging him again. "What happened to your face? Oh my God, were you in a fight?"

"Uh, no, Mom. I stepped on a broken bottle and slipped on the glass."

"This little bag is all you brought? Where are all your other clothes?"

"I....I have some of them in storage and others are at the Y," Pedro responds, opening the car door and sitting inside.

Sandra returns to the driver's seat and they leave the station, headed for home.

"Are you hungry? I'm thinking of making arroz con pollo. When was the last time you ate that?"

"It's been a while."

"You look so skinny. You haven't been eating, have you? How do you eat at the YMCA? They don't even have kitchens in their rooms, do they?"

"No. It's just a little bedroom and they, um, have a cafeteria downstairs, but I don't like the food there."

"Well no wonder you're so skinny. I'll how can you eat like a normal person in a place where you can't even cook your own food? What have you been doing for the past few weeks, mijo? Why haven't you called us? I was about to drive to the Y to look for you."

"Mom, uh, I've been trying to work things out. I've been depressed because of school and I was embarrassed to come home."

"You don't have to be embarrassed with your own family. You're supposed to ask us for help."

"I....I know, but I couldn't. Dad was so upset the last time I spoke to him about leaving school. He was right that I was making a big mistake and, uh, I was so stupid for not listening to him."

"Wow, I didn't expect you to say that. He'll really be shocked if you say that to him. You never agree with him and you always act like we're wrong and you know better."

"I know. Uh, I've been thinking and I want to go back to school. I went there today to talk to an advisor about reentering, but he said it's too late for the fall semester. I have a chance of getting into the spring semester, though."

"Why don't you apply to one of the schools in our area? You could go to Nassau Community College or SUNY Old Westbury. That way you could live at home and it would be so much cheaper than SVA. That school is too expensive, and other schools teach art too, you know."

"I....I know, but I really wanted to go to SVA."

"Well, you've already spent a whole lot of our money and you're not in school and you don't have a degree. Maybe you're not the kind of person who should be in a four-year college. At least if you go to one of the schools close by you might be able to transfer your classes and get an associates degree at least. Then if you still want to stay in school you should, but at least you'll have some kind of degree."

"Let me think about it," Pedro says with resignation.

His mother might have a good point, and it would allow Pedro to stay out of New York until people forget about Steve.

"What do you feel like eating?"

"Whatever you make is OK."

"What? You haven't been here in weeks and there's nothing you're craving?"

"Not really."

"I guess you don't really miss me as much as I miss you."

"I missed you, Mom, really."

"Well then why didn't you call me? It's been two weeks. If any more days had passed I would have called the police. Some days you don't know how much I cried worrying about you and what had happened after you had the fight with your papi last time you were here. Please don't start fighting with him when he gets home."

"Uh, he's the one that starts the fights, Mom. I don't want to fight with him, but he's very, uh, critical and always complaining. He doesn't like me."

"Mijo, he loves you and he worries about you. You're his only son, so of course he has high expectations and he wants the best for you. He doesn't want you to suffer and he's afraid that you'll end up with an art degree and no job."

"Luh-, lots of people who major in art get jobs in New York City, Mom. It's the, uh, art capital of the world and there are lots of jobs for illustrators and people like me who like to draw and paint. They're good jobs."

"Is that the kind of job you had since dropping out of school?"

"Mom, I don't want to talk too much about dropping out of school. I already feel bad about it and it just makes me feel worse."

"OK, mijo, I'm sorry. I'm just wondering what kind of job you've had since January. How are you supporting yourself in New York? That's a very expensive city."

"It really is. Uh, I didn't have a regular job. I worked at an art store for a while selling stuff there and then at a restaurant as a busboy. It was OK. I also had a part-time job painting fabric designs in the fashion district. That was a good job but it didn't last past the summer."

The only part of Pedro's brief job history that wasn't a lie was the fabric design painting. He'd landed that job at the end of the fall semester last year through the jobs board at the school. It was a good gig, just painting a variety of floral designs for a fabric company on W. 39th Street. It didn't require getting up early because they expected him to come after school and they paid a good amount for the painting it required. Unfortunately, when all the designs were done for the season the job ended and Pedro had to return to scamming with Steve.

"Well at least you're putting your artistic talent to good use. That's a positive step. I still don't understand how you were able to live in the YMCA and support yourself with temporary and part-time jobs."

"The Y isn't expensive and I'd eat at cheap restaurants."

"Junior, we paid so much money for you to stay in the dorms and eat there, so I'm having a hard time believing that you were able to work in the city and pay for a room and meals with such unstable jobs."

"Mom, uh, I wasn't living a very comfortable life. I didn't really have a lot of money. I didn't say it was a good eight months that I've had."

"I guess not, since I was wondering for a while if you'd ever come back after the last fight you had with your father. I'm begging you, don't get into it with him. If he's nagging, just listen and don't argue with him."

"He's always trying to tell me what to do, like I'm still a baby. I'm….I'm an adult now?"

Pedro's profession of maturity sound more like a questions as Sandra pulls into their little ranch-style home. Walking into his home, Pedro feels a cloud of failure descend. The place he wants so badly to escape is now a last refuge. Every knick-knack in his mother's living room is a reminder that he fled New York City, the only place he dreamed of living since early high school.

"I'm going to start dinner. Do you want me to wash any of your clothes?"

"I'll wash them," said Pedro, who didn't bring as many dirty clothes as he would have liked to have washed because he didn't plan on coming home. "Where's Nidia?"

"Your sister got a summer job and she works until 6 o'clock, so she won't be home 'til later."

Pedro goes to his little bedroom, which was cluttered with household items like a laundry basket, an ironing board and some shoe boxes. The room's walls are bare because Pedro took his Jesus and Mary Chain posters to the dorms and he threw out his old high school artwork, embarrassed by it.

His bedroom's empty walls remind him of the room at the Y. There isn't much in his bag to put away. He pulls out his extra change of clothes that aren't really clean and removes those he's wearing. His dresser still had lots of old clothes, so he puts some of those on and carries the little pile to the washing machine. He can hear mom singing along to the radio in the kitchen and he's reluctant to come out of the garage and sit with her in there.

"I'm gonna have to tell her something about what I've been doing. Shit."

Walking into the kitchen, Pedro sits at the little bar counter opposite Sandra, who's chopping some onions and peppers. "Uh, how have you been, Mom?"

"I've been sick with worry. I was thinking of calling the police to file a missing person's report. I didn't know what else to do since it was almost two weeks since you called. You at least called me once a week and when I left you messages at the Y they told me you didn't always rent a room there. Where are you staying when you're not at the Y?"

"I stay at different friends' places."

"Who are your friends? I used to know all of them when you lived here and now I don't know a single one that I can call to find out if you're OK. You have to give me at least one of your friend's phone numbers so I can check on you in case of an emergency. Mijo, it's New York City, anything can happen and I need to have an emergency contact number for you. Why aren't you staying in your room at the Y? Are you having money problems?"

"The Y's not expensive, but sometimes I don't have enough money because, uh, I quit the restaurant. It wasn't enough money for all the work."

"So why didn't you call us? Why didn't you come home where you don't have to pay rent? It's crazy that you're suffering in New York when you could just live here and use your money from a job for school. How would you even have time to do your homework if you go back to school and have to keep working? Mijo, you tried living in the city and it didn't work out. It's time to come home."

"I love the city, Mom."

"Why? What's so great about it? I grew up in Brooklyn and it was a horrible, run-down dump. Your papi and I busted our butts to get out of there so that you and Nidia wouldn't have to suffer. We move to a nice area and as soon as you're old enough you want to go back to that horrible city. I don't understand you."

"The city inspires me."

"It inspires you? What has it inspired?" Sandra asks, couching her voice with maternal affection and a mild reproach, resisting the urge to raise her voice. "Did it inspire you to drop out of college? Why would you do that when all you talked about in high school was art college and for the last year of high school all you talked about was SVA. We could barely afford that kind of school and we took out those loans to send you there. And what was your inspiration? To leave after just a year and a half. That's not even enough for a two-year degree, which you couldn't get at that school anyway because you insisted on attending a four-year school."

Pedro's mind freezes. There is no body of work he can point to as evidence of the inspiration he's alleging. It's been months since he painted. He doesn't even carry a note book in his bag, much less sketch in it as his first-year SVA teachers instructed freshmen to do.

"Nuh-, New York City is one of the centers of art in the country and that's where I….I want to be for my career," says Pedro, his stammering growing worse with a rising anxiety from his mom's questions.

"Mijo, you don't have a career, at least not yet. I want you to have a career, but you're not working on one right now. I don't know what you're working on. What are you doing in the city?"

"I don't know, Mom. I'm. uh, trying to figure it out," Pedro says abruptly, getting up and going into the garage to check on his laundry.

The washing machine is still in the spin cycle and Pedro sits on an old folding chair, his mom's questions echoing.

"I'm in the city because I'm an artist. It's the place for inspiration."

Pedro mentally searches for the most recent example of his work. No luck.

"I haven't been able to draw or paint recently because there's so much going on and I can't keep my supplies at the Y because I don't rent by the month."

Other reasons for Pedro's lack of creative output flash through his mind. His inaction stirs anger. "Shit."

The washing machine's buzzer knocks Pedro out of his noxious reverie and he puts the clothes in the dryer, returning to his chair, reluctant to go back in the kitchen for more questions. They'll keep coming all night long, especially during dinner. Pedro goes to his room to look through his dresser drawer where he stores his art supplies. At the top of the drawer is a sketch book that he opens to review some of his high school art. He leafs through the book sitting on his bed, recalling the rock stage silhouettes inspired by hours of viewing MTV. The spooky renderings of his former high school's hallways elicit a weak smile, but his landscapes of local parks do not. He reaches the last page with drawings, arriving at a blank page. Grabbing a pencil from the cup on his nightstand next to his bed, Pedro puts the tip to the paper and pauses. Staring at the paper, nothing happens. He's draws a straight horizontal line and pauses, waiting for an internal force to emerge and guide his hand around the page. Nothing. Minutes pass. Still nothing. He finally moves the pencil again, connecting the end of the line with a parallel, but rounded line that connects to both ends. A short, vertical line and and handle to the left of the vertical line and he's drawn a knife. He rips the page from the sketch book and puts it in his bag.

He gets up to retrieve the laundry. Packing it his bag, along with more clothes from his dresser, he returns to the kitchen and takes the same seat at the bar.

"You're so skinny," says Sandra, chopping some iceberg lettuce. "Where did you eat if there's no kitchen in your room? How could you afford restaurants every day?"

There were many other maternal questions. Pedro answers every third or fourth, but they come too quickly to answer all of them. It's almost six o'clock, the time Pedro, Sr. arrives, and all the questions will be asked again, with his mother comparing the answers, seeking inconsistencies. Nidia arrives first, calming and cheering Pedro a bit.

"I can't believe you! Where have you been?" Nidia asks as Pedro follows her into her room. "Mom and dad were bugging out."

"I know. I didn't feel like talking to them. They ask too many questions."

"What do you expect? They didn't know where you were. Where were you? What happened to your mouth?"

"Now you're asking questions? I stepped on some broken glass and slipped and fell on the ground and busted my lip."

"It looks like you were in a fight. We were worried. Or they were worried. I figured you were OK and you just didn't want to talk to them. What were you doing, anyway? New York City must be so exciting."

"It is. There are lots of awesome things to do, museums, art galleries, parks and great stores."

"How's your art going now that you're not in school? Are you ever getting your own art gallery show?

"It's been hard for me to work on my art since I moved out of the dorms because I don't have a place for my supplies and I can't really do it in my room at the Y. That's one of the reason's I'm thinking of coming home. So I can get back to that.

"You're moving back!? I thought you'd never come back to New Hyde Park. Don't you hate it here?"

"Well, yeah, but it's really hard living in New York City without a good job, and since I haven't finished school yet, there aren't that many good jobs I can get."

"I guess you're right. So what are you gonna do?"

"Uh, I'm gonna reapply to SVA so I can finish my degree and maybe I'll live here and just ride the train in for classes."

"Won't that be really expensive with the train?"

"Probably. But not as expensive as living there. And I can try to get all my classes on just a few days so that I don't have to go to New York every day, maybe just three days a week."

"Did you tell papi and mami?"

"I told mom, but not dad yet."

"What did she say?"

"She wants me to live here and go to Nassau Community College or one of the other schools around here. I really want to finish SVA."

"Well, I'm glad you're moving back. I miss you."

"Uh, I didn't say I was moving back, not yet. I wanted to talk to mom and dad about it first. Maybe dad won't want me to move back in."

"Yes he will, he just might not say so."

"I don't know. You know how much he yells at me. We might not be able to live in the same house any more."

"Oh, my song's on."

Nidia jumps to turn up the radio, which begins playing Milli Vanilli's "Baby Don't Forget My Number." She sings and dances for Pedro, who watches a bit and then with a dismissive wave of his hand walks out of her room. "I hate this pop radio shit."

Pedro returns to his room and sits on the bed. He looks at a framed photo of himself with his parents at his high school graduation and studies the smiles on everyone's faces."

"What am I doing here?"

An uncertain time passes, finally interrupted by Sandra's call from the kitchen. "Papi's here. We're having dinner!"

The familiar knot tightens within Pedro, sending a pang of nausea through his gut. Pedro opens his drawer where some of his art supplies are still stored, then he quickly closes it. He reaches for the closet door, but doesn't open the door. He goes into the bathroom to wash his hands. Looks in the mirror, runs his hands through his black, wavy hair, trimmed close at the sides and longer on top with long sideburns. With a wet hand he pushes the hair back from his forehead. His lip isn't so swollen any more, but it's still noticeable, especially to a parent.

"Tito, come on," Nidia yells to him, using the nickname for her brother.

Pedro draws a breath and leaves the bathroom, heading down the stairs.

"Hi dad. How are you?"

Pedro hugs his father as Nidia and Sandra watched expectantly.

"I'm very surprised to see you after all this time with no calls. I guess you didn't forget about us after all. Have you been fighting with someone?"

"I could never forget you. It's only been about three weeks since I saw you"

Pedro nervously fidgets, unsure where the conversation is heading.

"I slipped on some glass and fell on the ground."

Pedro Sr. say nothing as he walks into the dining room to sit down. Everyone follows silently to take their seats and they begin serving themselves.

"So do you still like arroz con pollo, or do you only eat junk food now?" Sandra asks, passing the main dish.

"I still like it, mom. I haven't eaten it in a while."

"It looks like you haven't eaten much of anything in a while," Pedro Sr. says bluntly. "What are you doing in the city?"

Sandra and Nidia nervously look down at their plates as they wait for Pedro's answer.

"Uh, I've been looking for an art job and working part-time jobs. I haven't had much luck," Pedro responds. "That's why I came home...um...to talk with you and mom about me going back to SVA."

"Hmm, First you want to go, then you don't, now you want to go again. I feel like you're just wasting your time and my money," Pedro Sr. says with restrained impatience.

"I, um, I don't think I was ready last year. I'm more prepared now," Pedro responds nervously, unsure what to say to keep the conversation from heading in a direction he dreads.

"How are you more prepared, Junior?" Pedro Sr. asks, putting down the fork piercing a piece of chicken thigh. "How have you changed? I get the feeling that I'm still looking at the same boy I saw last time you were here."

"Uh, I'm different, Dad. I've changed in the past few months. When you're not in school and just working or trying to find a job you realize how things are. I had it good in school and it was a mistake dropping out. I couldn't handle the freedom in the city, but now I've got that under control."

Nidia looks at Pedro and then at her father, not daring to say anything that could start a fire. Sandra offers her husband some red beans, hoping to ease the rising tension.

"You've got it under control? How can I believe that when we're not sure where you live. You don't have a phone where we can call you. Last time we spoke you were living at the YMCA, which in my mind is a place for winos and people who can't get their acts together."

"It's not like that. A lot of, uh, normal people who can't afford apartments live there."

"OK, what have you been doing in the past two weeks? I'm curious how you're different. Tell me what's different. Are you really living at the Y?"

"Um, I've been doing a lot of things. Like, I was painting for a fabric company and then I worked, uh, at the art store. I...was...working on some sketches. I, um, I don't know. I can't remember everything I've done."

"Where did you work yesterday or on the weekend, Junior?"

"I…I haven't worked in the past few days."

"Why not? Don't you need money to pay for your expenses?"

"Yeah, but I took some time off," says Pedro, aching to leave the table.

"A few months ago you told us that you quit the art store. Are you working at the same art store that you quit?"

"Yeah…uh….they hired me again because they needed extra help."

"What kind of job is this that you can quit and start working again and then take so many days off? And how are you paying your rent if you're taking so many days off?"

"Dad, you're asking so many questions. I….I came home to see you and Mom and talk about going back to SVA and you're asking about, uh, all these things that don't matter."

"Junior, I'm asking how you're working and what you're doing. I feel like I don't know anything about you and I don't understand how you're living in the city because it doesn't seem like you work that much or that you're making much money. How could you if you're living in the Y?"

"Dad, I don't want to talk about money. I, uh, came home to talk about school and maybe moving home so I can reapply to SVA."

"School is money. What you're saying tells me that you really don't have any money and that you don't understand money or school. For the past year you acted like living in New Hyde Park was the worst thing in the world. Maybe you've changed, but I'm still not sure how."

"Are you done, Papi?" Nidia asked, hoping to change the topic.

"Sí, mija, gracias."

Nidia takes her plate, her father's and goes in the kitchen, eager to escape the questioning. She starts washing some of the dishes in the kitchen to avoid the confrontation in the dining room, still listening intently.

"Junior, going back to school is a money issue. Maybe not for you, but for me it is. I spent a lot of money sending you to SVA and I don't want you to go back because it already didn't work out."

"But this time it's gonna be different. I, uh, don't think I was ready the first time. Now....I, I think I'm more focused."

"You think you're more focused? What are you focused on? You're so focused that you haven't called us for two weeks. We don't know if you're alive or dead because you're focused on something else. What are you so focused on?"

"If you want to come home and go back to school, of course you can do that," Sandra interjects, annoyed that her husband doesn't immediately endorse Pedro's idea. "Why don't you come home right away and then we'll discuss SVA. You don't even know if they'll let you back in, and they might not let you in right away, so you might start taking classes at one of the community colleges here and who knows? Maybe you'll like one of the schools here just as much or better?"

"Uh, I don't think any of the schools here are better than SVA, mom."

"Tienes razón. Your mom's right. Come home, Junior and we'll figure it out. What's important is that you come home because we miss you. But let me tell you this: You're a grown man now and I expect you to act like one, even if you do go back to school. I expect you to start looking for a job right away. You won't just waste our time and money like you did when you were at SVA. Understand?"

"Yeah, things are gonna be different this time," Pedro says unconvincingly, rising from his seat and taking some of the used glasses into the kitchen for his sister.

"You're coming home!" Nidia whispers excitedly to Pedro when he enters the kitchen.

Pedro forces his facial muscles up and back, but the smile he cracks is more pained than celebratory. Relieved that there is no fight and only a little humiliation, Pedro goes upstairs to his room, leaving his parents in the dining room, where they sit silently.

"What am I focused on? What kind of job am I gonna get around here?"

Pedro takes his sketch book again and opens it to a blank page, gazing into the emptiness. After some time, he puts a pencil's edge to the page, awaiting inspiration. After another period, the pencil doesn't move.

"Tito, do you wanna watch TV. My shows are almost on," says Nidia, yelling into Pedro's room.

Pedro puts down the sketch book and enters his sister's room, joining her on the little love seat in front of a small television just before "Who's the Boss" starts.

Pedro watches the show without speaking, followed by other inane comedies that don't interest him. The shows some how help him forget about the previous days. Eventually Pedro feels the weight of sleep and he goes into his room without bidding good night to his parents, who are watching television downstairs.

Chapter 13

The garbage truck outside makes its piercing, clanking sound as it pulls in front of the century-old tenement building. The garbage men noisily fling bags of garbage into their truck, loudly banging cans on the sidewalk. Sonny's eyes open grudgingly to glance at the clock-radio, which he didn't set last night. It's only 8:30, so there's no danger of arriving to work late. He lifts himself a bit, but then settles back into bed, staring at the ceiling.

"What am I wearing tomorrow? I've got to find something."

Sonny looks over to his big table and sizes up the mound of invitations that he set aside for tonight. There are easily 1,000 that he has to give out, and Trix isn't a big space, so he'll have to spend a good amount of time standing near the exit as people leave to ensure that they know about his party. The pile of invites on the table sends a pang of anxiety through Sonny.

"What if not enough people come? What if only the boring people come and none of the fabulous ones?"

In a sudden jolt of panic, Sonny rises from bed and walks to the closet, looking in for nothing in particular. He stands there for a few minutes, only the noise from outside registering.

"I've got to serve something good and I have almost no money."

Sonny kneels at the pile of clothes on the floor spilling out of the closet and he rifles through the garments. He pauses for a few minutes, looking at the pile on the floor kneeling, as if pleading for a smartly coordinated ensemble to rise from the wrinkled mess. From a distance he appears to be in prayer, worshipping some covert altar inside his closet that's dedicated to an indifferent, self-absorbed god that isn't prone to bestowing any miracles, visions or revelations. He gets up with nothing in hand and walks over to the table to look at tonight's outfit, one of the few neatly flooded garments in his apartment.

"I need more scandal."

Sonny rifles through a laundry bag in a corner to assemble his day look. The shirts in the "clean" bag are also wrinkled, but since they're mostly stretchy t-shirts, there's no ironing required. Once he puts on light green jeans with a yellow t-shirt, Sonny goes back to the closet in search of a Wednesday look. After about 10 minutes Sonny gives up, exasperated.

"Maybe I'll get inspired at work or something new will come into the store."

Frustrated, Sonny applies some under-eye cover and finishes his hair so he has enough time to order an egg sandwich and a Diet Pepsi at the bodega. He takes a quick look in the refrigerator just to ensure that there's nothing in there that he could eat so as not to spend anything, but, as usual, it's empty. The blazing sunshine hurts his eyes even through big, dark sunglasses. The day's beauty doesn't register with Sonny, as he mentally rifles through his closet, imagining each top with his collection of hot shorts and shoes. He's worn virtually all his going-out clothes at least once in the past month because he's worked the scene, going out as often as possible, even when he only had five dollars or less in his pocket. It's important to be seen at all the right parties.

Sonny usually buys his breakfast at the deli just around the corner from Runway, so he can get to the store and either eat his sandwich, sitting on the entrance steps or in the back room if the day's manager arrives early, which often doesn't happen. The deli was empty except for the workers just before 10, but the short order cook was still at his little station where he makes breakfast for the neighborhood rush-hour crowd. Sonny orders the egg-on-a-roll sandwich, the cheapest option on the breakfast menu because it only costs $1. The Diet Pepsi is 50 cents, so the meal is a bargain. He waits by the cash register for his sandwich, impassively surveying the store and scanning the newspaper rack. His eyes then bulge slightly after one of the tabloid's covers registers. He walks closer to the rack, though he needn't get closer to see the bold headline declaring DEADLY DISCOVERY. Quickly grabbing the paper Sonny excitedly leafs through the paper's front section until he finds the story about the incident, reading the lurid details with a dribble of excitement and an incipient smile on his face.

"Drama!"

Checking the front page to determine the price, he decides to buy it and pays for his purchase, rushing out of the store with purpose, thrilled at the prospect of retelling his subway tale tonight at Trix.

"People will gag when they hear this."

Darnell is already at Runway and the front door is open to allow for fresh air. Sonny sits on the steps outside the store, eats his sandwich and reads the murder story once again. The gruesome details fill Sonny with a sense of jubilation. It's confirmed that he's witnessed a murder — and he's delighted.

"This newspaper is perfect for tonight's outfit! Everyone will ask me about my look and they'll flip when I tell them what happened on Saturday!"

"Sonny, get inside. It's past 10 and you're not getting paid to decorate our front stoop. I need you to refold all the clothes on the racks and then help me hang the new merchandise. You've got a lot to do," Darnell barks to Sonny, after realizing that he's sitting outside.

"OK, I was just finishing my sandwich. You don't want me eating inside the store, do you? I could get stains on the merchandise."

"You should eat before your shift starts."

"I lost track of the time. I was reading the newspaper and you'll never believe what happened."

"If I want a news report, I'll watch TV. Please get started on the folding. If Sharon was to drop in right now, both our asses would be chewed out. This place is not the way she likes it," says Darnell, referring to Sharon Gold, the store's owner.

"No, you must hear this. You WILL GAG! Remember how I told you that I was walking through the subway on Saturday night and I saw that crazy looking homeless guy in the tunnel? Well, I wasn't lying! There really was a knife in his hand and he killed somebody! It's in the newspaper," says Sonny, waving the tabloid paper at Darnell.

"The cops found some homeless guy's body right in the area where I saw the scary homeless man when I was exploring. I could have been killed because he followed me! Isn't that crazy-doodles? I had a near-death experience! It's FABulous!"

"Let me see that, child."

Darnell grabs the paper from Sonny and takes a couple of minutes to read the story as Sonny fidgets from the excitement over the attention this will draw to him. He skips around a table displaying shirts and then twirls a shirt over his head in triumph.

"Stop that! I was certain you were bullshitting us yesterday, but there's no way you could have faked this. Call the police."

"Call the police? I'm not calling them. Why should I call them? What if they accuse me of killing that guy? I don't even really remember too clearly what the killer looked like. I was too busy trying to get away from the monster."

Sonny runs around the table again, imitating Tokyo residents fleeing Godzilla.

"Mon-sta! Mon-sta!"

"How could you witness someone killing someone else and not speak to the police? What's wrong with you club kids?"

"I didn't see him killing anybody. I heard some yelling. It was dark in there and I was more worried about saving my own ass. I'm not calling the cops. It's not my job and I don't know who that dead guy is anyway."

"What if that was somebody you knew? Wouldn't you want a witness to step forward and tell the police so that the killer could be punished?" says Darnell, his usual theatricality dampened by Sonny's indifference.

"I'm not calling the police. I have too many things to worry about. My party is on Thursday, I have to go out the next two nights and pass out thousands of invites. What if the police find out I'm giving away ecstasy at my party? They'll arrest me. My invite is subtle, but it's not that subtle."

"Why does every party the club kids throw have to involve drugs or ecstasy? Can't you just have fun dancing and drinking?"

"Ecstasy is the new liquor, and anyway, many of us aren't old enough to drink, so it's easier buying ecstasy than liquor since the dealers don't want to see your ID, tee-hee-hee!"

"Well, I still think you should call the police, but we can't discuss this any longer. We have work to do. You have to refold everything on the shelves and then we're opening the new deliveries. Get moving," says Darnell, resuming the imperious trill in his voice."

Sonny begins in the back of the store since it's early and there will be few customers in the first two hours of the day. The back is less messy because many customers come into the store, look in the front part and then leave. Scanning the shelves, Sonny grabs disheveled pants and tops, folds them carefully and neatly returns them to their spots. He starts silently rehearsing the story he'll tell people tonight at Trix. Sony often rehearses by day. It's his way of ensuring that he'll have something clever to discuss at night. Since he has short exchanges with dozens of clubbers, it doesn't matter if it's the same story, since virtually no one else in the loud space can overhear him.

Sometimes, when he can't think of a real story, he checks the calendar to see if it's some commemorative day. Any commemoration will do: Grandparents Day, Secretary's Day, National Hot Dog Day. The idea is to tell people you're observing that day and then invent some ridiculous tale around it that can be told in one or two minutes. Last month, on National Hot Dog Day, which is July 23, Sonny took a half package of hot dogs and some hot dog buns to the clubs, keeping the other halves at home for lunch or dinner. He put them in a little paper bag and went around the Tunnel telling his clubber acquaintances that it was National Hot Dog Day and he offered them a hot dog. To his surprise, two clubbers accepted the room-temperature snacks, though most rightly recoiled in disgust, the desired response all along.

Reviewing the lurid details in his mind, Sonny crafts a story that begins with a question, challenging clubbers to guess what he saw. Then he'll immediately reveal the gory details about the bum and his knife. Dramatic license dictates that Sonny saw it in the killer's right hand, with the subway platform's bare bulbs' light reflecting off the menacing blade's metal edge. Of course the north-bound train clanks its arrival, so Sonny has to not only run for his life from a killer, but from an oncoming train.

Naturally, everyone will ask why he was down there. The story he told Cookie and St. Helen, was cute, but not good enough. The graffiti alibi is better.

"I said I was spray painting my tag on the wall down there. I've got to do that tonight, otherwise someone might check it out."

Sonny makes a mental note to add the S-DEE tag to his story. His presence in the tunnel is a preparation for a tag party at the Tunnel, where he will spray-paint his tag on big sheets of paper and invite other club celebs to create tags for themselves.

"What a brilliant idea!" Sonny congratulates himself, still folding. "Maybe I can get Amanda to photograph my tags in the subway as an image for the invite. Or maybe I'll have a viewing party on the subway. I'll have people get on the train at 14th Street and ride up to 23rd Street so people can see my tags. That means I'll have to paint more than one of them. Well, I can at least paint one tonight so that my story is kinda true, and then I'll worry about the rest of the tags later. Anyway, I haven't even pitched a tag party, and if the balloon party doesn't go well on Thursday, I can forget about other parties. It will be a new trend, gay nightclubbing taggers. This will be so fabulous!"

Sonny's midway through the store by now, not just folding but examining each garment for its possible suitability as part of an outfit for Thursday night. Nothing appeals to him much, except the kelly green bolero with the feathers. He still hasn't asked permission to borrow it, and he's pretty sure the answer will be no. Sonny considers stealing it on Wednesday without asking.

"It doesn't matter if I get fired. I'm moving on to something different, a more glamorous life."

As he approaches the front of the store during the blitzkrieg folding session, he comes across a punk-rock style t-shirt with the traditional kidnap ransom-note letters cut from newspapers screen printed across the front. The letters spell BITCH. Sonny smiles and chuckles as he folds the shirt. Returning it to the table, a bolt of inspiration strikes. "I'm making my own BITCH outfit, but I'm making my outfit from the newspaper. All I need are a few more copies of today's newspaper and it will be fierce. Everyone will gag!"

The flow of creative juices help Sonny fold faster. He conceptualizes the look.

"Laminator? I put it under the sink and last week it worked perfectly. Do I need more lamination plastic? No, I still have the package from the Roach Motel earrings I made two weeks ago. If I take the letters from the newspaper and cut them up into separate words it will be easier to laminate them. I'll then use some safety pins to make it look like a ransom note on my shirt. I still have at least half a bottle of fake blood too, so I'll bruise up my face with makeup and then drip the blood on my face. No, it should be dripped on my chest or back because this guy didn't get stabbed in the face. Did he? I'll have to read the story again. What shirt should I use? I'll have to rip it and ruin it with the blood, so it should be one of the shirts I don't want any more. I'll be Night of the Living Dead goes to Trix on the subway. Should I wear a hat? Do homeless guys wear hats? The killer was wearing one, but what about his victim? It doesn't matter, no one cares about him. I'll be a fabulous diva murdered in the subway."

A customer interrupts Sonny's reverie to ask for a smaller sized t-shirt.

"We only have the sizes on the table. That t-shirt is almost sold out, sorry," Sonny responds, offering help with finding something else in an appropriate size.

By the time Sonny finishes folding and organizing all the

store's shelves, he's composed tonight's look. A rush of excitement courses through him in anticipation of making a big sensation, of being talked about, of provoking reactions that won't just be amusement, but maybe even actual horror or at least disturbed concern. All the attention this story will bring makes him giddy, and he's not usually so gleeful at the store. As the day progresses he's even solicitous and helpful to customers the minute they walk into the store. Such customer-oriented practices are not generally associated with Runway's sales clerks.

"Are you on X?" Corvette asks in the mid-afternoon. "Something's going on with you."

"I had a near-death experience this past weekend. I'm just celebrating LIFE, LIfe, life," Sonny responds.

"No, bitch, you're high, 'cause you're never this perky. You took one of the pills the club gave you for your party on Thursday, didn't you? I want one too!"

"Well, you don't have to believe me. If you escaped from the killer's clutches you'd be happy, tee-hee-hee!"

"I'm not sure I believe your little story. You club kids will say anything for attention."

"Well, I am telling the truth, I've got the newspaper to prove it and I told you this story before the newspaper got it. If you don't believe me, go there and look for my tag."

"I can't be bothered," she says, snapping her fingers at Sonny and walking to the back of the store. There will be no more words exchanged between them today.

As his shift ends, Sonny grows frustrated that his co-workers are relatively uninterested in his publicity coup. Neither Darnell nor Corvette bring it up after the initial review of the newspaper. Sonny starts wiping off costume jewelry in a display case.

"They're such selfish bitches. I can't wait to get out of this negative cesspool."

"Sonny, I need you back here to help me read the receipts," Darnell orders.

Sonny's glee dims somewhat since the early afternoon. He hopes some figures from the scene pop in so he can tell them his story, but none do, oddly. It just isn't one of those gossipy days when friends drop by.

"It figures that on the day I have big news to tell people, no one comes into the store. But when it's really busy customers, then all my friends want to drop by and chit-chat."

The shift ends with nary a scene queen dropping by so that Sonny can give someone an advance scoop. Nonetheless, when Sonny leaves work he again feels the glee rising and he races to the newsstand on Second Avenue to buy two more copies of the paper. He then rushes home, whips out a pair of scissors and heats up the laminator.

Tonight's outfit is an easy production because it's mostly a sloppy look. No need for tailoring or fine details, just blood, messy makeup and shredded clothing. Sonny carefully cuts the headlines, sub-headlines and letters from other headlines to make his own expressions. He takes two of the front page headlines in their entirety, laminates them and pins them on to the front and back of his white button-down shirt with one of the sleeves ripped off. He tears a few spots on the shirt and smears blood all over them. He also laminates two of the photos of the shrouded corpse on a stretcher and puts them under the headlines on his shirt. Then he carefully reserves some of the cut headlines that have words like unknown killer and murder so that he can glue them on his face. He pairs his shirt with black bondage shorts so that he can tie the sleeve he ripped off his shirt on to his left knee, which will then be bloodied. He digs out the can of day-glo pink spray paint he used last month to spray paint a pair of old shoes. After shaking it he determines there is enough paint in it for a big tag in the subway. Checking his flashlight before putting it in his Hello Kitty backpack, Sonny ensures that there's battery life for a late-night subway adventure.

Exhausted from a day at work and sleepy from the two slices of pizza he had for dinner, Sonny throws himself into bed for a disco nap, comforted by the fact that he now has two looks ready to go for tonight and tomorrow. A big smile spreads across his face as he thinks of tonight's reactions when he tells people about the subway killer.

"I could never make up something like this."

The alarm rings at 10 p.m. and Sonny rises sluggishly from bed. He feels tired, but the tonight's prospects are so exhilarating that he quickly dresses. No need for a shower, he decides, since he's slathering himself with blood and ghoulish make up and then stomping through the nasty subway tunnels for his tag. The shower will be required when he comes home. Trix is on 19th Street between 10th and 11th avenues, so it's not really an expensive taxi ride, Sonny decides. He arrives at the club around 11:30 before the big midnight crush begins.

"You're looking messy tonight, darling. Are you now working at a butcher shop?" asks Cookie, Trix's doorwoman.

"I was almost butchered, Miss Thing. Remember that story I told you on Saturday at the restaurant. The one about me in the subway?"

"Your little exploration?"

"Yes! That guy I saw in the tunnel killed somebody. This is the story and picture on my shirt! Didn't you see the newspaper?"

"No," said Cookie, scoffing at the notion that she'd read a newspaper — not that Sonny ever does.

"Well that homeless guy killed another homeless man, and then he started coming after me, but I got away. I was almost killed, tee-hee-hee!"

"Oh, well here's a ticket and I'll talk to you later inside," says Cookie turning away to size up new arrivals at the velvet rope, as if Sonny simply had told her he'd bought a great new wig or stubbed his toe.

Sonny doesn't take such abruptness personally. He understands you can't talk much at the door. It's more a time for air kisses and a quick outfit assessment, then you move on. The club is not that crowded yet, but there were people dancing, so Sonny pulls a stack of invites out of his backpack and begins walking around, handing them out. At one point he sees a clearing on the dance floor and he skips through the middle, hoping to elicit a little more attention for his ensemble.

"Sonny!" yells Amanda Watson, waving to catch his attention as he comes skipping off the dance floor. "Strike some poses."

Sonny recognizes Amanda as she brings her camera to eye level. Sonny puts both hands on his "wound" and winces in pain, the flashes go off, then he switches and puts a hand in his mouth, biting his fingers in pain, more flashes, then he raises a hand and starts walking menacingly towards Amanda as she takes more photos.

"I love your scary look! What's with all the blood?" she asks after repositioning her camera around her neck.

"It's my homage to the homeless guy that got killed in the subway tunnel. I actually saw the killer in there and I ran away from him when he started following me, tee-hee-hee!"

"Are you serious?"

"Yes, I was in the subway painting a tag and I heard some yelling, then I saw him and he saw me."

"Oh my God, did you call the police?"

"No, because I was afraid I'd get in trouble for tagging in the subway. That's a crime, you know."

"Yes, I know. I saw something about it on TV yesterday, are you sure that you saw the killer? That's so scary! You're a tagger? Isn't that scary too?"

"The killer was scary, but tagging isn't. I'm planning a tagging party in the subway when I'm done so people can see my work."

"That's so cool! Oh, I see a photo op. I'll talk to you later," Amanda says, running towards the bar after seeing Mount St. Helen with what looks like a little lamp shade on top of her wig.

For the next hour Sonny works the crowd, passing out his invites and explaining the concept behind his look when clubbers ask. When they don't ask, he asks them if they'd seen the news, which most haven't because current events are of no concern to them, except the gossip pages. After pumping the crowd with his account, Sonny spends a little time on the dance floor, stalking dancers to the beat and flailing around in a half-hearted attempt at voguing, the stylized dance performed by the uptown queens from Harlem, Washington Heights and the Bronx. By 1:30 a.m., satisfied that he told enough clubbers about his party on Thursday and his subway encounter, Sonny goes outside for an invite distribution blitz. He stands outside about an hour until he's given out all the invites, chatting with a few more clubbers on their way in to Trix. Cookie is too busy to talk, so Sonny keeps his distance.

"What's up Sonny? Cookie won't let you in?" says Eagle, approaching Sonny from behind.

"No, I was already inside. I'm just passing out more of my invites to the people going home. They're more likely to save them than if I give it to them inside," Sonny responds, defensively.

"At first I thought you were a homeless man begging the clubbers for money. Are you doing the homeless look?" says Eagle, shaking his head in either disbelief or disapproval, or both.

"It's my homage to the subway murder. I saw the killer on Saturday night when I was tagging in the subway tunnel. He saw me too and started following me!"

"You're tagging in the subway. That's funny. I have to find someone inside," says Eagle, not responding to Sonny's statement about the murder.

Sonny, crumples the invite Eagle gave him with his left hand. "It's time to go tagging."

Luckily, the subway station isn't too far from Trix.

"Which station should I go to, 14th or 23rd? What if there are undercover cops at 23rd Street waiting to see if the killer comes back to the tunnel. Killers sometimes do that."

Sonny stands momentarily on the corner of 19th Street and 10th Avenue, unsure whether to walk north or south on 10th Avenue. He's definitely not walking east because it will take him hear the housing projects on 9th Avenue. He usually avoids them because the residents are very hostile to people who they perceive to be gay, especially someone like Sonny. In the past residents have thrown eggs and more dangerous things at him from their apartment windows above, so he's learned to stay off those blocks, some of the many blocks in the city he avoids for similar reasons.

It's 1:30 a.m., Sonny's tired and he has to work tomorrow, so he decides to walk north to the 23rd Street station, since it's closer and it will be less of a hassle walking through the tunnel to paint his tag. He approaches the subway entrance with a bit of trepidation, but he summons all his inner strength.   It serves him well when he's walking into a club wearing a bloody outfit with newsprint clippings affixed to his clothing. By entering on the uptown side, Sonny figures he'll stir less suspicion because the murder occurred on the southbound side. Luckily, he has a token in his bag, avoiding the need for questioning looks from the token booth attendant.

He marches down the subway entrance steps quickly, trying to project nonchalance. A quick glance at the token booth confirms that the attendant is nodded off, so no worries there. Once through the turnstile he walks towards the south end of the platform, as other sleepy passengers awaiting the train look at him with puzzlement.

"I'm attracting too much attention. I should have worn my black tunic to cover up a bit. Why don't I just keep that in my bag at all times?"

A low rumble pierces Sonny's anxiety as he worries whether he's being watched. It's an uptown train. Sonny walks next to the wall and turns his back to the train, bending down as if to tie his boot. It's the only way he can partially conceal himself without looking too suspicious.

"Is a crouched figure in hot shorts and a Hello Kitty backpack inconspicuous?"

The train stops and the doors open, Sonny turns to face the the train, but he's still crouched in the boot-tying position. He scans the train and the platform for a cop and notices that he's caught the attention of a man on the train, but he's no threat, so Sonny keeps scanning as the door closes and the train begins pulling out of the station. Sonny suddenly rises to his feet and watches as passengers walk towards the exit. He waits for the last passenger walking from the north side of the platform turns towards the turnstiles and then he checks the southbound platform. He can't see anyone and quickly runs onto the small metal steps that lead into the dark.

Sonny's heart quickens its pace and he realizes that he forgot to pull out his flashlight, so after walking enough of a distance from the platform to ensure that he's hidden from view, he pulls off the backpack and fishes out the flashlight and the can of spray paint. With the flashlight on, Sonny looks across the tracks into the dark and then points his flashlight in that direction. He's close to the place where he saw the homeless guy with the captain's cap. The flashlight is good for illuminating the ground where he's stepping, but it doesn't reveal much across the tracks. Feeling a tingle, Sonny considers quickly jumping to the southbound tracks to see where the homeless man died, but the urge to get out as quickly as possible overrides curiosity. He has a tag to paint and it's got to be painted tonight.

"What if someone comes looking for it tomorrow? I told so many people about tonight."

Sonny turns his back on the crime scene, looking for a good spot for his own law breaking. He scans the walls in the tunnels, which are corroded with a dank effluent seeping into the tunnel from sidewalks above, or maybe from a sewer pipe. The years of dripping leaks create fetid frescoes on the tunnel's walls. The taggers don't even bother scraping off the accumulations when they get busy, which gives their murals a three-dimensional texture unappreciated by commuters as they whizz by on trains. Some of the good spots that catch the light from the not-too-distant platform are already taken, but after walking about 100 feet south on the northbound track Sonny sees a section of flat wall that has no graffiti on it, just the subterranean crust. Sonny mounts a small concrete rise in the tunnel to better reach it, but he's not close enough. He realizes that there is a metal rail near the wall, and if he grabs it he can stand on a narrow ledge on the wall. Gloves would have been a wise accessory to pack, but Sonny has none, so he rests the flashlight so that its light points up to the wall and grabs the bar, which is damp and slimy.

"I've got to hurry."

Recalling his renderings, Sonny draws a big S with a line at the top extending to the right as far as he can make it. The tag has to be about the height of a subway window. If it's bigger, commuters won't be able to decipher it. The DEE, hyphen and asterisk follow, hastily executed. Climbing down from the wall, Sonny grabs the flashlight to examine his handiwork and realizes that the strokes are not bold enough to be seen with a flashlight, much less by commuters gazing from a speeding train. He climbs back on to the wall and grabs the slimy metal bar again. He thickens the strokes on the letters while coughing and choking on the paint fumes.

"A mask would have been a good idea too."

Sonny runs out of paint before he finishes touching up the asterisk, but after stepping back he's pleased with the effect. It's not attractive like the ones drawn by the homeboys. It's actually terrible, but good enough. Anyone will be able to read the S-DEE, especially if they've got the lights from inside the subway train illuminating the wall.

Even though he's only been in the tunnel about 15 minutes and trains usually only run about every 30 minutes this time of night, Sonny gets panicky. He wipes his hand on his "blood-stained" t-shirt and runs towards the platform, tossing the empty spray paint can on the littered tracks. Without pausing to see if anyone is on the platform, he runs up the stairs and emerges into the light like a bloody corpse fleeing its tomb. No one sees him come out of the darkness as he quickly walks towards the exit, but he startles two passengers waiting in the yellow-marked safety area of the northbound platform near the token booth where people wait after hours. Once again Sonny looks to the clerk, but his head is still lowered. Passing through the turnstile, he hurriedly walks to the stairs and then runs up the rest of the way, into the street. He heads east on 23rd Street, relieved and flustered. Tired, Sonny considers hailing a cab, but instead keeps walking, hoping to reduce the cost of the ride. By the time he reaches Madison Square Park on Fifth Avenue and 23rd Street, he's calm and thrilled about his tag. What he told everyone tonight was now mostly true and he now had "proof" when he retells the story tomorrow. He turns at Broadway, walks to 22nd Street and continues walking east. It's a less conspicuous street to walk on.

Exhilarated by how every aspect of his tall tale is falling together, Sonny keeps walking until he reaches 1st Avenue, a safe street he can head south on without fear of harassment. He's exhausted but satisfied by the time he reaches home. It's a successful night because all he really spent was the $5 on the taxi, $1 in tip for the free drink he got at Trix and the token for the subway. In all it was an inexpensive night of party promotion that will yield big returns, Sonny assures himself with satisfaction once he's in bed drifting to sleep.

Chapter 14

"It's 7:30," Pedro Sr. barks at his son from the bedroom door.

"Wha-, What do you want?" Pedro asks, his voice cracking with grogginess.

"I want you to get your ass out of bed, take a shower and go out and look for a job. If you're gonna stay with us you need to be doing something every day. You're not just gonna sleep late every day while the rest of us work. Even your baby sister has a job and she's already up."

"Where am I gonna look for a job?" Pedro asks dismissively, not considering the seriousness of his father's tone.

"You're gonna get the same kind of job that every other teenager gets around here. I don't care if you get a job cleaning toilets at the mall, you need to be working and doing something, not just lying around being depressed, like other times you came back to stay with us. You need to get busy with something," Pedro Sr. says, getting an angry tone to his voice.

"I have to think about what kind of job I want," Pedro responds.

"You don't have to think about anything. Get your ass out of bed, take a shower, shave, put on some nice clothes and go to all the stores and ask them if they're hiring. Right now it doesn't matter what kind of job you want, you need to be working at something. You're not gonna just stay home watching TV. You need to get busy," his father responds.

Pedro doesn't rise from bed and he pulls the bed sheet over his shoulder, which his father rips off the bed after not getting the appropriate response.

"Get your ass out of bed. Now!" Pedro Sr. yells.

Alarmed, Pedro gets out of bed without saying anything. Standing in his underwear, he looks at the floor, then glances up to meet his father's angry eyes, then back at the floor.

"Alright dad, I'm up."

"Good, now do what I told you," Pedro Sr. says, walking out of the room.

Pedro picks up the sheet his father threw on the bedroom floor and throws it on the bed.

"I don't need this shit. I can't stay here tonight."

Pedro goes into the bathroom to shower. While dressing, he can still hear his father downstairs speaking with his mom in Spanish. They're arguing about something and they don't want the kids to know what it is, although it's probably about him. He's sure of that, but he doesn't try to listen since his Spanish is so bad he won't understand anyway. Back in his room, he makes the bed and puts on his clean clothes. After shaving he notices that the swelling on his lip is virtually gone, except for a little scab. His knees have bigger scabs and they still hurt slightly when he walks.

"How am I gonna look for a job when my knees hurt?" Pedro wonders, forgetting that he walked a great deal yesterday.

The Spanish-language discussion abruptly stops around 8 a.m. and Pedro hears his father come up the stairs again into his bedroom or the bathroom. Pedro stays in his room, hoping to avoid him. Nidia knocks on Pedro's door and then sticks her head in the room.

"Are you OK? I thought I heard dad cussing. Is he mad at you?"

"I guess. I don't know. Dad doesn't want me to sleep late, even though I wasn't planning on doing that. He wants me to look for a job today."

"So why don't you go to the mall and ask all the good stores there if they have any openings, or at least fill out some applications. It can't hurt and at least you can tell papi tonight that you filled out a bunch of applications."

"I don't want to work at the mall. That's the reason I went to SVA. To get away from something like that," Pedro says with a disdainful tone.

"You're not in SVA any more, Tito. You're back in New Hyde Park and if you need a job that's one of the only places you can look. If you don't want to work there, why did you drop out of school? You had it so good at SVA. Was it really that hard?"

"It's not that it was hard. I just, um, I got distracted," says Pedro, embarrassed about offering his younger sister excuses for failure.

"I have to go, papi's giving me a ride."

Pedro sits on his bed, staring at his boots. He puts one of them on, stopping and looking around the room. It's sunny outside and even though his shade is drawn, light still floods into the room. The outside glow offends Pedro because it's another reason for going out and obeying his father's order. After a few more minutes, Pedro Sr. comes into his son's room again. Without saying anything he walks over to his son and stares at him. Pedro, uncomfortable, rises.

"You know what you have to do, don't you?" Pedro Sr. says, half threatening and poking his son in the chest with his index finger.

Pedro doesn't say anything, he just nods in agreement.

"You know, right?" Pedro Sr. asks again, impatiently.

"Yea, dad, I know."

Pedro Sr. walks out of the room and calls to Nidia, telling her to meet him in the driveway. Pedro stares again at his belongings, focusing on his bag. He walks over to it and starts packing his washed clothes. He hears his father's car start and then the kitchen door closes loudly. He looks at the window and considers walking over to watch the car pull away, but he resists the urge, though he still listens intently as the car leaves the driveway and pulls away. It only takes about 60 seconds to fully pack the bag and he searches a couple of his desk drawers for anything useful, but there isn't. He also looks in the closet for any clothes he might want, but there's nothing there either. He hears his mother in the kitchen washing dishes or putting something away. Leaving the packed bag on the bed, he inhales and goes downstairs.

"Good morning, mijo. Do you want some scrambled eggs?"

"OK"

"I can't believe the summer is almost over. In two more weeks it's back to school for me. I'll miss our backyard," says Sandra, referring to her job as an elementary school teacher's aide. "So, papi said you're go job hunting today?"

"That's what he told me to do, but I don't think I'm gonna get any job around here."

"Not with that attitude, you won't. You have to be positive."

"Mom, I….I am positive, but I'm not ready to look for a job yet. I, um, need to go back to New York for a couple of days to get the rest of my stuff, then I'll come back and look for a job. What's the point of me looking for one today?"

"You just got here yesterday and you want to go back today? Why don't you stay here, and then maybe on Sunday we can go in the car to get the rest of your things? Isn't that a better idea?"

Pedro feels his heart palpitate and a choking feeling, as if he can't get enough air.

"Mom," he says with his voice cracking, "I, uh, need to go back, but I'll be back this weekend."

"Can't you just stay here and look for a job today? Why is that such a big deal? You said things changed and that you want to come back. Now you're telling me that you want to leave. What happened?

"I just want to empty out my locker and get all the rest of my stuff. There's no point in leaving it there. I, uh, wanna check with SVA about registering for the spring."

"Can't you just call them and find out? And what do you have in your locker that's so important? Why would it take you two days to do that anyway? Can't it wait until the weekend so you can look for a job? It's a good time to be looking for a job because a lot of the kids who have summer jobs will be going back to school in a couple of weeks and the stores will need new workers."

"I can look when I get back. It will still be a good time."

"Mijo, I just wish you would stay here. That place is no good for you. Why do you need to stay there until the weekend? If all you need to do is clean out your locker, why don't you just go there, clean it out and then come back this afternoon? It won't take a long time to clean out a locker."

"OK, mom, I'll just go there and come back tonight."

"Can't you at least go to the mall for a little while this morning to fill out some applications? That why papi won't be so upset when you get back, because he really wants you to start looking for a job."

"Alright. The stores won't open for about two hours. Can you drive me to the train station so I can go pick up my stuff and I'll go to the mall when I get back?

"How can you look for a job when you have all these bags with you? The managers will think you're a homeless bum."

"You're right, I'll go to the mall and fill out applications, then I'll go to the city to pick up my things. I should be back by 6 or 7."

"I wish you'd just wait until the weekend. It's a waste of money going to the city today. You don't even have any money, do you?"

"Not really. Can I borrow $20?"

"You're papi will be mad at me for giving you this," Sandra said, as she walks over to her purse, pulls out a wallet and fishes out two $20 bills. "Let me get myself together and I'll drive you to the mall."

Sandra goes upstairs and Pedro remains seated in the kitchen, looking at the $20 bills before folding them and putting them in his pocket. He looks up to the white and yellow checkered cafe curtains hung over the kitchen sink. The plastic flowers in a vase the shape of a rooster next to the sink stir a flight instinct in Pedro. He wants to run out of the house, but resists the impulse, feeling defeated.

"What's the use. I'll end up back here anyway."

Pedro remains seated, staring at the rooster vase, thinking about the Y, remembering Steve and the reason why he can't stay at the Y. There are too many reminders and it's time to fade into oblivion, and New Hyde Park is just as good a place for that as anywhere else. A tear falls from Pedro's eye, and then another. He quickly wipes them, not wanting his mother to see. Pedro finally rises from his seat, but only to move to the living room, where he turns on the television and stares at it blankly, not noticing what's actually on. Memories of Steve keep intruding and an unwanted craving also tickles beneath the nape of his neck. A vague panic passes through Pedro, causing him to shiver a bit.

He runs upstairs to his room to grab his backpack, and then decides that his mother has a good point. If he's collecting his belongings, why does he need a big bag with clothes in it? He turns to his dresser and he pulls out a canvas army green shoulder bag. It was likely used to store a canteen or some military supplies, but in high school Pedro used it like a supply bag for his art supplies. He unfolds it and takes some of the essentials from his big bag: a pair of socks, underwear, his drug gear in a little tin box, the switchblade, which he puts in a zippered compartment inside the bag so that it won't be seen if someone opens it. Set to travel lightly, he returns to the TV in the living room.

Sandra finally comes downstairs and goes into the kitchen to retrieve her purse.

"Are you ready?" she asked, shaking her car keys.

Pedro gets up without responding and he heads out the door.

"I'm so happy you're coming home," Sandra says on the way to the mall. "It will be very good for you here. You'll be able to start fresh."

"Mom, I want to tell you something," Pedro responds, haltingly, wondering how to tell her about his predicament. "I'm worried that no one is gonna want to hire me."

"Mijo, you need to be more positive. You're a grown man now and you can do anything you set your mind to. If you go with the attitude that they don't want to hire you, they won't. You're capable of anything."

"That's what scares me."

"Why should that scare you? You're very creative. If something happens, you can think your way out of it. If they ask you something during the interview, just improvise and be positive."

"Do you want me to drop you off by the JC Penny's or the Sear's?"

"It doesn't matter."

"OK, mijo, good luck and be positive. Call me later when you know what time you're coming home."

"Alright, I'll see you later," Pedro says, leaning over to kiss Sandra.

Pedro watches Sandra pull away and he goes into the mall, walks to a different exit and searches for the bus stop.

"Can I really stay here and look for a job?" Pedro wonders after taking his seat for the bus bound for the Long Island Railroad station.

He passes a number of strip malls, seeing the Sizzler and Red Lobster restaurants where he's eaten with his family.

"I don't know if I can stay here."

Pedro surveys the restaurants' empty parking lots, then recalls the bloody switchblade he wiped clean in the Y's bathroom. "I'll just cop one last time, then I'll come home with a little stash and start over."

Pedro breathes with relief as he walks off the train into Penn Station. He feels a bit of the old excitement he used to feel at arriving in the station when he first started college, almost causing him to smile. The bustle in the station also strangely comforts him, while the chain restaurants and stores in the station don't depress him quite the way they do in New Hyde Park. Pedro takes a deep breath inside the station, filling his lungs with a slightly unpleasant odor — he's home.

Pedro heads to the subway for a quick stop at the YMCA to assess how much of his locker's contents he's taking home and what he's throwing out. The humid summer day amplifies the Y's rank lobby. Pedro waves to the attendant, who recognizes him and waves back.

"You stayin' here tonight?"

"No, I'm moving my stuff out of the locker."

"We don't give refunds for unused rental time on lockers, you know."

"I know. I'm just cleaning out my stuff now and arranging my bag. I'm not leaving yet, probably later this afternoon. If I come back later this month, I'll just take another locker for the time I'm paid, OK?

The attendant nods distractedly, no longer looking at Pedro, who descends the stairs into the locker area. Arriving at his locker, something doesn't look right. The door is locked, but slightly ajar. Pedro hurriedly opens the lock and struggles to pull up the switch that unlatches the locker door, revealing to Pedro that someone somehow jimmied it open. When he finally opens the door, a jumble of rifled belongings spill onto the floor. As the surprise wears off, Pedro quickly rummages through the locker to check what's been taken. It's an impulsive response that quickly fades because Pedro remembers that he never keeps anything of value in the locker. It's the Y and it's not safe to leave anything behind. Some of his t-shirts, some pants, other clothing and a pair of sneakers are missing. His art supplies are all still there, as untouched by the thief as by Pedro.

Pedro sorts through his possessions. He resolves to preserve as many of his art supplies as possible, since he can take them home. Many of the clothes left behind by the thief aren't worth keeping. A couple of months of the junkie lifestyle left them looking raggedy. He tosses them into the locker room's large garbage can, except for one t-shirt and a pair of ripped jeans, in case he decides to spend the night in New York . He fills a carry-on piece of luggage at the bottom of the locker with as many of the art supplies that fit. Pads, paints, brushes, thinner, a scrapbook, pens. He unrolls a canvas in the back of the locker to look at an unfinished project from just before he dropped out of school. The idea was to finish it at the Y. He throws it in the trash. He puts his art supplies back in the locker and locks it again. He sticks his hand in his pocket to fondle the money Sandra gave him. A hunger tickles the bottom of his throat and his heart beats a little faster at the thought of getting high.

After double-checking that the lock is set and that the locker door is closed securely, he leaves the locker room and heads out into the muggy sunshine, towards Eighth Avenue and his abandoned alcove. What was dread and trepidation is now slight revulsion and nervousness, but the dealers await on Ninth Avenue. Why shouldn't he walk past the 8th Avenue subway station like anyone else? That's what he does, barely pausing to remember Saturday night. Steeled by the determination to find dope's numbing embrace, Pedro walks through the intersection with no trouble. He feels strangely free.

"Nobody is gonna find out what happened."

The projects are rather quiet except for the yelling of small children playing in a cement courtyard with a water hose. Pedro walks along 19th Street towards 10th Avenue and quickly sees one of the dealers sitting on an upside down bucket on the sidewalk. The dealer looks at Pedro and recognizes him as one of the regulars, nodding to him. Pedro already has the $20 bill in his hand and when he walks up to the dealer they shake hands, while Pedro presses the bill into the dealer's palm.

"Let's go for a walk," the dealer orders, rising from the bucket and continuing westbound. "What do you want today? I have Benz and Smiley."

The dealer calls his heroin by their street names. One of the packages has the Mercedes Benz logo stamped on the package, while the other one has a 1970s happy face. The stamps aren't necessarily a mark of quality. Pedro has tried all of the brands. The Benz made Pedro sick last time he bought it, so he chooses Smiley.

"I gave you a twenty," Pedro tells the dealer.

"I know, here's your two-pack," the dealer said as he slipped the drugs into Pedro's back pants pocket after they turn left on 10th Avenue. "Be cool, we gotta keep walking to 18th Street and back to the projects. The cops drove by this morning, so they might still be around."

The walk around the block ends when the dealer goes back into the projects, as Pedro continues to Ninth Avenue and then heads north. He decides to go back to the Y, since it's the only place he can think of where he can snort a little of his stash.

"You back again? You stayin' or leavin'?" the Y front desk attendant asks when Pedro walks back in.

"I'm probably leaving tomorrow and I'm throwing out my old stuff and packing up. I'm almost done," Pedro, as he hurried towards the locker room downstairs.

He locks the bathroom stall and then lowers his pants, sitting on the toilet so it looks like he's legitimately using it. He listens for any sounds and hears no one in the adjacent stalls, so he opens one of the packages and quickly snorts up the entire content with the other $20, which he's rolled into a tube. Nervous, he quickly crumples the wax paper package, throws it in the toilet, flushes it and unrolls the bill, wiping it on his shirt and folding it so it doesn't look like it's been used for drugs.

Pedro only has a few minutes to get out of the Y before the heroin high hits. He doesn't want the staff there to see him stumble out. Rushing, Pedro checks himself in the mirror and quickly ascends the stairs, waving to the front desk on his way out the door. Feeling as if he just slid into home base, Pedro smiles triumphantly as his head lightens and his knees weaken. He's got to get away from the Y, so he makes a quick turn north on Seventh Avenue and then a quick right at 24th Street heading east towards Madison Square Park. He doesn't make it, though. By Sixth Avenue, he feels an overwhelming need to sit down and does so on 24th St. It's not so busy on that block, so no one chases him away from the spot he's chosen, where waves of dizzy numbness crash on him.

After an uncertain amount of time, Pedro is able to rise and renew his trip to the park. Staggering slightly on the way there, he ultimately reaches a bench on the western edge of the park by Broadway and immediately takes a seat. Luckily it's in the shade, for now. Pedro puts his little canteen bag on his lap and folds his arms around it before nodding off.

The slow roast of his afternoon in the park rudely awakens Pedro, who's now covered with sweat. Groggy and disoriented, he moves to a shady part of the park, noticing that it's now almost 6 p.m. Hungry, he eventually walks to the Wendy's across 23rd Street from the park and orders a junior cheeseburger deluxe and a frosty.

He returns to the park to eat his meal and wake up some more. Pedro feels like going back into the Wendy's to use their bathroom and snort up the other packet.

"This is supposed to be the pack I'm taking back to New Hyde Park, unless I get more," Pedro thinks, doing financial calculations in his head.

"If I get more I'll barely have enough to get back to New Hyde Park. I didn't fill out a single application. Dad's gonna be pissed."

Pedro decides that the best course of action is to go to the Merry-go-round to make some extra money and maybe get a free place to sleep tonight. He holds off on snorting more of the heroin because he won't be successful at the merry-go-round if he's nodding off. It's not dark yet so Pedro goes back to the park for a little while. He doesn't feel like walking all the way to midtown, so he'll take the subway. That way he won't feel so tired while up there, in case it takes time to find a trick. Johns don't like the young guys who look so druggy. They want healthy or muscular guys, except for the johns who have the teen fetishes and prefer the skinny guys that can pass as high school students. That's the look the best fits Pedro, so he lies and tells the guys he just turned 18. The park's activity bores him. It's the time of the evening when residents in the surrounding apartment buildings bring their dogs for a walk after getting home from work. There are a few joggers too, but the sight of them running in the steamy afternoon nauseates Pedro, who already craves a shower after baking in the park all afternoon. The post-high funk sets in as a breeze kicks up. Pedro closes his eyes for a bit, and drifts off to sleep again.

"Reggie, get away away from that man!" yells a dog owner to his yorkie, which is drawn to Pedro's scent and runs up to him to rub his nose against Pedro's leg. The yelling and dod's soft rubbing on his leg awakens Pedro, slightly startling him. Disoriented, he's forgotten where he is. It's twilight in the park, so he doesn't recognize the surroundings.

"Where did I go after Wendy's?"

As the yorkie retreats, the owner waves and shouts sorry. Pedro waves back distractedly, looking around and then remembering that he's still in Madison Square Park. Looking up to the clock tower above the park, it's 8:30, so he's been asleep for about 90 minutes. The post-narcotic funk has worn off and he's in a near-normal mood, though the little package in his pocket beckons.

"It's time to make some money."

Pedro rises and walks to the Lexington Avenue line. It's dark by the time Pedro reaches the merry-go-round and many of the good perches are already taken by some of the regular toughs who work most nights. Pedro is afraid to approach them because they're unfriendly and some of them have even warned Pedro to stay away from their perches because they don't want the competition. Pedro notices the spot he used last time is empty, so he resumes his position there.

"It's not a bad spot. Last time I was here I got someone really fast, so maybe I'll get lucky the same way tonight."

Cars with older men are already circling and some of the older men walk around the block, summing up the meat rack. Pedro feels judged as the men passed, sizing him up. Nervous, Pedro averts his gaze, but then he remembers that he's here to meet someone, not ignore interested customers. He forces himself to look and nod at the men, repulsed by the effort.

"Is this really easy money? Is this easier than just begging in Times Square?"

Suddenly, a man in his 50s approaches Pedro.

"Hey there, what's going on?"

"Not much," Pedro responds, shrugging.

"What's your name?"

"Pedro," he blurts out before bothering to think up a fake name.

"Oh, a Spanish boy, what a treat. You don't look Spanish," said the man. "I'm Marvin."

"How are you?"

"I'm very happy to meet you, Pedro. Do you like to party?

"Yea, I like parties. Doesn't everyone?"

"Well, there are parties and then there is partying. I like to party hard. Why not, right? You only live once and it's more fun to party with a hot guy like you."

Pedro stares unenthusiastically at the street, watching other men pass, and they aren't paying as much attention to him now that one of the johns is chatting him up.

"What are you looking for tonight?"

"I'd like to party with you, Pedro. Are you into that?"

"OK, uh, where do you want to party?"

"I've got a hotel in Midtown that we can go to. We can take a taxi there if you want."

"You have to give me $100 and you can't fuck me," Pedro says abruptly.

"I figured you'd want something, Pedro. That's fine, let's go look for a taxi."

Pedro feels a nervous tingle while walking with Marvin.

"Who is this man? Will he kill me? Maybe he'll just be like the guy from the other night. It was disgusting having sex with him, but it was over fast and I didn't have to do that much for the money. If I begged in Times Square it could take two days to get $100. This will be faster."

Pedro gets in the taxi without questioning which hotel he's being taken to or without listening to Marvin as he instructs the taxi driver. Pedro remains silent in the taxi, as does Marvin. In less than 10 minutes they arrive at the hotel. It's on Lexington Avenue, but Pedro doesn't see the name of the place when they walk in and pass the front desk to the elevator. Pedro draws quick and deep breaths, as if he's riding up the steep incline of a roller coaster that's about to take the first big plunge. He feels that same roller coaster dread and the weight of gravity pulling at him, but none of the anticipated fun or exhilaration, just the pre-plunge dread.

"I suppose this room will do. I bought some gin and tonic at the store before running into you. Would you like some? I'll go get the ice," says Marvin, grabbing the ice bucket and walking out the door.

Pedro walks to the desk where Marvin left the pint of gin, noticing that it's a nameless, cheap brand. Pedro thinks he doesn't like gin, though he can't remember what it tastes like. He opens the bottle, sniffs, and recoils at the scent.

"It's not the good stuff," says Marvin walking in on Pedro. "They didn't have the good stuff in the small sizes, and the store where I bought must sell to a low-class crowd because their selection wasn't so good to begin with."

Pedro looks at Marvin, but says nothing.

"Do you like crank?" Marvin asks.

"Um, I don't know what that is," Pedro responds, his interest slightly piqued because he's still feeling an evil little tickle.

"Is is like coke?"

"It's similar, but it lasts a lot longer. I like it because it makes me horny. I had some earlier today, which is one of the reasons I came looking for you. Why don't I make a couple of lines so you can try it."

Pedro nods silently, unsure what to expect. He's vaguely heard of it, presuming it's some kind of speed or stimulant. Marvin takes a little baggie with a white powder and scoops some out onto a little mirror he pulls out of a little shaving kit he has in the bag with the liquor. There is a razor blade in the shaving kit that he uses to chop the powder and arrange it into little lines. He hands Pedro a cut piece of plastic straw also pulled from the little shaving kit.

"I hope you like it. It's pretty good stuff, so you don't need a lot to get off."

Pedro snorts up the two lines, one for each nostril, and then winces from the burning pain in his sinus. The sting is much worse than heroin, he thinks.

"That second line was actually for me," Marvin says. "That's all right, there's more," he said, scooping a small amount out of the baggie with the key and snorting the tiny mound right off the key. "Remind me to rinse this key off before turning it back in."

Pedro feels the sting subside, awaiting an effect, though

unsure what will happen next. Marvin takes two plastic cups on a little tray on the desk and pours some gin into each. He adds the tonic water and fishes a couple of ice cubes out of the bucket with his hand, dropping them into the fizzing cups. He hands one to Pedro.

"Cheers. This is the best taste of the summer. The funny thing is, I can't stand drinking these in the winter."

Pedro says nothing as he takes a sip from his. Again he recoils, making a frown that causes Marvin to laugh.

"Um, I don't know what's worse, the sting from this shit I just snorted or this nasty drink," says Pedro, making his first candid, unguarded remark since meeting Marvin.

"You don't have to drink it if you don't like it. Let's get naked. The crank is making me hot."

"I need the money," Pedro demands.

"Oh, yeah, I forgot about that," Marvin says, laughing, he pulls out his wallet and removes a wad of money, turning slightly so that Pedro can't see how much cash he has.

Handing Pedro the money, Marvin takes another gulp of the gin and tonic.

Pedro looks at the cash and quickly confirms there are five $20 bills before putting them in his front left pants pocket. He then begins to take off his boots, socks and then his shirt. As he removes his shirt, he feels his heart beating faster, but not from fear or dread. It's not sexual excitement either, though he feels a strange tingling in his cock. It certainly isn't in anticipation of Marvin's hand or tongue all over him.

"What a nice, lean chest," Marvin says admiringly as his bulging eyes consume Pedro's pallid flesh. "I can't believe you're Spanish. You're very white, though your arms sure are tan."

Pedro says nothing as Marvin first fondles his nipples and then works his way to Pedro's navel and belt buckle, unfastening it and then undoing his pants, which fall to the floor. Pedro avoids his gaze after briefly noting Marvin's overly tan beer gut and sagging pectorals. Sex is the last thing he wants, yet the drug is making him feel flush and strangely aroused, causing his cock to harden in his underwear as Marvin kneels down to help Pedro remove his pants. By the time Marvin removes Pedro's pants and turns his attention to Pedro's underwear, there's already an erect penis awaiting.

"See what I meant, this stuff makes you horny," Marvin says, rubbing Pedro's package and then pressing his nose to Pedro's crotch to take a sniff.

"You're very clean," Marvin said, as he pulls Pedro's underwear down to his feet. "I like that."

Marvin pushes Pedro towards the bed without saying anything. Marvin takes another big gulp of cocktail and then removes his pants and underwear. Pedro feels sweaty and hot as Marvin sits next to him on the bed, fondling his genitals greedily while playing with himself. Pedro feels confused by the drug's effect. He's aroused and repulsed at the same time, unsure how that's possible. An exhilaration besieges Pedro, his heart beating, his cock throbbing, while Marvin's grubby hands get their money's worth. Marvin puts Pedro's manhood in his mouth and excitement shoots up Pedro's spine. It's not the sex he had a couple of nights ago.

"This shit is incredible. How come I never did it before? It's way better than coke."

Suddenly Pedro shivers uncontrollably as his swollen dick releases its load into Marvin's slurping mouth.

"That a boy," Marvin says enthusiastically, barely pausing to swallow his prize.

Pedro barely hears Marvin because the orgasm sets off noise in his head. His brain buzzes, like the little steel ball shooting around a pinball machine. He feels short of breath and a wave of perspiration crashes through his skin, soaking his back and wetting the bed sheet. He feels another hot flash, producing another perspiration wave. Neurons fire rapidly.

"Oh, oh, I'm coming," Marvin barks, as a warm glob hits Pedro's belly, jolting him out of his adrenalin rush.

"It's really hot in here," Pedro complains, wiping his wet forehead.

"That's the crystal. It makes me really hot too, and this is good stuff. You want to do another line?"

Pedro nods, not sure what he's taking, but wanting to continue the rush. Wiping the cum off his belly with the bath towel Marvin brought from the bathroom before they got naked, Pedro walks over to the little desk where Marvin removes another amount of speed and puts it on the little mirror he left on the table. With the razor blade he again makes two fine lines. Before handing the mirror and straw to Pedro, Marvin snorts one of the lines.

"I won't make the same mistake as last time, I'm taking the first line. Fuck, this shit burns."

Pedro snorts his line and also winces in pain.

"You see what I mean about this stuff making you horny? You still have a hard-on. Or is it just that you like me?" Marvin asks, smiling to reveal a misshapen front top tooth.

"This stuff is great," Pedro exclaims, not particularly addressing Marvin while looking down at his erection, wishing it would dissipate. "Where do you get it?"

"I have special connections in California who get it for me. It's not that common in New York City," Marvin says with pride.

"I…I never met a dealer who had this stuff," Pedro says, licking his lips, which are dry.

Pedro walks over to the cup of gin and tonic and finishes the remaining amount to quench the dryness in his mouth. He no longer gags like he did with the first sip.

"I guess you're either getting really high or you've learned to love gin and tonic," Marvin says, again revealing the crooked tooth through his lips.

"I'm gonna go. Can I have some?" Pedro says abruptly, feeling an urgent need to flee.

"I might consider giving you some, but what do I get out of it? I just gave you $100 for a blow job. Now you want something that I have, so what do I get out of it? Fuck me for a bit and I'll give you some."

"I don't think I can come again," Pedro responds, not liking that option at all.

"Just for a couple of minutes. You don't need to come," Marvin says, grabbing a condom package and opening it. "Here, I'll help you."

Pedro lets Marvin put the condom on him and then lube it up. Marvin then lubricates himself before laying on the bed. He orders Pedro to climb on top and penetrate him. Disgusted, but craving more drugs, Pedro obeys and pumps unenthusiastically.

After about five minutes, Marvin asks Pedro to stop.

"I can't take it any more. I'm getting too excited. At my age I have to be careful about that," Marvin says.

Pedro walks into the bathroom, takes a quick shower and cleans the sticky mess off. The cold water succeeds in softening his sore erection. After drying himself, he comes back into the room to get dressed. Marvin is scooping some more powder on the mirror.

"Do you want a final bump before you leave?" Marvin asks, wiping the specks of a dry, white foam at the corners of his mouth with the back of his hand.

Pedro simply nods after putting on his underwear. He snorts the line, winces again and goes back to the pile of his clothes. After putting on his pants he checks the pocket to ensure that the money is still there, and it is. Once he's fully dressed, he walks over to the gin and tonic and pours himself another shot of gin and adds the tonic. I doesn't taste bad at all by now. He gulps it, feeling so thirsty.

"It's time for me to leave," he tells Marvin.

"I know. It was fun having you come over for a while. Too bad you don't feel like staying, we could party all night. Anyway, I made you a little to-go bag for the extra fuck. It was good," says Marvin, handing him the baggie.

"Thanks," Pedro says turning and heading for the door, trying not to look as if he's rushing out, though he wants out more than ever. It's not even Marvin, he just wants to go outside and walk around in the night.

"I'll see you around," Pedro says, turning to nod to Marvin, who's still standing at the table naked, licking the little mirror.

Marvin waves to Pedro, who walks out, his mind spinning at wild revolutions per minute. The elevator takes an eternity to arrive and carry him to the lobby, while Pedro anxiously pecks at the elevator's call button. Once in the lobby, Pedro feels liberated. With thoughts racing through his mind, Pedro walks into the night, not knowing where he'll go, but exhilarated by the possibilities.

Chapter 15

"Is today really my last day at Runway? Do I really hate my job that much? Yes. I'm quitting. Actually, they'll probably fire me when they realize I took the green feather jacket. So what. I'll get another job, or my club career will take off. I'll be a celebrity after tomorrow, and wait 'til they come to my tagging party. Yes, I'll buy spray paint cans and have everybody do a tag. It will be a whole crowd of people breaking the law. People will love that."

Sonny's morning reverie quickly ends with a glance at the clock. It's 9:10.

"Can't start the day late. I'm stealing from work today! Tee-hee-hee!"

There's no need for a shower since he took one after coming home from the subway. It's one of those mornings when appearances don't matter. Grab a t-shirt, some jeans, sneakers, a hat and some sunglasses. Apply makeup at work, if needed.

"I used to put so much effort into getting dressed for work. What was I thinking? Nobody there appreciates my looks anyway. They're all too into themselves."

Rushing out the door, Sonny drops a stack of invites to tomorrow's party into his backpack and he checks his pockets for the keys before locking the door and bolting down the steps to the street.

"What am I doing after quitting Runway? I could get a job at Bang Bang if I'm desperate. They'll hire me since I have a lot of experience selling clothes and they're always trying to copy Runway's style."

It wasn't so hard walking to work today, despite the fatigue, knowing that this is the possibly the last day.

"Maybe they won't fire me. Why should they? I'm an OK worker. I'm better than some of the drag queens who worked there. At least I come on time and I'm not bitchy. Maybe Susan will just forgive me or make me pay a discounted price for the jacket. I can work it off and she can take it off my salary. Still, once I get rolling in the party promoting, I'm quitting this shit job. I've had enough. I should get a sandwich, since I'll need energy to give my invites to everyone who walks into the store."

Sonny walks into the usual deli to order his egg sandwich and diet Pepsi. He scans the papers, but there's no mention of the subway crime on the front page and he doesn't want to look inside.

"They've probably found some new body somewhere else. That guy wasn't someone famous, so why would they keep writing about him? Why is my sandwich taking so long?"

Arriving at Runway's stoop, Sonny sits and eats, staring at the street.

"Do I really want to wear my joker outfit tonight? Is it outrageous enough? It is. People will like it, but will it motivate them to come to my party tomorrow night? What if nobody comes to the party? I'll be fucked. Shit, that and losing my job here for taking the jacket might cause me to lose my apartment. Is there something else I can wear?"

"Sonny, get your ass in here, it's time to work," Darnell shouts from behind the closed door, knocking on the glass door for emphasis.

Sonny sluggishly rises, turning to the entrance.

"This isn't the job I wanted. What was I thinking when I applied here?"

Darnell has a Sade album playing, which is his speed at that time of the day. Boxes delivered late yesterday afternoon sit on the floor opened but still unpacked. It's usually Sonny's job to take the invoices and match them to the contents to ensure that everything on the list was delivered, not the kind of job he relishes on a groggy morning.

"All those boxes need reconciliation," says Darnell, not specifically addressing Sonny but intending his command for him nonetheless. "Try to hurry up and do that before the customers start coming."

"Who's coming in at 10 on a Wednesday?" Sonny says aloud, not directing his comment to Darnell and getting no response.

"Everyone who matters is still asleep. Maybe there will be something in these boxes that might be cute for my outfit tomorrow."

There is nothing in the boxes that Sonny wants to wear to his party debut. Still, he is in a much better mood after finishing the box reconciliation. He walks to the rack where the kelly green bolero jacket hangs and he admires it, petting the black feather epaulettes and moving the lamé fabric so that it reflects the store's overhead lights.

"Nobody better buy you today, because I'll be fucked."

Sonny's fatigue causes the day to drag for the first few hours, until the magazine stylist Eva Cole drops by around 3 p.m.

"I'm styling extras for a video shoot for a client. I can't tell you who the client is because of a confidentiality agreement, but it's a famous client and we're looking for some wild looks to spice up the extras. What's new in the store?" Eva asks Sonny, mostly looking past and around him as she speaks, scanning the shop for inspiration.

"I just opened some boxes, so I'll show you the new stuff first. By the way, did you know I'm having a party tomorrow at the Tunnel?

"No, what kind of party is it?"

"It's in the basement of Tunnel. I'm having a balloon toss, and there will be surprise ecstasy pills inside the balloons. Here's an invite for it. Basically the idea is to get people to fight with each other over the balloons. It will be an out-of-control frenzy, outfits will be ruined and make-up smeared, tee-hee-hee! Then we all get high. What good party doesn't end that way? Tee-hee-hee!"

"That sounds like fun, but I might be busy planning the video shoot."

"Who are the extras?"

"They're people we found in the clubs. We went to Trix and Outré to find some of the wildest club kids and fashion victims."

"I'm going to Outré tonight. I'm wearing a joker outfit that I made out of playing cards."

"Sounds cute," Eva says absentmindedly as she looks through merchandise, creating a pile of clothing she elects to buy for the video.

"I'm taking Friday off, since my big party is on Thursday. I don't really have anything planned for Friday," Sonny says expectantly.

"It sounds like you'll need a day off after a party like that," Eva replies, without looking at Sonny. "These are the shirts I want. I'm using a credit card."

Sonny cracks a disappointed smile.

"Great, I'll ring them up. These will look great in your video," says Sonny, feeling a flash of anger, like the time he found out he was not invited to the Class of 1989 photo shoot organized by Magazine, a cheaply produced publication that celebrates up-and-coming club creatures and the venues they frequent.

Eva's visit puts Sonny in a funk and increases his worry that not enough people will come to his party. Powerlessness melts into self-doubt as he continues with the many little chores at Runway. Fold the clothes, which will be unfolded by the next few customers. Wipe down the front door, where later on the customers will invariably put their greasy hands on the glass. His most humiliating chore is going outside with a broom and dust pan to pick up scattered trash on the sidewalk and in the gutter, including dog shit, lest the store get a ticket for not maintaining the area. It's the chore Sonny does the fastest, lest someone see him.

"I don't understand why I always have to sweep the street. It's cruel punishment and we should take turns doing it. It's not fair!" Sonny complains to Darnell.

"Listen, you stuck up little queen. The day before yesterday I listened to you brag about trolling through the sewage-strewn subway tunnels and tagging shit, but God-forbid someone should see you keeping our city clean. Don't even try it, bitch. You're sweeping the street tomorrow and every day after that," Darnell says, snapping his fingers.

"Well, I won't be here Friday, so you'll have to do it."

"No, honey. There will be more for you to do on Saturday, end of dis-cus-sion," Darnell says, throwing his right hand in the air and walking into the back of the store.

The day drags, with Sonny carrying a few of his party invites in his back pocket, offering them to everyone who walks into the store. A European tourist walks in to look at the front t-shirt display, and Sonny swoops in to offer assistance.

"This is my favorite one," Sonny says to the guy, who's in his early 20s and is kind of cute. "I like it because it has bombs falling on these stilettos. It's funny. Bomb the drag queens!" Sonny says, cracking a rare smile at work.

"I thought it was for girls," says the tourist in an accent that Sonny can't identify, but it's not British.

"Most girls don't wear those kinds of shoes. It's mostly men who dress like women that like such high heels, tee-hee-hee!"

"I guess you're right. I don't think it works for me."

"OK, you seem a little butch. How about this shirt," Sonny asks, holding up a shirt with meat cleavers on it, somewhat in the style of an Andy Warhol silk screen with knives on it."

"I like it," says the guy, smiling at Sonny, who suddenly feels nervous.

"You should wear it to my party tomorrow at Tunnel. It will be an outrageous SCAN-dal"

"I don't know where the Tunnel is," says the tall, pale tourist.

"The address of the club is on this invite. See it on the

bottom? You should go out tonight too. I'm going to Outre to hang out and promote my party."

"Where is Outre?" the tourist asks, furrowing his brow, which sets off his blue eyes under wavy brown bangs.

"It's on the corner of 17th Street and Broadway. You can't miss it."

"What time does the party start?"

"The clubs usually open around 10 but nobody goes that early. Usually the fabulous people start arriving around 11:30 and it stays open until 4."

"OK, I want to go. Should I wear this shirt tonight?"

"Yes, it will look cute on you," Sonny says, embarrassed by his attraction to the stranger. "What's your name?"

"I'm Dieter."

"That's a weird name. Are you from England?"

"Germany."

"Oh, I don't know anything about your country, sorry," says Sonny, not wanting to admit that the only thing that pops into his head is Adolf Hitler.

"Well, that's because your an American," says Dieter, smiling at Sonny and lifting his dark eyebrows a bit, which make his blue eyes all the more piercing.

"Are you doing a show at your party?"

"Not really, but we're having a spectacle. Around midnight I'm releasing more than 100 balloons with an extra special surprise in some of them. There will be a riot on the dance floor."

"A riot? Why?"

"Because of the extra special surprise, you know, EX-tremely special."

"I don't understand."

"There's X in the balloons," Sonny tells Dieter with a bit of frustration, lowering his voice to a whisper when he says X, even though there's no one in the store who would care.

"Oh, I think I understand," Dieter says. "That does sound like fun. Is the music good?"

"It's alright. I don't have any control over the DJ, but I usually don't pay much mind to it because I'm often busy in the clubs working it."

"You work in the clubs?"

"Well, kind of. I'll be working tomorrow, but tonight I'll be working it because I have to promote my party at Outre."

"I will come to Outre and join you. Maybe you can give me a tour," says Dieter, smiling at Sonny.

"OK," Sonny responds nervously, shaken by the smile and involuntarily glancing towards the back of the store.

"Am I keeping you from your work? I should go," Dieter says, picking the cleaver shirt off the table and handing it to Sonny.

"Alright, I'll ring it up for you," says Sonny, embarrassed by his attraction to the foreigner.

After processing the sale and exchanging some more awkward pleasantries, Dieter leaves the store.

"Are we planning some after-hours customer service?" Darnell asks in a queeny school-teacher tone.

"Oh, please. He's not my type."

"Don't play me. I can tell you like him. He's cute and I'll bet he's good in bed by the way he walks," says Darnell, lowering his voice into a husky baritone when he says the word "walks."

"Why does everything with you and the other queens in this store have to do with sex? We're in the AIDS crisis and no one should be having sex. Sex is passé. I don't have sex; I do ecstasy."

"Sex is a natural drug, but you young folks don't understand."

"Darnell, we understand and we know sex is too dangerous. That's why we have our fun in other ways. It's not about fucking. It's about being creative and expressing yourself in a fun way. That's what I believe, anyway. I don't need sex," says Sonny, snapping his fingers dismissively.

"You're full of shit. Get back to work and start counting receipts. There's only two hours until closing and the sooner we get the morning and afternoon squared away the faster you'll get out of here."

The reminder of quitting time sends Sonny to the front of the store to check on the coveted jacket.

"How am I getting this out of the store without Darnell seeing me? This will be hard."

Sonny walks back to the register, grabs the biggest shopping bag under the counter and puts it in a closet next to the dressing room.

"I'm doing it. I don't care. They can fire me, or I'll just pay them later or they can take it out of my paycheck. If I ask to borrow it they'll just say no. Just Say No works for the drug war, but not for me."

After the final customer leaves and the accounts are settled, Darnell announces with a wave of his hand that Sonny is free to go. Sonny goes downstairs to get his backpack, knowing that Darnell will also come down at some point. He waits downstairs in the little employee bathroom, hoping Darnell descends for a moment, so that he has his chance. As he hears Darnell's footsteps, Sonny emerges from the bathroom, grabs his bag and bids his boss farewell as he walks up the stairs.

"Don't forget to check that the door is locked behind you," Darnell orders.

Reconsidering his next move, Sonny abandons the hidden shopping bag because Darnell might hear too many footsteps below and get suspicious. Walking past the clothes rack, he simply grabs the coat off the hanger without interrupting his gait and heads for the door, greedily clutching his prize. Checking the door, Sonny escapes with his showpiece, triumphantly.

With no shopping bag for his prize, Sonny stops every two blocks to fold and refold the coat, not wanting to muss the feathers. Worried that he might damage the feathers, he does not visit the corner pizzeria to buy some dinner.

A few hours later, a nervous jolt zaps Sonny when he awakes from his disco nap.

"Oh shit, it's 9:30 and I haven't even eaten."

Sonny looks through the small cupboard above his sink for a dinner substitute. There are no provisions for actually making a meal, so it's odd bits: a mostly eaten box of Triscuits and a can of SpaghettiOs. While eating dinner, Sonny makes his bed and then carefully lays out the joker outfit for final appraisal and embellishment. He never finished the back of the vest, he now realizes.

"I don't have time for the entire back, maybe if I just do a line across by the shoulder blades, that won't be too hard and then people will see my cards as a line matching the line that goes across my top hat. What choice do I have at this point? It's a style element!"

He gets busy with the back of the vest, working as fast as possible while scanning the kitchen counter next to the sink where he keeps much of his make-up. Some of his face will be covered by the cards, so he won't need as much as usual. By 10:30 the back of the vest is done. It takes longer than anticipated, so Sonny opts for a bold make-up look using big blotches, so he doesn't have to worry about fine, time-consuming details. The first layer is clown white, which he applies with a dish sponge, since he's run out of make up sponges.

"This sponge works pretty good, though it would be better if it weren't the same one I use to wipe the counter. I boiled it, so technically it's sanitized. When it's clown white, having a fine sponge doesn't matter. I'm buying these from now on for the clown looks. They're cheaper. That might make a good story for tonight. The make-up queens will gag over it."

After the clown white, Sonny removes two little round stickers from his cheeks. He blots spirit gum on the unpainted flesh and he places little pieces of playing cards that he glued together yesterday. They're winning hands: royal flushes. A uni-brow will work best for this look, so Sonny takes the black grease stick and draws a straight black stripe from his left temple, across his eyebrows, to his right temple. The rim of the top had will just just above that black stripe. He also uses the stick to draw a vertical black stripe under his nose and above his lip for a fake Charlie Chaplin mustache. Using a liquid eyeliner, Sonny draws lines on his eyelids and applies heavy, black mascara. Kabuki red lips complete the look.

By the time the lips go on, Sonny's in a panic. It's almost 11:15 and he's not dressed. It's not cool getting to the club early, but there are invites to be distributed, and the remaining stack is at least 1,000 flyers high. He quickly puts on the outfit, covers himself with the black graduation gown that he bought in a thrift store, puts the invites in the Hello Kitty backpack and runs out the door, almost forgetting his keys. Luckily, Outré isn't far from the apartment, so all he has to do is walk fast.

Sonny's attempt at covering up is hardly inconspicuous as he walks down 13th Street heading west, the black gown ruffling with every quick step. There's still the issue of the top hat, the backpack, the facial decor and make-up.

"Are you graduating from clown school tonight?" yells some asshole who passes Sonny with a group of his friends, all snickering.

It's better not to respond and Sonny continues quickly walking through the East Village. Even though it's kind of scary, he likes walking down East 13th Street because it's dark and rather deserted. That means less encounters with idiots. The idea is to walk quickly, look straight ahead, try not to be nervous and be aware of anyone walking behind.

"Bang, bang, bang, bang, bango. Bango. Bango. Bang, bang, bang, bang, bango," Sonny chants to himself, singing the repetitive sample from Todd Terry's Bango (To the Batcave), the big club hit last year. Like a Hail Mary or some other prayer, Sonny finds the song comforting and it excites him at the prospect of the coming thump-thump. The song often alternates with the Batgirl theme song. A few taxis slow down as they pass Sonny to check him out. It's not unusual for the taxis to slow down, thinking that he's a prostitute, but once they see the clown white, it's a turn off and they speed away. He arrives at the club without incident, having taken the darkest streets to remain as inconspicuous as possible.

"Work the gown, work the clown gown, bitch," Sonny tells himself as a skips across the street toward Outré's entrance.

"Clear a path, clear a path! Yeaaa!" Sonny shouts as he arrives at the velvet ropes, which really had only four people standing and waiting.

"Hello Sonny, why are you so covered up? That's not like you," says Solange, removing the rope from its stand and looking at Sonny with an amused and puzzled expression. "Usually you're more....exposed."

"Oh, I am, I just graduated from clown school and then ran over here to celebrate," Sonny replies, taking a complimentary admission ticket from her.

"Well congratulations on your graduation. I'm glad some of you club kids stayed in school and graduated. It's still a bit quiet inside, but I suppose you'll stir things up," Solange said before turning her attention back to the people who were waiting before Sonny arrived.

Outré usually doesn't get crowded until midnight, and most of the clubbers schedule their arrival to that time, because the club quickly goes from empty to full. There are few people on the dance floor when Sonny enters, but he avoids it, quickly bolting into the bathroom to remove his gown and put it in the backpack. While pulling a stack of invites from the bag, Sterling walks in.

"There you are! I was wondering what had happened to you. I figured you were staying home to get your beauty rest for the big party tomorrow. What do you think of my look?" says Sterling, who was wearing a silver sequined vest with a black, fishnet, long sleeved shirt, black hot pants, fishnet hose and black combat boots that laced up to just below his knees.

"You look fabulous, and mine?"

"Very colorful. I like the playing cards. I have a pack of Uno cards that I don't want. Do you want to turn them into your next look? Or perhaps I'll give you my deck of Old Maid, that would suit you just fine, hiaaah!"

Sterling touches up the sliver stripes on his face with a little brush he pulls out of his lunchbox.

"Can you help me pass out invites tonight? I still have a lot to give out and the party's tomorrow."

"Again? All this work for just $75? It's less than minimum wage!"

"Sterling, you know that we have to make a special effort on this party because it's my first and..."

"Oh, don't start with that. I'm sick of hearing that. Gimme a small stack, bitch."

"Thanks. Let's go out there and work the dance floor before it gets crowded."

"OK, but just for a minute, because I'm supposed to be dancing on the box near the bar."

"You're working here now?"

"Yeah, I got a call from Solange today telling me that they needed another go-go dancer and she asked if I could do it. Of course I need the money so I said yes. You're not the only one who's moving up in the club scene, hiaaah!"

"That's great," says Sonny, wondering why Solange didn't call him.

Sonny quickly forgets about Solange not calling when one of his favorite acid house songs begins to play: 101's "Rock to the Beat," which is almost a year old but still fun for dancing. Sonny and Sterling began spinning around, then doing their computer programming dance, in which they face each other and repeatedly punch imaginary buttons with an intense concentration, as if operating some giant console that controls the weather or nuclear weapons.

"Rock to the beat, rock to the beat, rock to the beat, rock to the beat," the female singer coos, never saying anything more. It's a five-minute song with just four words and lots of druggy sound effects. On ecstasy it makes perfect sense and it doesn't even seem like a long song, but in his present, sober state Sonny worries that he's been in the club for 20 minutes already and hasn't given out a single invite.

"I've got to get busy. I'll dance later."

"That's OK, I'm supposed to be dancing on the box anyway."

Sonny skips off the dance floor in the direction of the bar. He walks past the people near the bar, all of whom look at him to check out his look. He uses those curious gazes to hit them up with his invite.

"Come to my party. Come to my party," Sonny says, handing each patron an invite.

"I can't give out all these invites unless it gets crowded in here. What time is it?"

"Is that you Sonny? You look incredible," says Dieter, grinning at Sonny's appearance. "You look so different from earlier today."

"That's supposed to be the point. I'm not coming out wearing a day look."

Dieter smiles, unsure what Sonny means.

"This club looks like so much fun. Do you come here every week?"

"Not every week, but pretty often. My party tomorrow will be better. Things never get too crazy here."

"I don't understand what you mean by crazy."

"It's the people who come here. They don't cut loose as much as we do in the basement of the Tunnel, where you can pretty much do what you want. Here things are more controlled."

"Oh," Dieter replies, smiling again but still not sure what Sonny means.

"I have to hand out more of these invites. Do you want to

help me?"

"Yes"

"OK, just follow me around and if you see someone who I haven't given an invite to, give them one," says Sonny, handing a short stack to Dieter and then motioning for him to follow.

Sonny heads for the perimeter of the room.

"When I'm passing out invites, I like to work the edges of the room because that's where people tend to hang out. That way you're not constantly going around too much," Sonny says to Dieter, who can't really hear.

After working his way around the room once, Sonny heads over to the entrance and begins passing out the invites to the new arrivals, while Dieter stands next to him.

"How long will you pass out those invitations?"

"Until I run out. I need to get as many people at my party as possible. Oh, I like this song, let's go dance," Sonny said, as the screaming sample from Blackbox's "Ride on Time" shakes the club.

Sonny and Dieter reach the dance floor as the screaming continues. Sonny flails his arms wildly as he mimics Loleatta Holloway's booming lyrics.

Dieter laughs while watching the wacky joker sing a rousing number.

"You're a good dancer," he screams into Sonny's ear, putting his hand around Sonny's waist and touching his back.

The touch startles Sonny and breaks his dance floor concentration, but he resumes flailing his arms, without as much gusto as before. When the song ends he motions to Dieter towards the bar, and he starts passing out the invites again until Sterling approaches.

"Who's your new boyfriend. I saw you dancing with him and now he's following you around. He's so cuuuute,"

"It's Dieter. He's not my boyfriend. I just met him at the store today."

"That's great, then I'll take him! Hello, I'm Sterling. What's your name?"

Sterling takes his index finger and runs it across Dieter's chest, startling him a bit.

"I am Dieter," he says, pulling away.

"I like your shirt. Did you get that at Runway? It looks

familiar."

"Yes, I bought it there today. That's where I met Sonny and I came here to see him."

"Oh, you came to see Sonny, how IN-teresting," says Sterling, waving his right arm extravagantly in the air and then passing his palm under Sonny's chin.

"Would you like to fuck him?"

"Shut up, Sterling. You're such an asshole," Sonny yells, pushing Sterling slightly. "Don't you have work to do? You're a paid entertainer tonight. So go entertain someone."

"With pleasure, my audience wants me anyway. See you later, Dieter, darling," says Sterling, grabbing his fishnet sleeve and snapping it when he says "darling."

"He's very funny," Dieter says, turning to Sonny. "Is he always like that."

"No, he's much worse, usually."

"Do you want to dance again?"

"No, I need to pass out more invites. I really need to get rid of more of them. Come with me," says Sonny, grabbing Dieter by the arm before he can reply.

Sonny parades around the club, unable to pass out any invites because he's dragging Dieter by the arm behind him, once back by the coat check, assured that everyone saw him with Dieter, he returns near the club's entrance to pass out the invites. The pile has gotten a bit smaller, but not enough.

"Do you want a drink, Sonny?"

"No, I'm not drinking any alcohol tonight because of my party tomorrow. It'll be a busy day and night."

"OK, I will get one for myself. I'll be back in a little while."

"Hey Sonny, nice look," says Eagle, after walking through the door.

"Why thank you, I made it myself, tee-hee-hee!"

"I can tell. It looks very homemade," says Eagle, adjusting his purple fedora hat with a big black feather sticking eight inches into the air.

"Wait until you see my outfit tomorrow, you'll love it," said Sonny, basking in Eagle's attention.

"I'll see you inside. I see you still have work to do," Eagle says, walking away before Sonny can respond.

Sonny returns his attention to the new arrivals.

"Come to my party tomorrow, it's at the Tunnel."

"Come to my party tomorrow, you won't regret it."

"Come to my party tomorrow. It will be an event you'll never forget, or remember!"

The clubbers take the invites while processing Sonny's look, but he isn't sure if they're listening, or if they are listening, maybe they can hear him? Many of them mouth OK, but it's hard to tell if they mean it.

"Excuse me, can I have a word with you by the coat check?"

Sonny's whipped out of his momentary self-doubt and he follows the conservatively dressed woman.

"I'm Christine Sharp, Channel 9 News, and I'm doing a report on some of the wildest New York City parties, and you look incredible. Do you work at Outré?"

"Well, hellooooo, I'm Sonny Delight. I don't work here, I just come here a lot, but I do work at The Tunnel and I'm having a huge, wild party tomorrow. Do you want to come?" Sonny asks excitedly, offering the reporter an invite. "Where is the camera?"

"He'll be here in a few minutes. He had to park the van and I just came in to scope out the place. I'd like to do an interview with you when he comes in. I've got to get your outfit on camera. You're one of the wildest looking people in here, and I want to ask you about that."

"Sure, just let me know when you're ready."

"Christine, there you are," yells Solange, shooting an annoyed look at Sonny. "Let me introduce you to some of my most fabulous guests."

"Well, I've already started with Sonny, so let's meet the rest."

"No, darling, I mean real VIPs, the fashion crowd, not the club kids. We just let them in for the comic relief," Solange says dismissively, taking Christine towards the back bar.

Sonny returns to the front entrance. Dieter is sitting at a sofa nearby and he rises when Sonny returns.

"I thought you might have gone outside, but I didn't go because I had this drink."

"I was talking to the reporter. I'll be on TV."

"Why?"

"She's doing a special report on the most fabulous people in New York City, and you happen to be talking to one of them! Tee-hee-hee!"

"That's so interesting. I'm glad I met you," says Dieter, brushing Sonny's forearm lightly.

"Well, you're lucky that you did. That means you'll get into one of the best parties of the year tomorrow," Sonny says, smiling and looking back towards the bar for the reporter.

"I better go check my make-up before the camera guy shows up. Come on," Sonny says, pulling Dieter towards the back of the club.

Sterling is in the bathroom when Sonny enters. Other queens are in there too, all examining their make-up, even though it's barely midnight. The club hasn't even reached a temperature where anyone would sweat, except for those on coke or X, who are already sweaty messes.

"Hello, love birdieees," Sterling teases.

"Shut up. Did you know that the Channel 9 news is here. They're doing a show about this club and other wild parties. They might come to my party tomorrow."

"Yes, honey, we know. Why else would we all be in here?"

"You're in here all the time and there's almost never any TV cameras in the club!"

"Yes, but there are cameras. At least Amanda's. We still have to look good for her."

I just came here for a quick check, and it's too crowded, see you later," says Sonny, leaving with only a brief look at his face, which looks fine. Nothing moved out of place. No need to panic.

Sonny walks towards the dance floor, then stops and heads back to the entrance when he feels the weight of the stack of invites in his hand. He motions to Dieter to follow.

"Come to my party. Come to my party," he repeats mechanically as the club fills with patrons, many fashionably dressed in designer clothes or flashy disco shirts.

While looking around the entrance area, Sonny sees some of his invites on the floor. He involuntarily touches his face to make sure his glued on cards are still attached. Unlike Sterling, Dieter actually makes an effort to put the invites in people's hands, Sonny notices. After another half-hour passes, the club is packed and Sonny decides that he'll pass out the rest of the invites in his backpack outside as everyone is leaving. The duo returns to the dance floor, where the music suddenly stops as the show begins. The television reporter stands with her cameraman to the left of the stage, and Sonny grabs Dieter's arm and quickly pushes his way to the front and center of the stage.

"Look at all you fabulous people," Solange says through a microphone. "I'm having a fashion orgasm just looking at you! And you know, I can have many orgasms, so work my pussy!"

The crowd yells in agreement as Sonny wildly waves his arms in the air, coaxing people behind him to yell louder.

"Tonight we have, back by popular demand, Lady Kahlua, who will gag you with her beauty and talents. She just came back from Las Vegas, so she's ready to serve it up dirty Harlem style. Please welcome, Lady Kahlua!"

The crowd yells in anticipation and some patrons move away from the front of the stage, thrilling Sonny because he has an unobstructed view of the cameraman. Lady Kahlua appeared at least twice before at Outré, to much scandal mongering because of her nasty stage tricks. One trick involves sticking a cigarette in her pussy and blowing smoke for the patrons. Those are the kinds of talents that appeal to Solange and she often brings in strippers and other erotic performers.

The dainty pings from Anita Ward's "Ring My Bell" begin playing as a figure in a hooded floor-length robe enters from stage right, her bare legs visible beneath the robe. The woman has her back to the audience as the song cranks up. She writhes with her arms wrapped around her body so it looks like someone is hugging her. She starts slapping her ass and then she pulls a little mallet out the robe's pocket. Hitting her ass cheeks to the beat of the song. Then she turns around, still writhing, and rips off the robe, exposing her deep black, nude body. All she's wearing is a gold thong and pasties on her nipples that have little chains dangling with tiny gongs at the end. With the little mallet, she strikes the little gongs during the song, caressing herself as the audience squeals with amusement. Sonny is also banging imaginary gongs, following Lady Kahlua's lead and shooting furtive glances towards the cameraman.

"Can they show her on TV?" Sonny wonders, imagining how they will censor the performer.

As the song winds down — it's the radio edit — Lady Kahlua sits on the stage and strikes a suggestive pose with her legs crossed to better show off her gold fuck-me pumps, which match the little gold colored gongs dangling from her pasties. The audience applauds wildly as the song ends and Lady Kahlua bows her head, awaiting the next song, which starts after the applause dies down. She's dancing to Salt-N-Pepa's "Push It" for her next routine. As the suggestive refrain begins, she tugs at the little chains each time "push it" is repeated. When the song gets going Lady Kahlua leaps up and starts dancing, thrusting her hips as she rips off one of the pasties to another roar. She throws the pasty into the crowd and there is a minor commotion as the clubbers scramble to catch it. The cameraman turns on his overhead light to capture the frenzy. Spotting the cameraman's action, Sonny jumps up and down, motioning to Lady Kahlua that she throw him the next mini-gong. The dancer ignores Sonny or she doesn't see him while continuing her erotic gyrations. She then rips off the second pasty, sending another ripple of yelling into the crowd. Spinning it she throws it past Sonny's head, though he unsuccessfully tries to catch it. Sonny suddenly realizes where this performance is going, so he opens his mouth and wags his tongue suggestively, peering from the corner of his eye to check whether the cameraman's attention is back on the performer.

As song enters its final stage, Sonny starts writhing, waving his tongue while his mouth is wide open. With her breasts sufficiently fondled, Lady Kahlua squeezes her left breast on one of the final refrains of "Push It", squirting a stream of breast milk into the audience. Sonny jumps up trying to catch some of it in his mouth, while turning his face slightly to the left, but the warm stream hits his right eye instead. Blinded, Sonny blinks rapidly as the audience screams in delight, disgust or some combination of both. Lady Kahlua squeezes her right breast at another refrain of "Push It," and squirts a few more patrons. The audiences yelling grows louder as Lady Kahlua steps away from the front of the stage, picking up her robe and blotting her nipples to the beat. She tosses the robe over one shoulder and takes a bow, to more screaming.

Distracted, Sonny loses sight of the cameraman in his breast-milk induced blindness.

"Are you OK?" Dieter asks.

"Yes, I got some milk in my eye. It stings a little, but it's only milk, I hope."

"Ladies and gentlemen, give it up once more for Lady Kahlua!" Solange booms over the loudspeaker as "Push It" fades out. "How can anyone here top her talent tonight?"

"I've never seen anything like that," Dieter said to Sonny. "That was crazy."

"It's funny, right?" I knew she would do that because she did it last time she was here, but not to that song. I don't know how many times she can get away with the trick, but it's a good one for the camera, though I doubt they'll put it on TV. I have to go to the bathroom."

"I can't believe that reporter didn't want to speak to me," Sterling tells Sonny when he walks into the bathroom.

"How do you know. Maybe she will," Sonny shoots back, checking his eye and the surrounding makeup for any damage, and finding none.

"I asked that bitch if she wants interview me and she said she has enough material. I don't think so," Sterling complains.

"Maybe she'll change her mind and do it tomorrow. I think she's coming to my party. I told her about it."

"I doubt that. Anyway, do you really want a reporter filming you giving out a hundred balloons with drugs inside them?"

"She won't know. Who'll tell her?"

"She'll figure it out, stupid. She's a reporter!"

"I don't care. No publicity is bad publicity. It will be all the more scandalous if she does figure it out, tee-hee-hee," says Sonny, waving his arm in the air and walking out.

Sonny takes Dieter by the arm to the dance floor and they stand there looking for an empty spot and for the cameraman. Sonny picks a spot and starts moving his hips distractedly, until he sees the cameraman plowing through the dancers, getting close-ups of their faces and bodies. Sonny begins swinging wildly, grabbing Dieter and pretending to go down on him. Confused, Dieter plays along timidly. As he rises from his crouching position, Sonny sees the cameraman near enough, and he starts fondling himself like Lady Kahlua. The cameraman focuses on Sonny, pans him up and down and closes in on his face, then walks away. Sonny faces Dieter again, but once he sees the cameraman step off the dance floor he loses interest. He half-heartedly finishes the song and grabs Dieter's arm to bring him off the dance floor.

"Are you tired already? We haven't danced that much."

"No, I just have to check the time, because it's getting close to the time that I have to go outside to pass out the rest of the invitations. And I don't want to do that yet because the reporter said she wanted to interview me."

"Hi Sonny," says St. Helen as she bends over to give an air kiss. "Having fun?"

"Yes, it's fun here tonight and there is a reporter from Channel 9 who's doing interviews about the club scene."

"Oh, I was wondering who she was. I just got here. Has she been here long?"

Helen is working the geisha look tonight with a black wig and white paint on her face.

"I don't know. She's been here at least an hour, because I spoke to her when she came in. I'm gong to talk to her again. Right now, dammit, tee-hee-hee!"

"Oh, there you are, Sonny. Let's go by the entrance where it's a little more quiet so we can interview you."

"Oh, OK, no problem," Sonny says with feigned nonchalance.

Once by the coat check, the reporter explains her report.

"I just want to ask you a couple of questions about why you dress up this way and what the most fun club is."

"Sure," Sonny answers while waving to Dieter.

"Let's roll. One, two, three. I'm here with Sonny Delight and he's a creature of the night out for a good time at Outré. It's of the hottest parties in the city that attracts outrageous clubbers that give this party its cutting edge flavor. Sonny, why did you come here dressed like this?"

"This is all about self-expressing and living your fantasies. I'm a creative person and I like to hang out with other creative people. I also work in the clubs, so you do have to stand out and be somewhat outlandish because that's part of entertaining people."

"So your a performer?"

"Yes and no. I do go-go dance at The Tunnel, but mainly I'm a party promoter, so I host parties and make sure people have a good time there. And if that means I have to dress like drunken Ronald

McDonald, so be it. Garbage men wear uniforms, so why shouldn't I?"

"What are the best parties in New York City?

"Well, my parties are among the best and I'm having one Thursday night at the Tunnel in the basement. We'll have extra special party favors and fabulous music!"

"Thanks Sonny. You heard it people, The Tunnel, where we'll go for a peek at another one of this scene's hottest venues. I'm Christine Sharpe reporting from club Outré in Chelsea."

"Thanks Sonny, we're coming to your party tomorrow. I'll call the club in the morning to get the OK, which I'm sure they'll give us. I'm looking forward to seeing what kind of party you throw."

"Sure Christine, I'll see you then," Sonny says as the journalists walk away.

"That was quick," Dieter says.

"I thought they would ask me more questions, but I guess they don't want to bore people."

"How dare you upstage me! Hiaaah! What did you tell them?" Sterling yells as he hops over to Sonny and grabs his arm. "Did you mention me?"

"No! I was being professional and I promoted my party. They're coming tomorrow. We'll be FA-mous!"

"Holy shit, I've got to come up with a better outfit. I'm the first person they'll see when they come in to the party since I'm in charge of the ropes."

"You see, you thought I was giving you a horrible job."

"It is a horrible job, but it won't be so bad tomorrow because at least the cameras will be there. Good job, Sonny."

Sterling pets Sonny on the arm as he would a pet.

"OK, now I've really got to pass out the rest of these invites."

Sonny pulls off the backpack to retrieve the rest of the invites.

"Do you want me to help you?" Dieter asks.

"I'm going outside because I want to catch the people as they leave. You can stay in here if you want."

"OK"

Sonny goes outside and picks his ideal spot, where no one leaving can miss him. After about 30 minutes, Dieter comes out.

"What's wrong, weren't you having fun?"

"I came here tonight to spend time with you," Dieter responds, smiling.

Sonny drops the shrunken stack of invites.

"Ooops, the other clubbers can throw my invites on the floor, but I never do that!"

Sonny stares at the ground while Dieter helps him collect the invites.

"Are you almost done? I'll help you pass them out."

"OK."

After about 10 minutes the stack is gone. It took a week to get rid of them, and Sonny smiles to himself.

"Do you want to go back inside the club?" Dieter asks.

"No, I have to go home because I have a lot to do tomorrow. You can go in."

"No, I'm going back to the hotel. Do you want to come with me?"

Instead of responding, Sonny looks at Outré's entrance.

"Do you want to go back in the club?" Dieter asks again.

"No, I'm tired and I need beauty rest. I have to go home," Sonny says, turning and walking east on 23rd Street.

Dieter joins him in the walk to the corner. Sonny says nothing until reaching the corner.

"I'm taking a taxi home because I'm tired. I guess I'll see you tomorrow at my party."

"Let me know if you need any help in the day. I'm staying at the Hilton Hotel on Sixth Avenue and 53rd Street. My room is 620 if you want to call."

"If you want to help me, come to the Tunnel around 1 o'clock. I'll be there decorating."

"Sure, I'll see you there," says Dieter, touching Sonny's arm as he gets into a taxi. "Good night."

Sonny waves at Dieter through the window and looks once again after the car pulls away a good distance so that Dieter can't see him looking back.

"Tomorrow will be incredible!"

Chapter 16

"What should I do? I can't go to the Y like this."

The awesome tingling in Pedro's brain has him panting and sweaty while walking south on Lexington Avenue from the hotel. At 34th Street, he turns right and walks west. After a few steps, he stops, and then walks back to Lexington and pauses at the corner. When the light changes he crosses Lexington and then stops at the southwest corner of the intersection. He continues south, then abruptly turns and heads west again.

"This is good stuff. It's incredible."

Although he generally avoids 34th Street, Pedro's walk tonight is fun and he's laughing to himself. The store windows between Fifth Avenue are full of wonder, even when it's just a bunch of women's clothes. The mannequins stop Pedro, who then scrutinizes their empty stares.

"Shit. They're looking at me."

Pedro continues his walk, his heart beating a little faster because of the mannequins' gaze. By Seventh Avenue, he's lost interest in the windows now that Madison Square Garden's in sight. There is still a flow of people coming in and out of there, so Pedro heads towards the Seventh Avenue escalator. Unsure what to do once inside, he goes to the men's room for a look around. He first discovered the men's room at the train station shortly after entering SVA and commuting home for the weekends. Though many of the men by the urinals are old and unattractive, there are sometimes really cute young guys in there too. There aren't too many men in the bathroom and about half of them look over their shoulders from the urinals to check out Pedro. The stares unnerve him, and Pedro searches for an open stall. He tries to urinate, but can only summon a weak trickle. After releasing a few drops, he zips up and hurries out of the bathroom, taking the Eighth Avenue exit from the station. Outside again, he sees the post office across the street and is reminded of one of his favorite hangouts.

"I'm sure I'll see someone there I know."

Pedro heads west on 31st Street towards the elevated train tracks between 30th and 31st streets between Ninth and Tenth avenues. The unused tracks are a hangout for many homeless people, who go up there to get away from the police and the street. A broken gate in the middle of the block is the passage to stairs leading up to the tracks. It's almost always unlocked despite the city's efforts to secure it. Someone just cuts the lock or chain. Pedro carefully feels his way up the stairs. It's pitch black in the stairwell, but he hears the distant sounds of talking and laughter, recognizing a heavily accented, nasal whine.

"Who's th-ah?Papi! What a sa-prize!" yells Twinkie, waving Pedro over to him. "Sit next to me, Pedrito."

Twinkie is wearing a red baseball cap, a too-tight black t-shirt and cut-off jeans that reveal too much of his skinny legs, which had been shaved but are now stubbly, though it's not that noticeable on the dark, abandoned train tracks. Pedro only notices them after Twinkie intentionally rubs his right leg against Pedro's left arm after Pedro sits next to him, causing Pedro to inch slightly away from Twinkie.

"Look at yoooo! It's been a while, where have yoooo been?" asks Twinkie, who purses his sticky, glossed lips, though not closing them completely and revealing his irregularly shaped and discolored front teeth.

"I've been staying at the Y and at my parents' house. I'm trying to decide what to do, because I can't be hanging out any more. I've gotta get my shit together," Pedro explains.

"Good for yoooo. I'm planning on doing that. I'm moving, maybe to Miami, where it's not so expensive. I'm tryn' to save money, but, ay, it's hard. Business is terrible."

Pedro says nothing in response, a little tremble passing up his spine at the thought of paying for sex with Twinkie.

"Where's your homeboy, Stevie? You-ah not friends anymore?"

"I haven't seen him in a few days. I don't know where he is," Pedro says defensively.

"Oooh K, I see, he left you for someone else."

"Shut up."

"Oooh K, let's have some fun. Do you haf any money? Let's get some beer and make a little party! I'll pay haf and you'll pay haf.

No one asks about Steve again, and Pedro doesn't think about him, not with the Twinkie floor show about to kick off for an all-night engagement.

There is a group of four up there, the two other guys familiar to Pedro from the soup kitchens and the overnight shelters. He never really talks to them, though, and he isn't about to start now, since can barely speak anyway from the tweak.

"I need a stay-age. I can't pa-form without a stay-age," Twinkie announces. "Pedrito, you gonna to help me. It won't be hard. All we haf to do is go to the store and get some of the cardboards they-ah throwing out."

Pedro just nods, unable to speak, but eager for an adventure. Hopefully it won't end like the last excursion with Twinkie, when he got in a fight with punk rockers near Thompkin Square Park after one of the punks called him a faggot while they were in the park trying to score some dope. Twinkie took a bottle and broke it over one of the punks' head, forcing Twinkie, Pedro and Steve to run and then fight off one of the punks who caught Steve and started pounding on him. Luckily, Twinkie is from the South Bronx and got ghetto on Steve's attacker, smashing him on the side of the head with a garbage can on East Ninth Street, which allowed the three to continue fleeing. Pedro was terrified during the altercation, but it now all seems like a fun war story to share with friends.

"Let's go," Pedro tells Twinkie.

"We should go to the bodega on Eighth Avenue. That way we can get some cardboard and beers. I need a big box, or maybe two or three big boxes so I can do special show."

It isn't hard finding used cardboard on 30th Street, especially between Eighth Avenue and Seventh Avenue, where all the fur and other businesses leave their trash at night. After getting the beers, Twinkie and Pedro explore the trash. Twinkie is choosy, so it's not a quick errand, but he ultimately chooses three big boxes that have been flattened for disposal. He puts them on top of his head and steadies them with his two outstretched arms, causing all the drivers heading east on 30th Street to slow down slightly as they passed the pair heading back to the tracks. Twinkie spreads the flat boxes around on the ground, giving him a clean surface for his show. Twinkie removes his sneakers and starts twirling to the beat of the little cassette player he carries in his backpack. He moves suggestively to the initial crooning, while the other guys watch.

"Hey you, over there, everybody, everywhere, to feel good, yeah, say I like you."

Twinkie sings off-key instead of just mouthing the words. His abrasive, honking voice provokes laughter, which further drowns out singer Phyllis Nelson's voice. Released in 1985, "I Like You" reminds Twinkie of better days, when he first started going out to gay clubs before he started getting high all the time and before his mother kicked him out of the house when she found out he was gay.

"And later on when you need someone, don't you hesitate to call me on the phone, I like you, yes I like you," Twinkie sings as he writhes on top of the cardboard, pointing at his audience.

It's the extended disco mix, so the performance lasts about six minutes, ending with Twinkie in a sweaty, vulgar vogueing pose that he imagines to be sexy. More performances follow. During the "intermissions" Pedro gets up, paces a little bit and then sits back down to talk with Twinkie. Twinkie insists on being the center of attention, which means that the intermissions don't last that long. Twinkie sometimes goes off with some of the strangers to the end of the tracks where he can't be seen, but eventually comes back, clearly altered. Between the performances, there are arguments, cursing, one man storms off. When the sky begins to lighten, Twinkie announces that he's bored of the tracks.

"Let's go to the pee-uhrs and we'll watch the sunrise over Manhat-an," Twinkie announces.

Pedro nods. They emerge from the dark stairwell into a growing light, in search of the afterhours party.

Chapter 17

The ringing phone can't be for a guest list request. Not at this hour. Sonny lets it ring.

"Did you accidentally take something home with you yesterday? I noticed that the green jacket is not here and I don't remember seeing a sales slip for it. If you took it, there will be consequences," says Darnell, hanging up abruptly.

"Good morning to you too."

Sonny jumps out of bed to get dressed. Grabbing the duffel bag filled with decorating supplies, he rushes out the door. After a trip to the party store, Sonny arrives at the Tunnel by 12:30, sweating under the pressure that he won't be finished in time. The Tunnel's basement smells like disinfectant from the cleaning crews' mops. He starts inflating the balloons with a little plastic pump from the party store. He inserts 25 ecstasy pills into the opaque balloons and slowly blows those up, adding them to the balloon pile. Nearing the end of the balloon blowing, Sonny takes a break, sitting on the basement's small stage by himself. The cleaning crew come into the basement, mop and quickly move on to the rest of the club.

"No time to rest, I've got to tie up the balloons. How will I do that?" he wonders while pulling a large net out of his duffel bag.

"I have to hang the balloons in a net above the stage so I can untie the front and have them cascade on to the crowd. I'll have to figure it out. Sterling's obviously not showing up."

"Sonny? Are you down there?"

"Yes, I'm down here," he replies, not sure who's calling him. "Sterling, is that you?"

"No, I'm Dieter," says the tourist as his upper torso becomes visible coming down the basement's stairs. "I looked around the club, but I did not see you. None of the workers who I spoke to know you."

"Tonight is my first party, so they haven't gotten to know me yet. They will. Are you here to help me?"

"Yes, I said last night I would help you."

"I know, it's just that other people said they would help me too, and here I am by myself, as usual. The club scene is full of unreliable people."

"You are lucky then that I am not part of your club scene," says Dieter, patting Sonny on the arm, which recoils a bit at the touch.

"I guess I am lucky," says Sonny, his little smile getting bigger. "So, I'm almost done blowing up the balloons and I need you to help me put up this net so we can put all the balloons inside. I need you to hold the net while I staple or tie it to the ceiling, OK?"

"Yes, I can do that. Will there be a show tonight?"

"Kind of, we'll probably have some of the club kids dancing up here on the stage and then during a break we'll have the show. It's not really a show, but people will like it anyway. I'll get on stage and introduce myself, then I'll explain that the contest is starting. I'll release the net and balloons into the crowd, and then announce that there are 25 ecstasy pills inside the balloons for anyone lucky enough to pop the balloons and find them, tee-tee-hee."

"Really, there are ecstasy pills in these balloons?

"Not in all of them. There are just 25, so people will have

to pop the balloons to find the pills. It will be MAY-hem!!"

"It will be dark in here. Won't people have a hard time finding the pills? I think someone could get hurt if there is fighting over the balloons."

"It's not supposed to be safe, Dieter. Safety is boring! Boring! Boring! The more people that get hurt, the better, tee-tee-hee! People will remember the party that way, and really, what good party is there that doesn't end in some kind of injury? Last month at an outlaw party thrown in a public park I cut my knee on the fence while trying to climb over it. It left an ugly gash that only now healed, but every time I looked at that gash I remember how crazy that party was. Everybody was talking about it, and that's what I want for my party. Otherwise, nobody will care or remember."

With the net up and the balloons inserted, Sonny tests the release, which is less than effective. He's force to push out about half the balloons by hand.

"It does not seem like it is working, Sonny"

"It'll work. I'll have the club kids up here push the balloons into the crowd. It WILL work."

After securing the balloons above the stage, Sonny and Dieter blow up more balloons, which Sonny marks up with smiley faces, the symbol of the acid house movement and the current youth symbol for ecstasy. He begins attaching them to the walls around the basement and up the stairs.

"Are you really getting paid for this?" Dieter asks after about two hours. "How much do club party promoters get paid?"

"They're giving me $400, but I spent $250 on the ecstasy and then another $50 on the supplies, like balloons, the net and some other supplies for the past week."

"That is not a lot of money you are making."

"I know, I actually would have made more if I had been hired to go-go dance all the night's I've gone out to promote this party, but no one is hiring me and I had to go out and promote the party. Oh, well. This is an investment. I'm trying to build up a reputation so that I can make more money next time."

"I understand. I hope your party tonight is successful."

"It will be. Everyone will talk about it Friday. You'll see. Are you around on Friday? When are your going back to Germany?"

"I am on holiday until Wednesday. Do you want to have a

lunch with me?"

"OK, maybe this weekend. I have to work on Saturday or Sunday, but I may not have a job when I show up on Saturday."

"Why?"

"Because I took a jacket from work for tonight's party without permission. I had asked to borrow it and they told me no because it's too expensive. We're selling it for $300 and it's a one-of-a-kind creation by Tax Evasion, so my boss didn't want anyone wearing it. I took it yesterday at the end of the day and I might get fired for that."

"That is terrible. Why did you do that?"

"I wanted something fabulous and I'm tired of making stuff. I'm always making my outfits and they don't look as good as some of the wild stuff at Runway. Tonight is so important that I didn't want some impromptu ensemble I hot glued together. It has to be fierce since those scene queens will be judging me. It will actually be good for my standing if they hear that I stole the jacket from Runway, tee-hee-hee!"

"Why would you want them to think you are a thief?"

"I don't want anybody to think I'm a thief. This is just a one-time thing. I want them to know that I had the balls to take the jacket from Runway even though I was told that I couldn't. Believe it or not, people respect that."

"I don't understand."

"I'm serious. At the last voguing ball I went to at a Chinese banquet hall last month on East Broadway, one of the House of Extravaganza's competitions was mopping, that's when you steal from a store. They had people who had taken entire designer outfits worth more than $1,000 with the price tags still on them. It means you're fearless."

"I still don't really understand why that is considered good. It is stealing."

"I know. It's the outlaw factor. People love outlaws and rule breakers, they admire them, and that's why I took the jacket. I'll give it back to the store on Saturday."

"What if they want you to pay for it?"

"Then I'll just pay for it. They can take a bit out of my paycheck. All that matters is that people think I stole it. They don't have to know I later returned it or paid for it."

Sonny runs out of balloons by 5 p.m. He only bought 500 and the goal was to plaster the basement with the remaining yellow balloons, all of which now have smiley faces. As a lure, Sonny has the idea of attaching an explosion of the smiley faces on the walls at the top of the stairs leading into the basement. Sterling will stand at the velvet rope framed by a balloon arrangement leading to the basement below. Sonny stands at the entrance admiring his handiwork as he and Dieter leave.

"I think it looks good enough. Anyway, they'll get popped by the first hour. I'm sure of it," Sonny says.

"I am hungry. Are you? Would you like to have a snack?" Dieter asks expectantly.

"Alright, but it will have to be quick because I'm meeting the press tonight. I can't be late," Sonny says, smiling again as the two walk east on 27th Street.

Chapter 18

Faces and names at the pier-queen scene frequently change, but the atmosphere is consistent: Young men and a few young women congregate there in the pre-dawn hours with boom boxes, drinks and drugs. One contingent is the collection of young gays from the outer boroughs who don't want to risk going back to the Bronx or deep Brooklyn by subway in the dead of night because of the dangers. The other contingent, which can also include members of the outer borough queens, are the hookers who are done tricking for the night. Most of them get high nightly to prepare for their hustling, so the pier is an after-work happy hour. The third contingent includes the homeless or shelter queens and gay druggies scamming their way through New York with as little effort or work as possible. The pier queens spend the pre-dawn hours dancing and talking, since many of them are coked up or on some other stimulant. The scene often perks up around sunrise. That means the cops, who rarely stop by anyway, can't disperse the groups if they're too loud because they are doing their shift change. Nobody lives around there, so a bunch of screaming queens on a pier don't garner much attention, even when their dinky stereos are playing full blast.

Pedro and Twinkie arrive at 7am. It's prime time. Jose, a tall, lanky black queen from the South Bronx stands atop a cement barrier that's supposed to keep the public from falling off the pier. For the moment it's his stage.

"Catch my moves, bitch-assss! Catch dis," Jose yells, with the nasal whine shared by many of the pier queens.

Jose strikes a faux gymnast pose; he's on a balance beam.

"I'm in da uh-lympics, Twinkie. Wass my sco-ruh?"

"Ten, ten, tens across the board for yo-ah gym-cunt realness, eeoaw!" Twinkie yells back, making a cat scratch motion with her left hand. "Now do uh back flip when you jump off."

"Fuck you. How bout I flip my ass on yo-ah face, bitch?" Jose yelled back in the hostile-jokey way he and the other queens address each other.

"Don't you charge the trolls, like, 50 cents for that? Or do I get the Welfare-ah discount?" Twinkie shoots back, eliciting amused cat-calls from another pier queen who also gives Twinkie a high-five.

That kind of talk sometimes scares Pedro. He isn't sure when they are just joking and when they are really mad. If they are mad there could be trouble, since he's seen angry queens break bottles on guys' heads for trivial offenses that didn't warrant a felonious assault. It's just their ghetto response to perceived slights.

Jose jumps gracelessly from the concrete barrier towards Twinkie. He offers her an air kiss and says "muwah, muwah."

"Wass your friend's name uh-gain?"

"Dis is Pedro. Don't you remembuh him? He's come here befor-uh with me," said Twinkie, waving her hand under Pedro's face because she's sure that Jose is checking out his pale good looks and goatee.

"Yea, I remembuh him. You-ah so cute," Jose says, brushing Pedro's arm suggestively.

Pedro's too tweaked to respond.

"You wan' some Zima?" asks Jose, picking up a paper bag near the concrete barrier.

Pedro notices the smeared pick lipstick on the corner of Jose's mouth.

"No, thanks," Pedro says as Twinkie grabs the clear carbonated alcoholic drink and takes a swig. S' Express's "S-Express" starts blasting from the boom box.

The queens start yelling.

"Ayyy. Wooooork!"

They launch into a dance. With lots of room, some of them start walking an imaginary, pacing back and forth across the empty pier as the other queens cheer them on and curse at them. A voguing battle erupts as three queens then simultaneously walk down the pier together, arm in arm, only to break apart when they turn. One kneels, the other throws a kung-fu kick and the third pretends to powder her face with her fingertips. Others join in the fray, walking back and forth, striking poses, flaying their arms in the air, around their faces. The concrete barrier becomes a prop as the queens hump it, lie on it and caress it.

After about an hour, Twinkie tells Pedro that she needs to freshen up and she suggests they cross West Street because one of the porn stores is open 24 hours. Pedro, still mostly unable to speak nods in agreement. The Riverview Video Shop is conveniently located across West Street from the queens' hangout. The video shop's owners don't welcome them if they're just looking for a bathroom. Twinkie already knows this, so she explains to Pedro that when they come in the store he's supposed to follow her to one of the "buddy" booths. The booths are designed so that a partition between the plastic windows rises when someone puts a quarter in the booth's slot. The idea is that the two men in different booths can then see each other jerking off on the porn in the little television sets mounted inside the booths.

Instead of going inside separate booths, Twinkie and Pedro go in one booth, which is a violation of the rules, but many customers do that. At this hour the attendant isn't so vigilant anyway. The booth can barely contain one person comfortably, since it's even smaller than an airplane's bathroom.

"OK, time for a little touch-up," says Twinkie, who's pressed against Pedro face-to-face inside the booth. Pedro is vaguely revolted by having Twinkie so close, but he's fiending for more crystal.

Pedro fishes for the baggie, which he put inside the little pocket on the right side of his jeans. Hunching his right shoulder awkwardly, Pedro manages to pull out the little baggie plus the piece of straw that he keeps there too. Since there's not so much space in the booth, he then carefully manipulates his arm to bring it up to his chest area, only to drop the baggie.

"Shit. I dropped the bag."

"I got it. I got it," says Twinkie, accidentally elbowing Pedro as she tries to stop the baggie from falling on the floor.

Her actions only hastened the baggie's fall to the booth's floor.

"Don't open the door," Twinkie says. "If the clerk sees us we'll get kicked out. I can bend and get it. I've done this before."

She isn't exaggerating. In fact, Twinkie has done it many times before, pushing her back against the booths wall and sliding herself down to give tricks blow jobs. There isn't much room for maneuvering, but enough for a head to rock back and forth. Slowly Twinkie slides herself down until she's squatting and her head is at Pedro's groin area. Taking advantage of the situation, Twinkie presses her face against Pedro's crotch as she feels around the floor with her hands. One hand lands in a viscous glob, which she immediately wipes on Pedro's pant leg, though she suggestively caresses his leg while she rubs her fingers clean so he won't realize what's happening. Findnig the baggie, she then slides herself back up, which isn't as easy as going down.

"I need help. Lift me," Twinkie orders.

With no choice, Pedro puts his left hand in Twinkies underarm and pulls her up, wincing at the squishy stickiness from the unwanted compression of their flesh. Once she's up, Twinkie expertly pops the baggie open with one hand and Pedro removes a bump of the power to put in Twinkie's nostril. He then serves himself a bump and, wet from perspiration in the booth, which smells of disinfectant and body odor, they open the door and clumsily exit, taking deep breaths on their way out of the video store.

Back at the pier, the queens are no longer dancing. Juan is "testifying." That means the others are listening to some story, most likely some encounter with a trick earlier in the evening, or maybe a fight Juan or some other queen had. Even though Pedro and Twinkie are still across the street, they can hear Juan yelling about something.

"Whaaa's he on?" Twinkie asks. "I want some."

By 11 a.m. the party is ending. The piers' subway commuters left before the morning rush hour crush. The hookers leave around 9 a.m., when they start getting hot and their foundation begins to slide around their faces, revealing unattractive men with unsightly stubble. Twinkie and Pedro sit with Coco behind a

Dumpster the city left near the pier, which because of the sun's angle, casts the only shade. Even thought the dancing and testifying lasted hours, Coco's not done yet because she's found people who haven't heard her story yet about the eccentric john who picked her up in the Meatpacking district around 2 a.m. earlier. The tranny hookers hang out by 13th Street and Washington Street in the meatpacking district, where the tricking tends to stop around 4 a.m. as the workers for the meat companies start arriving to load and unload the beef that will stock New York City's supermarkets and restaurants. Many of the meatpacking trannies are crazy to some degree, either from recreational drug abuse or from the hormones they take without medical supervision. The chemicals fuck with their minds and make some of them very mean and belligerent. Despite their belligerence, they still attract customers.

Coco is one of the nice ones and she actually looks like a woman — from behind, and from a block away, at night. Her street-walking demeanor is flirty and shy, a strategy that contrasts with some of the pushier, and uglier, queens, who run towards the johns as they cruise around the block to get at their cash first. Coco doesn't need to run. They come to her, though the johns that come to her are just as wacky as the ones that go with the ugly queens that obviously look like men. Crazy has a different definition on 13th and Washington streets because the meatpacking trannies have a different concept of eccentricity. Still, some of them are surprised when confronted with an unexpected request.

"Once I start fucking him is when he gets freaky," Coco recounts. "He picks up the phone next to the bed and calls a friend. Then he wants me to talk to his friend. I don't know what to say. He hands me the phone and all I can say is, hello?"

Coco's voice grows dainty, but crackly from too much smoking. The greeting sends Twinkie into a fit of laughter.

"Oh shit, you sick bitch. What did you say?" Twinkie demands.

"I di-n't know what to say. I said 'What's your name?' He said his name was Frankie. Isn't that cute? Then I ax Louie what he wants me to tell Frankie. He tells me to start pumping his ass and tell Frankie about it. Can you imagine?"

"Oh my God. How could you even keep from laughing?"

"I couldn't laugh, it was too weird, so I started groaning

and telling Frankie, 'Your friend Louie's pussy is tighter than mine. I'm plowing him with my she-male and he's tingling. His nipples are getting hard.'"

"Get it, Coco," Twinkie yells, waving her arms in the air and punching Pedro in the arm playfully.

Pedro, unable to speak, smiles, but his intoxication only allows him to pull his lips back and push out his two front teeth.

"Then Frankie axes me to give the phone to Louie and he tells me to pump hard. So I'm still pumping and he's talking to Louie, who's making this serious face and saying oh, oh."

"What were they talking about," Pedro asks, managing a few words.

"Baseball, I don't know. I was getting bored and wanted to get out of there. It was wei-ud. Louie was jerking himself off with one hand with the phone in the other, telling Frankie, 'she's fucking my ass. I'm a dirty pussy, I'm a dirty pussy.' I'm thinking that he better not cum on my Fredericks of Hollywood bra. It's new. Then he grabbed one of his socks he left next to the phone, put it over his cock and came into it. That was it. He got off me and and told Frankie that he'd call him later. I axed him if we were done and he said yes, so I went in the bathroom to wash off and put my clothes on as fast as possible. He was trippin' on something."

"At least you got 200 daw-lahs," Twinkie says, feigning the Bronx queens' pronunciation.

"Did he put the sock with cum back on his foot?" asks Pedro, summoning some more words.

"I don't know. I got the hell outta there," Coco says, huffing.

Satisfied with her tawdry tale, Coco readjusts her sunglasses and the trio get up from behind the Dumpster. On West Street, they watch Coco get into a cab for her ride uptown. Pedro and Twinkie walk towards Eighth Avenue. It's almost noon, which means lunch at the soup kitchen on 30th Street. Block after block, Pedro serves as Twinkie's audience as she stares men down and makes suggestive comments. The walk is a running commentary on the store windows, the passing men, the women, their clothes and how terrible she thinks they look. All this chatter erupts from a sweaty, disheveled and somewhat emaciated man with erratically tweezed eyebrows.

By the time the duo reaches 23rd Street, Pedro feels none of the apprehension from earlier this week. He walks near his abandoned lair without pause. It's easy crossing the intersection with Twinkie, laughing dumbly at her ceaseless chatter. Sunday morning's memory barely registers. Pedro smiles slightly and passes one of the stairwells leading into the 23rd Street station. He looks behind him, and down the stairwell. The sight arouses nothing.

"I'm going into the Y to pick up some of my stuff and maybe take a shower. It's so hot."

"You'll miss da lunch."

"I'm too high to eat. I'll just get something later. It was great hanging out with you. Thanks."

"For what? I di-n't gifff you anythin'."

"For being such a trip."

"You know it," Twinkie says, snapping her fingers as she continues along 23rd Street past the Y, turning once to wave good bye.

Chapter 19

The dinner snack with Dieter means that Sonny doesn't get home until 7 p.m. and he's feeling panicky. He hasn't even done his guest list yet and the answering machine is blinking. He spends about 30 minutes preparing the list and listening to the messages, many from people who he's not really friends with but who he urged to call in the past two weeks. The calls from strangers warm Sonny and reassure him that his event will be successful. It doesn't matter who they are, so long as they come.

It's difficult moving around Sonny's apartment because of the bags and other party preparations lying about. Sterling is supposed to come over around 9 p.m. Sonny clears space on the bed and carefully puts the green jacket on the bed and combines it with the black hot pants and knee-high black combat boots. He finds a pastel green t-shirt that contrasts with the jacket's kelly green lamé. Kneeling in front of the closet, Sonny paws through the bags on the floor, searching for head pieces. He finds a black motorcycle helmet he bought at the thrift store. For a previous outfit he glued little round mirrors about 1 inch in diameter to the helmet. None of the mirrors are broken or cracked, so the helmet joins the ensemble.

With a helmet, there's no need for a hairstyle, so the accessory is a time-saver, which he needs for his guest list preparation, as the phone continues to ring.

By 8:30, Sonny gets a call, and it's not for the guest list.

"Hello Sonny, it's been at least two weeks since you have called us. Why are you so cruel to your mother?" asks Sonny's father.

"Hi Dad, I'm sorry, I've been very busy. My big party is tonight and I have to make a good impression for the sake of my career."

"What career is that? Working in a clothes shop is not a career. You should be focusing on a real career instead of wasting your time with parties."

"No, Dad. I'm talking about my club promotion. I'm trying to get out of the retail business and get into something that will make me more money. If my party goes well tonight, that will be a big, new start for me. I'll move on to something better. I'm not working in stores anymore. I'm fed up with retail anyway."

"How are you? It's been so long since you've called us and your mother is very worried."

"I'm fine. I've been very busy getting ready for my party and I've had to stay up late in the past week promoting it and passing out invites. Sorry I didn't call you. I've just been very busy and I can't really talk right now either."

"You don't have time to speak to your mother?"

"OK, put her on."

"Sonny? How are you?"

"I'm fine, mom. I'm working tonight at a nightclub as a party host. It's a big step up from the dancing I've been doing there and if the party goes well I'll have a new job and I'll quit working in the clothes store."

"Have you been eating?"

"Mom, I'm not starving myself."

"I don't know. Every time I see you, you are so thin. It worries me."

"I eat to live, mom. You know I'm not a big eater."

"I know. I don't understand why you never liked my food."

"I like your food. I've eaten it all my life."

"Come see us this weekend."

"Maybe, I'll come on Saturday night after work, but I can't stay for Sunday because I have to work."

"Why are you always too busy for us?"

"I'm getting ready for a big party. It's my first promotion for the Tunnel, so I've been working very hard on it, going out every night to promote it. People are talking about the party and they're noticing me."

"Why are you spending your time of parties? Your cousin Murat just got a promotion at his accounting company. He has only worked there nine months and he is promoted."

"Mom, I'm not interested in that kind of work. I'm a creative, artistic person and I need a career that lets me to express my personality and originality."

"Artists do not make much money and they have to suffer for their art. Do you know that?"

"Yes, I've already been suffering at Runway. I think my suffering will end tonight. It's an important night and I've got to finish getting ready, Mom, so I've got to go."

"Sonny, we just want you to know that we love you and we're worried about you. Be careful. I'm praying for you."

"Thanks. Pray that my party is a big hit. Good night, mom."

"Good night. I will see you this weekend, insha'ala."

Sonny looks at the clock and his heart jumps. It's almost 9 and he hasn't applied make-up. He darts over to the kitchen sink where he's mounted a mirror. Tonight's look is not so complicated. The clown white foundation goes on first, followed by a straight black bar across his eyebrows. He then glues black feathers to his upper and lower eyelids that project towards the sides of his head. A little pot of kelly green grease paint matches the jacket perfectly, so that goes on as his evil , jagged clown grimace.

Sterling arrives as Sonny finishes his face.

"That's some beat. How on earth will you keep that from smearing?"

"I'm a professional, darling. I won't smear my look, and I have little travel pots for my lunchbox in case something goes wrong. Don't you-hoo?"

"Yes, bitch, you learned that from me. Clear the mirror. I've got a look to assemble!"

"Sterling, you've really got to hurry. It's 9:30 and we've got to get there by 10:15 at the latest. That means you have 15 minutes to top yourself off, or we'll be late to our own premiere and our close-ups with the TV crew. So hurry."

"I'll only be a second," Sterling says as he throws his overcoat on a chair and opens his lunch box on the sink counter.

After tying his boots, Sonny puts on the stolen jacket, caressing the lamé on the sleeve after he buttons it, only to unbutton it nervously. He puts his lunch box in his backpack, and clumsily puts his arms through the backpack's straps, careful to not damage the feathers on the epaulettes. Checking himself in the mirror, the pink backpack sits awkwardly on his back.

"Does this backpack look terrible?"

"Yes, why are you wearing it? Can't you use a lunch box?"

"I need it for the party supplies. I didn't want to leave them at the club because things tend to disappear or get moved, and then how would I find them?"

"That's true. Somebody took my Keropi lunch box when I went there to pick up fliers during the day last month. I was furious! You can't possibly wear that backpack, it ruins the jacket's lines. Just stash it in the basement DJ booth."

"That's the plan since I'll need access to it through the night. Hiromi's DJing tonight and he can't refuse me anyway, since I'm the party's host. Are you done yet?"

"Yes, I am, behold and learn it, bitch!" Sterling snaps his fingers while putting the sliver sequined top hat on his head, which matches perfectly with the big silver tinsel eyelashes he just applied.

Sterling waves his hand around his stretchy silver vest over a spandex black t-shirt. Black leggings with platform shoes he sprayed painted silver completed his look.

"Fabulous, Sterling, you're the best looking doorman ever, tee-hee-hee."

"I'm a legend, hiaah!" Sterling replies, framing his face with his hands, puckering his kabuki red lips and sucking in his overly rouged cheeks.

"OK, legend, lets go. We're late!"

"Fashionably late!"

"No, just late. Remember, the sooner we get there the sooner we'll have our interview with the reporter."

"The press can wait too. They're not paying us."

On the street, Sonny remembers his inconveniently empty wallet.

"I've spent most of my money on the party and I don't have enough to get to the Tunnel. How much do you have?"

"Uh, oh. I'm down to my last three dollars because I was counting on my pay tonight to get me through tomorrow and my weekend gigs."

"Well, we'll just take the taxi as far as we can go, just like last time we took a taxi to the Tunnel."

"We can't arrive at our party by foot. That's so embarrassing! I won't hear of it!"

"OK, you don't have enough money to ride all the way there, do you? We have to walk. The reporter will be there. A fight with the taxi driver is not the kind of scene I want to create when we arrive."

"All I can say is that you shouldn't have spent all the party budget on supplies. Getting to the club for your big party is a legitimate expense, you know."

"I lost track of how much I spent. Just get in the cab!"

Sonny climbs into a sedan after Sterling, not bothering to remove the backpack, so as not to risk damaging the epaulettes.

Chapter 20

Nobody greets Pedro when he walks into the Y and the front desk attendant isn't there. He goes into the locker room to check on his belongings. There's a note taped to his locker door that says "Call your mom." He tears off the note, opens the locker and rifles through the locker's art supplies. He throws a few more away, and sets a sketchbook and pencils aside. Tossing clothes from a bag, Pedro finds the switchblade he hid in the bag earlier this week. The blade's metallic casing glistens in the locker room's florescent lights, plunging Pedro into the subway's darkness. Staring into the locker, Pedro nods off and drops the blade, which springs open upon hitting the floor. The blade flips open on his foot, waking him out of the micro-sleep. Frightened, Pedro picks up the blade, folds it and puts it in his backpack.

"I need to go home."

Pedro has been awake about 30 hours. He gathers other school items that he didn't take home on Tuesday and puts them in the school bag, then he takes the remaining contents and dumps them in the locker room's big garbage can.

"I don't need this shit. It's time to start fresh."

He enters the bathroom and hides in a stall to snort the last bit of crystal in his baggie. He then flushes the empty baggie.

"That's it. No more snorting anything. Ever. It's time for a new life."

Fortified, Pedro walks out of the stall and checks himself in the mirror. His dark brown eyes are bulging out of his head and there are dark crescents under his eyes. He notices a little bit of white foam at the corner of his lip, which he wipes with a paper towel. His nostrils show no trace of powder.

On his way out of the Y the desk attendant, now back at his post, calls out to him.

"Hey Pedro, can you call your mom and ask her to stop calling here? She's been calling all yesterday and this morning and it's really pissing me off. She needs to stop. Call her," says Toby.

Unsure how to respond and in the grip of a new tweak, Pedro stutters.

"F, F, if, uh, she calls again, tell her I'll be home tomorrow."

"Sure, I guess you shouldn't go back today since you're looking pretty burned out. Maybe you should get some sleep. You look like shit."

"I, uh, I'm goin' to the park for a little nap."

"It's a nice day for it. Make sure you check for dog shit in the grass before you lie down in it."

"Ye-, yeah, good idea."

Since he doesn't know what to do, Pedro heads to Madison Square Park. He pulls a newspaper of a garbage can and carefully spreads the pages on the grass under a tree on the north side of the street to get away from the bustle of 23rd Street. Seated, Pedro pulls out his sketch pens and lays them out, but then realizes that he's left his sketch book in the locker at the Y.

"Why do I always forget paper or pens?"

He lies down on the papers just to rest his eyes for a bit.

Hours later, a police siren awakens Pedro. He opens his

eyes and looks around. It's twilight.

"I guess that stuff wasn't as strong as I thought it was."

Pedro's clothes are damp from perspiration and his heart is racing, even though his brain shut down for a few hours. Fearfully, Pedro feels his pockets. The money is there, as well as the acid, which he pulls out to examine and considers swallowing the two tabs. His tongue and throat, dried by the crystal, make swallowing anything an impossibility. He heads over to the Wendy's on 23rd Street for another Pepsi. Sitting in the restaurant's dining room, he puts the tabs in his mouth after guzzling half the soda. Pedro still feels a hunger that food can't satisfy.

"Fuck it, I'm getting one last baggie. I need to wind down before going home."

Pedro leaves the restaurant and follows a comforting trail towards the projects. Looking up at the clock tower above Madison Square Park, Pedro notices that it's 9 p.m.

"At least one or two dealers have to be on the street by now."

A vague tingling creeps down Pedro's spine as he arrives at the projects, which pulse with menacing tension. The acid is taking effect, causing the grimy public housing's walls to pulsate unpleasantly. Pedro's throat gags as if he wants to vomit, but his throat is too dry to heave anything.

The homeboy he knows as Pee Wee is standing near the courtyard mid-block. Pee Wee nods to Pedro.

"You lookin' for sumthin?

"Benz," Pedro replies, referring to the heroin packet with the Mercedes Benz logo on it.

"I got it. Follow me," Pee Wee orders, walking towards 10th Avenue.

Pee Wee leads Pedro behind a plywood pathway on 10th Avenue set up to shield pedestrians from construction on a building's facade. With the street swaying, Pedro concentrates hard on following Pee Wee. Pedro pulls the $20 bill out of his pocket and holds it in his left hand conspicuously until they reach the back of the corridor between the plywood and the front of the building.

"How much you want?" Pee Wee asks, noticing Pedro's bug eyes and sweat-matted hair under his hat.

"I want $20," Pedro says, holding up the bill.

Pee Wee takes the bill, turns slightly and puts the bill in his pocket. Pedro feels another wave of swaying. A passing car's distorted bass echoes through the swaying construction chamber. Pedro turns to the plywood and recoils a bit, thinking he's seen big roaches crawling about. After his double take, he feels his jaw snap towards the plywood, cracking forcefully into his right ear. A flash of white blinds him and he falls against the plywood. "Roaches" scramble across his face, biting fiercely. "Rats" scramble across his body, also biting and squealing in a high pitched, painful siren. As the white flash passes, Pedro finds himself crumpled against the plywood, all wet. Wiping his mouth, it leaves a red streak on his arm from his bleeding lip.

"Shit! That fucking dealer jumped me! He took my money!"

Pedro wobbles as he rises from the littered passageway. Pedro stumbles from the passageway towards Ninth Avenue, feeling the throb on his jaw, amplified by the acid. A siren begins ringing in his ear, adding to the pain.

"I'm gonna kill that asshole."

He rifles through his bag and finds his knife, which he moves to his front right pocket. Before reaching Ninth Avenue, a group of three homeboys approach and surround him.

"You need to get out of here or you're gonna get fucked up," one of them says.

"Pee Wee took my money," Pedro slurs through his mouth, still crooked from the blow.

"Get the fuck out of here before we tear your ass up," the other homie says as he shoves Pedro, almost knocking him down again.

Frightened, Pedro turns around and walks towards 10th Avenue, as one of the homeboys kicks him in the ass.

"Run, fucking faggot."

The acid-amplified panic moves Pedro's legs faster as he hears a menacing laughter. He flees the confrontation, turning north at 10th Avenue, not sure where he's going.

"Fuck. Should I go to the Y?" Pedro's eyes water with anger and fear. "I should have cut one of those assholes. Why didn't I just slice him? He deserves it. I should jam my knife in his fucking gut. I stabbed Steve. I couldn't stab those thugs? Why did I cut Steve and not those fucking jerks?"

By the time he reaches 23rd Street, the bleeding stops. It's a cut inside his cheek where the flesh smashed against his teeth. Pausing at a corner, he considers walking to the Y.

"What am I gonna do there? They're gonna see my mouth and ask a bunch of questions. Fuck them. It's time to go home. Fuck New York. I don't care what happens."

Pedro continues northbound on 10th Avenue. Hallucinations torment his jaw, forcing it to relive the sucker punch with pulsing, painful flashes. On the next block, crack, another white flash. The wincing makes Pedro stumble at 26th Street, where he pauses for a moment.

"I should go back to the projects and just get anybody I can. They all deserve it for ripping me off tonight and other times I came here and they sold me shit."

Pedro sees a taxi stop at the southwest corner of 27th Street. A big queen with silver boots and a top hat emerges from the taxi. Pedro forgets his pain. Then he sees another queen with a green jacket and a pink backpack.

"It's that faggot from the subway."

Pedro walks towards the pair as they cackle about something and rush west on 27th Street.

"He's laughing at me again."

"This is not the way I envisioned your party promotion debut, hiaaah," Sterling proclaims while straightening his top hat. "I'm embarrassed to show up on foot. I was expecting a limo!"

"Oh shut up. You can barely afford the subway. If anybody asks, just tell people I was showing you my tag in the subway because we're planning my graffiti art subway exhibition. It'll be genius! GEE-NEE-US! That's what you have to tell the reporter if she asks you anything. It's our alibi! Tee-hee-hee!"

"OK, but don't expect me to shower your little idea with all kinds of praise. I have to save that for my parties. I'm telling her about my party too."

"You don't have a party. What party?"

"It's my silver party. That's it, I'm calling it Silver Wear. I may as well use my trademark as a party theme. It makes perfect sense. I'm pitching it to the party promoters tonight. Too bad I don't already have a date to give to the reporter."

"That's not even a real party with any kind of theme. You're basically using your outfits as a theme. I think you should use a little more creativity."

"Don't tell me about creativity. You go in the slimy subway tunnel and spray paint some shit on the wall and now it's an art exhibit. You're so full of shit. My outfit theme is just as good as any spray paint on some grimy wall. Anyway, my party will have lots of spray paint too, just all silver like I did with my shoes."

"OK, just don't inhale too much of those paint fumes, or you'll think you're a big time New York City party promoter! Tee-hee-hee!"

"You think you're so clever. You're lucky I'm working for you tonight, or I wouldn't put up with your sass."

"That's right, don't forget you're working for me! Tee-hee-hee!"

"Please, why don't you practice your lies and exaggerations for the reporter?" Sterling says, waving his hard imperiously to order an end to the repartee.

"There she is! I see her with the camera guy. Oh shit, let the show begin!" Sonny proclaims, running towards the journalist, lest the camera shoot a frame without him.

"Don't run! You have to play hard to get!" says Sterling, running after Sonny.

Christine Sharpe stands next to her cameraman outside the velvet ropes, where a small crowd of early birds already waits for admission. The cameraman pans his camera back and forth across the waiting patrons, the light slowly crawling over their outfits. Sonny jumps on a parked car about 50 feet from the club's entrance.

"Christine! Christine!" he yells, jumping on top of the car's roof.

Once Christine looks his way, Sonny jumps onto the car's hood and then onto the trunk of another car parked in front of the first car. He then jumps on the second car's roof. The camera's greedy light shines towards Sonny, documenting his thoughtless vandalism. Sterling walks past the parked cars, trying to get himself in the frame without having to climb on top of the cars.

"Let the games begin. You are about to experience a party like no other. Prepare yourselves for a night of ecstasy! A night of sin! A night of sheer decadence you'll never forget, or remember!

Tee-hee-hee!" Sonny yells as he jumps off the car and prances toward the velvet ropes. "And those of you not dressed right, go home! You can't get in!" Sonny waves his hands, laughing towards the street. "You're not fierce enough! Tee-hee-hee!"

"What's so funny?" asks Pedro, stepping from amid the crowd.

Sonny recognizes the captain's hat, but he's stunned into silence.

"I'm not a fucking joke!"

The switchblade clicks open and Pedro jabs it into Sonny's lower chest, slipping the blade sideways between bone, then pulling out. A clubber at the rope screams.

"He's got a knife!"

Another clubber yells and the crowd rushes away from Pedro.

"Why?" Sonny yells with a garbled voice at Pedro.

A dark stain spreads over Sonny's new jacket and the cameraman illuminates the growing stain with his floodlight. Pedro stands there with no answer for Sonny. A bouncer kicks Pedro to the ground and stomps on his hand, cracking bones and kicking the weapon away.

Sonny turns to the reporter and then to Sterling.

"Call the ambulance!" Sterling says to the doorman. "The police!"

"Sonny, sit down until they come."

Sterling guides Sonny to the sidewalk as the camera's light follows.

"My list."

Blood drools over Sonny's clown grimace, coughed up from his left lung. He takes the papers out of the jacket's inside pocket and holds them up for Sterling, who takes them.

"Sonny, who's that crazy guy? Do you know him?"

Sonny nods, looking for the reporter, but unable to see her because of the blinding camera. People rush about and he sees a bouncer approach who he takes Sterling's place, laying Sonny down.

"Christine," Sonny gurgles, unable to get the word through the blood bubbling up his trachea.

The camera's white light finds Sonny again. The bouncer's hands push down on his wound to stop the bleeding, but the force also pushes the remaining breath from his chest. Sonny mouths to the reporter as he touches the mirrors on his helmet with his left hand to ensure they haven't fallen off.

"When is this on TV?"

More blood trickles out of Sonny's mouth. No one hears his question. Sonny looks towards The Tunnel and the camera's light dims.

CPSIA information can be obtained at www.ICGtesting.com
Printed in the USA
BVOW08s1816040615

403271BV00013B/100/P